C. LEE MCKENZIE

Evernight Teen ®

www.evernightteen.com

C. LEE MCKENZIE

DEDICATION

Because No One Noticed has been a long time coming. It would still be on my C-drive if I hadn't had insightful readers convince me I should send it out for publication. My critique partners gave me encouragement and much-needed suggestions, so thank you, Yvonne Ventresca, Heather Couthard, and Mel Higgins for those early assists. And thank you, Gabi Coatsworth, Liz Morten, and Gillian Foster who read the later version and helped me bring it across the finish line.

A special shout out to Denise Leffers, MFT. She pushed me in the right direction to re-write a key character, and that brought the story together when I'd almost given up.

C. LEE MCKENZIE

BECAUSE NO ONE NOTICED

C. Lee McKenzie

Copyright © 2024

Prologue

"The world is a dangerous place to live; not because of the people who
are evil, but because of the people who don't do anything
about it."
– Albert Einstein

Saturday, The Day Of

Sirens slice through the early September morning silence. It's only eight-thirty, and already Saturday has switched from a calm first day of fall to one charged with danger. The sounds speed down the highway where accidents happen most of the time, then veer into the center of the small town of Las Animas.

Fire trucks, police cars, and EMT vans converge

on the town's lone strip mall in a crescendo of ear-splitting shrieks until the parking lot is a solid din.

People who'd planned on a late start shove bed covers aside and peer out windows. Those already savoring their morning coffee set down their cups and go onto front porches. Early joggers stop, cocking their heads to determine where those emergency vehicles are headed.

Clifford Mott's boss grumbles as he opens the convenience store door, and the full force of the noise shatters the last shred of his good humor. The man's beginning to regret hiring the slow-witted high school dropout who called in sick and pulled him from his girlfriend's very warm and lovely bed. He'd fire the jerk if anything like this happened again.

In seventeen-year-old Lula Banes's house, her father—the General—sits at the kitchen table, folding the Wall Street Journal in half and trying to ignore the annoying noise. Upstairs in her bedroom, Lucille, his wife, pulls out earplugs from her nightstand, and, stuffing them into her ears, buries her head under the silk-covered pillow.

Win Knight's father is in what Las Animas town dwellers refer to as Knight's Castle. He and his latest girlfriend have spent the night together. Kate's there, too. The housekeeper sets aside the skillet of sizzling bacon to turn on the local news.

Marty Skolinski's dad, on his way to open the hardware store, slows the car to peer at the crowd gathered on the street. The sirens have stopped, but the emergency lights still flash like a manic light show. He shakes his head, frowning, but then drives on because he has a sale this weekend, and customers will want in by 9:00 AM.

Both Dina Strong and her cousin Brittany left

their house early, freeing up two slots for the one shower in the crowded home. Dina's parents, her aunt, and her uncle will have to vie for bathroom time. Each of them looks forward to those extra few minutes alone with soap and hot water. Anticipation of this small luxury keeps them too occupied to pay much attention to the noise coming from the street.

In the old upscale section of town, Blossom Henley's mother is just finishing her morning shower, but she still hears the blaring horns and screeching sirens. She hopes someone hasn't been hurt, but from the sounds, something serious is happening. She turns off the water and grips the safety bar. The night her husband was killed in a car crash, she'd heard sirens and never thought they had anything to do with her. She'd been so wrong. Now whenever she hears sirens, they almost stop her heart with dread.

Soon everyone in Las Animas will know what has happened in that strip mall at the Saturday morning hangout called Blendz and Moore. In the future, whenever sirens wail, they'll halt whatever they are doing, remember this morning, and share that heart-stopping dread with Blossom Henley's mother.

Chapter One

Blossom
Two Days Before

Mr. Jason called time and then walked down the row of desks toward Blossom. When he reached her, he shook his head and slid the paper from under her hand. "Blossom, I said, pencils up."

She'd guessed at most of the questions because no matter how many times she'd gone over the chapter, nothing stuck. She might as well have been taking a test about Greek, not cell division. Her face flushed, already seeing the F that was sure to be at the top of her paper when she got it back. It was embarrassing to fail a biology class when you were the daughter of a marine biology professor.

The rest of the students had handed their tests forward, and Mr. Jason added Blossom's to the stack before tapping it on his desk and evening the edges. At the bell, with their backpacks over their shoulders, students scrambled to make it out the door and to lunch.

Lula moseyed across the front of the classroom and plunked herself on Blossom's desktop. Studying her nails, she said, "Piece of pissin'-tart cake."

"Yeah." Blossom grinned at yet another of Lula's *creative* swear words, but, she didn't look up while she stuffed some papers and a pen into her backpack. Her face would be all about that F she was guaranteed to get, and Lula would pick up that something was wrong.

"Want to grab a burger across the street?" Lula asked.

"That's great. Sure." Blossom hoisted her backpack onto one shoulder and followed Lula's leggy stroll out the door and down the street toward Best Burger.

Why was everything so easy for Lula and so hard for her? She sighed, and Lula glanced at her.

"That was soulful. Something wrong?"

"The usual." Blossom kept her answer vague. She couldn't—wouldn't—let Lula know about the failing grades that kept piling up in Mr. Jason's book. Even her English scores had dropped from Bs to low Cs, and her last report in social studies came back with a solid C minus. It wasn't that Lula would use it against her. Lula was hard, but not mean. It was that Blossom didn't share things that she was so ashamed of with anyone, even her best friend. And this was one of those things.

"Parents?"

Blossom stopped but kept her eyes focused ahead.

Lula took hold of her arm and squeezed it. "I'm sorry. That came out before my brain went online."

She stood next to Lula with the familiar ache lodged in the center of her chest. That ache came and went as it had since the January day her dad had been killed in the accident. How long do you ache after someone you love dies? Maybe forever.

She touched Lula's hand, which still gripped her arm. "That's okay. I forget sometimes, too. It's only been a few months. But you're almost right. The problem is I've got one parent. My mom." Blossom walked on, thinking that if she could only stop all the turbulence inside her head, she might be able to concentrate on school again. But every day was a new challenge. It was so hard to be with her mom, to try to talk to her, only to find the mother she once knew was missing. The absence of her real mother made her dad's death that much more difficult to handle.

"She still's not connecting with any of her

friends?" Lula asked. "Or you?"

Nodding in slow agreement, Blossom said, "But once in a while Mom'll ask about what's going on at school. Just not much."

"That's kind of normal for my parents, but I'm sorry." Lula threw an arm around Blossom and pulled her close to her side. "It's going to take a while for her to get over the accident. Hang in there with her."

"I'm trying to." Blossom dug her nails into her palms and stopped the smarting in her eyes.

They crossed the street and had started past the convenience store when the door opened and a display rack was rolled out to the front.

"Keep going," Lula said, pulling Blossom along more quickly beside her.

"What's the rush?"

"I don't like being near that Mott person." Lula jerked her thumb in the direction of the lanky figure who stood staring at them.

Blossom glanced over her shoulder. "Clifford Mott?"

"That's the one."

He'd been on campus last year, but she hadn't seen him there since the new semester. He always reminded her of someone who was lost, the way he roamed the halls without seeming to have a destination. He was still gripping the side of the display rack, but he seemed to have forgotten what he'd set out to do with it as he stared at her and Lula.

"Is he okay?" Blossom asked.

"Not hardly."

"What's wrong with—"

"Later. I'm starving." At Best Burger, Lula swept ahead and pushed open the door.

Win sat in a booth at the far end, alone. Without

thinking, Blossom unbuttoned the two top buttons of her sweater. She'd worn her dark green one today with a creamy lace chemise under it. Unlike Lula or most of the girls at Las Animas, Blossom didn't wear deconstructed jeans or tees. She didn't wear tennis shoes, but sandals or boots. Yes, Lula teased her, calling her Retro Girl. She was, but she liked having her own style. It made her feel special, and that made up for some of the rottenness, like those F's in Jason's class, her dad, her mom. And here she exhaled long and slow. It made up for Win. The rottenness of how he treated her.

Lula went straight to Win and dropped onto the seat across from him. "Mind if we fill up the empty side?"

Blossom took her time following, then waited next to the table a moment before easing herself onto the vinyl bench next to Lula. As much as she wanted to be near him, she dreaded it, too. She dreaded that he'd finally tell her to steer clear of him. He'd done that to other girls. He'd just done it to Melinda Bailey.

Win slid one of his menacing looks at Lula, and then with a slightly less hostile expression, he locked onto Blossom. She glanced away, pretending to read the menu above the cash register. Those hard looks of his hurt. Just once, she wanted his eyes to be warm when they met hers.

"You ordered already?" Lula asked him.

Win cracked his knuckles. "Nope."

"Gross." She pointed to his hands.

He cracked them again. Louder.

"You're such a Neanderthal, Win." Lula pushed herself up and waited for Blossom to move. "Come on, Blossom. Let's get something. I'm starved."

Blossom stood up, and without connecting with Win's stare, went to the counter. "You rile him on purpose," she said, leaning close to Lula.

"Nah. I'd never do that."

By the time they'd placed their order, picked it up, and returned to their seats, Win had taken off, leaving the booth empty.

"Such a social creature that Baldwin Knight." Lula took the seat Win had vacated and removed the paper wrapper from her burger. She paused before taking a bite. "He's got the hots for you, you know."

Blossom choked on her fries. "About as much as he has the hots for my goldfish." She shook her head and swallowed. "You're talking crazy."

"Just saying." She waggled her finger at Blossom's sweater. "His eyes aim for you, and they land just about there every time you come near him." She grinned. "He's hot for what you got in that sweater." She started to bite into her burger again, but stopped, staring at the door. "Marty's here."

Blossom laughed. "Talk about having the hots for somebody. Marty's wherever Lula Banes is."

Marty trotted across from the door and bounced onto the seat next to Lula. "Got something for you." He held out his fist.

"What's that?" Lula asked.

"Guess."

Lula speared her dill pickle with a plastic fork. "I'm not into guessing while I eat."

"When you were ten, you used to be fun. You are not fun anymore," he said.

"Shoot me."

Marty aimed an index finger at Lula and clowned "Kapow!" Then he opened his fist and held up a chain with a silver rabbit's foot the size of a peanut dangling at the end. "It's a present."

"For?"

"Actually, it's a bribe." Marty glanced up at the menu. "I'll be right back as soon as I rustle up some grub. Back in a sec."

Blossom leaned across the table. "Now that is weird."

"Marty's weird. What can I say?" Lula finished her fries and sipped the last of her Coke before Marty returned with a plate piled with greens. Marty was always in training, even at Best Burger.

"What are you, part rabbit?" Lula asked him. She dangled the silver rabbit's foot. "A relative?"

He ignored her question. "My mom's baking cakes again."

Blossom caught Lula's eye, and with grins nowhere near cheerful, they shared their common plight. Lula's mom had never cooked a thing in her life, let alone baked a cake. And Blossom's mom had always worked, so the Henley food came from the deli and the local bakery.

Marty didn't catch their exchange and kept talking. "I've got to cut back on the carbs when I can." He didn't wait for Lula to ask about the bribe. "Now for the important stuff. I need an alibi," he said. "I need you to give me one."

"Hmm." Lula jiggled the ice in her cup.

"I've got a chance to talk to the gymnastics coach at Gladford. My mom and dad are 'No Way, Jose'' whenever I even mention gymnastics, so I kind of don't. It'll only be like a few hours, but I'll miss dinner. All you have to do is back me up with something like I was at your place doing homework. What about it?"

Lula took her time to chew and swallow, then reached over and picked up Marty's water and took a gulp. "When?"

Marty grinned. "Saturday night. Thanks," he said

before he jabbed his fork into his salad and started munching on lettuce.

Lula pulled the chain over her head and let the rabbit's foot dangle between her breasts. "Nice bribe. I'll see what I can do."

Marty nodded and chewed while he stared at the silver rabbit's foot and licked his lips.

Blossom caught Lula's attention and smiled.

Chapter Two

Win

Win kept his eyes on Lula as she walked to the order line at Best Burger. How could she be such a bitch and still look like a Teen Vogue model, the perfect face, all glam?

He had something to ask Blossom, but not in front of Lula. The problem was Lula never failed to be where Blossom was. Were they glued at the hip?

He stared at the lunch crowd from the high school, eating and ordering until everyone became a smear of colors. Maybe his plan wasn't the greatest. He shook his head in a private communication with himself, emphasizing what he knew was true. It was a rotten idea. Stupid. What was he thinking? But he was freaking tired of the mess girls like Dina and Melinda caused. He didn't want another Las Animas High girl mucking with him the way those two were. Hell, he didn't want another single person making his life miserable. He already had his dad doing an A-1 job.

And right now, all he wanted was to do was get out of the booth before Lula and Blossom came back, so he got to his feet, jammed his hands into his sweatshirt pockets, and fled Best Burger.

Before he went back to class, he'd grab some chips and a soda, something to cool down and make him burp. His stomach always burned after being around Lula Banes. They had a history that went way back, and she was one person he'd be very happy to say goodbye to when he left Las Animas for the last time.

He pushed his way into the convenience store next to the hamburger joint and walked to the refrigerator section at the back. The happy retail store music playing seemed so wrong for the way he was feeling at the moment.

It wasn't until Win had retrieved a cold soft drink that someone called, "Hold on. I'm coming."

When he looked toward the rear of the store, Clifford Mott had stuck his head out from the swinging doors marked employees only. The guy always gave him the creeps, the way he looked at you, but didn't really connect.

Mott came toward Win, his thin arms clutching a stack of candy cartons. He slouched inside his clothes as if he'd dressed in somebody else's pants and shirt, somebody much bulkier. His dark blond hair was gelled into short spikes, adding more of an edge to his angular frame. When he turned his head, the black ear gauge in his left earlobe resembled a round third eye.

Win waited for Clifford to step behind the counter, then he set the can down, grabbed a bag of chips, and pulled out his wallet.

"Is that all?" Clifford asked, making it sound as if Win should have added at least one more item to make it worth his time ringing the sale up.

Without answering, Win fished out a twenty and slid it across the counter.

"Hmm. Got something smaller? I'm low on change." Apology tinged his voice, but there was something else Win heard. Bitterness. When Win looked up, he caught that same apologetic resentment on Mott's face.

Win had heard the Clifford Mott stories that circulated Las Animas High after he dropped out of school, and he'd seen a few online chats about the guy. Mott was creepy, but he had a hard time believing the creep could be deadly.

Win dug into his pocket, pulled out a small wad of ones, and dropped three on the counter.

"Thanks, man." Clifford counted the change into Win's palm, one coin at a time all the while staring up at him.

As Win stuffed the coins into his pocket, Marty shoved open the door and hurried inside. Win turned to leave, but Marty blocked his way.

"Hey, have to ask you something," Marty said.

"Sure. Ask away." Win dodged around him and walked toward the exit, but he didn't get far before Marty caught up and trotted alongside.

"Don't tell me you're in a rush to get to class because I know that just ain't so." Mary laughed.

Marty was right. Win was in no hurry to get to class, but he'd had enough of Mott and the convenience store music. Lula had put him in a bad mood, and he intended to stay in it for a while. Marty had a way of clowning you out of scowls and into smiles. He didn't feel like smiling.

He ignored Marty's outstretched hand and kept moving, banging the door open with the flat of his hand and setting off the buzzer.

Finally, Marty grabbed Win's arm to stop him from walking out. "I just want to make sure you're on the early shift at Blendz and Moore this Saturday."

"Yeah. I start at eight."

"Great! That means Lula and Blossom will be there, too, right?"

Win shrugged his resignation. "They usually are." Silently, he cursed Lula again.

"Perfect. See you Saturday." Marty walked back inside the store.

Not so perfect, Win thought. Just once it would be nice to see Blossom come into the coffee shop without

19

C. LEE MCKENZIE

Lula.

Chapter Three

Clifford

Clifford braced his hands on the counter and tracked Win as he jogged across the street to the high school. Funny how some days could be so interesting and others dragged out like all the ones that came before. Today had been a good one. First, his boss had left for a long lunch with his girlfriend, so that gave Clifford a chance to have a real break. And now Win Knight had come into the store—the catch of Las Animas High. Clifford heard that more than once from girls who came in the store or who sat in front of him at the games.

How would it feel being that rich and that tall with sexy hair and a perfect nose? He imagined his face different and himself rich, famous even. Without thinking, he brushed a finger along the side of his jaw, pausing for a second at the scar—still raw when he touched it after so many years. That scar always stirred up the anger in his belly, and he didn't want that showing in public. He reached into his pocket for his phone, then typed Win's name into Notes and added: "Get rich. Look good."

When Marty set a bottle of orange juice on the counter with a thump, Clifford switched his attention away from Win and onto the high school's head cheerleader. He was another one always in the spotlight, all eyes on him during half-time at the games. This guy had rubber bands instead of bones under that skin of his. All those backflips and handstands. That's how he made people notice him. And he hung out with the in-crowd.

How would that feel?

He took his time making change while Marty

shifted from one foot to the other.

He never stands still. That would drive a normal person crazy.

When Clifford slapped the change on the counter, Marty flinched.

"I hear Blendz and Moore's the happening place for Saturday mornings," Clifford said. He never missed picking up bits of information about what the high school kids had going on. It kept him connected, made him feel like he was still part of the action.

"Yeah. Most Saturdays." Marty swept up the change and stepped back to stuff it into his pocket. "I don't drink coffee myself. Lula—she's my girl—can't get enough caffeine. She hangs out there with Blossom. That's why I go." He spoke fast, and Clifford noted the tiny beads of perspiration above Marty's upper lip.

All that energy build-up.

Laughing, Clifford said, "That's the best reason for showing up anywheres."

"You bet." Marty reached out to grab his orange juice and hurried toward the door as more students drifted in.

Clifford went to the window and kept him in sight, watching him hurry off, his feet springing up and down on the pavement. He watched Marty until he disappeared behind the school.

Clifford turned away and took care of another high school customer, then he set to restocking the candy display and neatening the magazine rack. Kids from the high school were slobs, so he'd have to clean up again after the lunch crowd left, but he didn't like leaving the store in a mess even for a few moments. It was important to keep those displays and racks in order. That gave him a sense of control over something and helped the time pass faster. His boss liked when Clifford was on duty and said so. Clifford wanted to keep it that way. He wanted to keep this job until he didn't need it anymore.

He wiped up a small pool of spilled Coke and swept up a crumpled Snickers Bar wrapper some idiot had dropped. The damned trash can was right next to the door, but did they use it? Not much. He could deal with most of the mess, but cleaning up gum was the worst.

"Hey," he said to the kid wearing a gamer t-shirt and about to drop a wad on the floor, "put the gum in there." He pointed to a trash bin.

"Back off, gramps." The kid laughed, but he spit his gum into the bin before pushing his way out through the door.

Clifford made a mental note of the "gramps" comment and the one who'd said it. He was only a couple of years older than that punk. Stupid kid. One day he'd be sorry.

This is a temporary job, he reminded himself as he sprayed cleaner on the glass door and rubbed off fingerprints. He peeled away the old ad clutter, ripping the last of the sticky-backed paper from the window. *Temporary, like everything.*

Lunch hour was almost over because the students who'd hurried off campus now slow-walked their way back toward it. Some hung in groups. The freshmen guys jostled each other like a litter of pups, and the girls walked in tight bunches while they crossed the street, their heads close, laughing and talking non-stop. The juniors and seniors were cooler, but they still hung together.

He'd been in that herd once, but when he'd been in high school, he'd never been part of the pack. He'd always been the one kid crossing the street by himself and going into class alone.

No one understood him. That was why. He made

another swipe at a gluey spot on the glass.

And there was nobody smart enough for him to talk to anyways. They were all jerks.

He spotted Dina and Brittany, the pair he'd nicknamed the Thin Twins. They'd come into the store a few times, and he'd chatted them up to see if there was anything interesting about either one of them. There wasn't. He couldn't decide which one was more boring. Both were under-a-rock pale. Even their personalities were washed out. They made wood fascinating to watch.

When he'd asked if they were twins, they'd laughed. "No. Cousins," they'd said.

Well, he'd been right. They shared the same gene pool. "Are there any more at home like you?" He'd hidden the sarcasm and looked interested when they'd giggled and said they were each only children.

"Like me," he'd said, all the time thinking, *but so not like me*. He shuddered even considering how it would feel to be related to those two.

He was about to go into the back to take another break before his boss returned, when two other girls he always paused to watch crossed in front of the store. Two so different from the Thin Twins that he leaned against the window and gave them his complete attention for the second time that day. The leggy, dark-haired one with the superior sneer was Lula Banes. He knew her from when she'd come to Las Animas High as a freshman. It had been his junior year, the year before he'd finally bailed.

Her dark huntress looks excited him, and his chest tightened when he thought of the first time she'd burned him with those eyes. She had to be the Lula Marty was talking about. How many Lulas could there be in this town? But Marty's girl? No way.

The shorter one always seemed to be with her, but he'd never taken the time to study her before now. Lula, knotted into seventeen years' worth of insolence, upstaged anyone he saw her with. But not today. Today, he focused on the girl walking next to her. Even from this angle, he could see that this one had a blonde sexy look. She was gesturing with her hands when, right in front of the store window, she stopped to face Lula, giving him a chance to see how animated she was, eyes wide and her face like a flower open to the sun. Whatever she was saying, it was important to her.

He didn't believe in all the mystical junk about light shining from inside people, but she seemed to glow, and looking at her made his chest ache. No other girl had stirred this kind of feeling in him before, and that confused him. He didn't have a girl in his plans for the future.

He slid his fingers along the window pane, imagining the softness of her cheek and her warmth through the glass. A girl filled with sunshine. He wondered whether he could draw her face and if he could show all that warm light. Probably not. He didn't have the right kind of pencils. He didn't even know what the right kind were. He should have gone to more of his art classes, but he hated that teacher.

His hand shook as he took out the phone from his pocket and typed, "Blonde one who's friends with the huntress", adding this to his list under Win's name. And what was the other name Marty mentioned? Petal. No. It was Blossom.

He wrote that name, and next to it "Find out if that's Blossom —Call her Sunshine. Need to know more about her. Blendz and Moore. Sat. 8 A.M."

He lingered at the window until the two girls crossed the street and disappeared into the crowd returning to campus. Then he closed his eyes, keeping that one girl's image in his memory. She was special, and he wanted her to notice him. He let out a long, slow breath. "Sunshine."

Chapter Four

Marty

Marty settled into his desk, ready to take on Mr. Cochran's English class now that his plan was in place. If Lula came through and gave him his alibi, his mom and dad wouldn't worry. Plus, he'd get to scope out the men's gymnastics practice at Gladford and talk to the coach without feeling too guilty.

The very best thing he'd accomplished today was putting that lucky rabbit charm exactly where he longed to nuzzle, right between Lula Banes's perfect breasts.

And speaking of those breasts, here they came. His dark queen strode into English, ignoring the peasants at their desks, even ignoring Mr. Cochran who never failed to notice Lula. Marty itched to punch the old lech in the chops for that leer. Instead, he cleared his throat, and when Mr. Cochran looked in his direction, Marty made it clear he'd seen all.

His teacher quickly switched on the overhead projector with the outline of their assignment. "Get those devices on, people. Papers are due next week, so get to work. If you have questions, I'm here."

Branch Redford tapped Marty on the shoulder and leaned forward. "You think Lula and Cochran are doing it?"

Marty swiveled to face him. "Shut up, jerk off. You're an idiot."

"Whoa. Kinda touchy, Skolinski."

"Just watch your mouth." Marty turned to face front, his hands balled into fists.

Behind him, Branch laughed but didn't say anything else.

Blossom hurried through the door behind Lula. Sweetness. Light. Kind. That's what Blossom brought into any room she entered. Marty liked that she sat across the aisle from him. He loved those vibes of hers, and she didn't distract him like Lula did. He could get some work done in this class with Blossom close by.

Win came in just at the bell. Win always came in *just* at the bell.

If Lula had a brother, which she didn't, it would be Baldwin Knight. What would it be like to be the male sex magnet of Las Animas High? Marty closed his eyes and imagined himself tall, very mysterious in a dark, sexy vampirish way—rich and buffed. He imagined himself the exact opposite of how he was. Still, Win never seemed to have any fun, and Marty couldn't imagine being like that.

He sighed, and it was louder than he'd meant it to be.

"Got you worried about Lula and Cochran?" Branch said from behind him.

"I told you to put a cork in it, Branch."

"Absolutely. But I can imagine, can't I? *That* I do real quiet."

Marty flipped Branch the finger over his shoulder, then he typed in his password. I <3L U L A and opened the file for his English term paper. The History of Cirque du Soleil.

His dream was right there on the screen, to become an acrobatic performer in the Cirque.

He whispered the word, "Cirque."

"What?" Now Branch was over his shoulder again. "What the hell is Cirque?"

"Piss off. And keep your eyes on your own screen." Marty reached behind and pushed Branch away. "What don't you understand about personal space, man?"

"I'm a twin, Skolinski. I got no such thing as *personal space.*" He shoved Marty's back gently. "Ease up. I'm only kidding."

Branch wasn't a jerk, but today Marty was on edge. And that had everything to do with lying to his parents about this weekend. Okay, he was weird. He loved his parents. And from what he'd heard, other kids at school didn't think that was normal. Normal meant you'd rather hang by your thumbs in a dungeon than talk to the two people responsible for your existence.

But he loved Cirque, too. *Cirque*, he said to himself this time silently. That's what those who aspired to auditioning and being chosen called it. Thinking about all it meant to be a part of that troupe of acrobats gave him goosebumps.

He shielded his screen from Branch by turning it slightly to the side.

Competition was stiff, so he had to be a top gymnast in a top gymnastics program. He'd have to make sure the talent scouts noticed him from his first year in university, and he had to be at the right one for that to happen. For him, that was Gladford, the number one school in the state for men's gymnastics.

The problem was his parents had other ideas. Junior college first, then college. A school close by, so he could still live at home—and not too expensive. Business. Safe. Definitely not a profession where he could plummet from the sky and hurt himself.

"Not too expensive. Safe," he said to his device screen, then he grinned because he'd pulled up a YouTube video about the Cirque's shows that were still touring. Since he'd seen this video a lot of times, he fast-forwarded to the part about the resident troupes in Las Vegas.

From behind, Branch whispered, "Hey! You

planning a trip to Vegas?"

"Will you stop spying over my shoulder?"

"I'm bored, Skolinski. My paper's done. You're my entertainment."

"Study your quarterback plays, then. The big game's this week, and you're the hope of Las Animas High."

"I got my plays memorized. Now, about Las Vegas."

"Yes. I'm going there ... one of these days." Marty hit mute and sat back to watch the performers. The hurdles he had ahead dimmed as he imagined himself flying over the stage on golden rings or performing on the vault just the way those guys on his screen were.

He tried to ignore Branch's breath at his back.

BECAUSE NO ONE NOTICED

Chapter Five

Blossom

Blossom returned Marty's smile when she came into Cochran's class. He always made her feel special. He was such a sweet guy. She wished Lula treated him better, but Lula tolerated him, and that was way more than she did for others who tracked her orbit around school. No one else seemed to exist to Lula. Maybe it was because she was so tall. She could look over most of the other students' heads and never notice any of them as they parted like a field of wheat to let her through. She was a seventeen-year-old Demeter at Las Animas. That's how Blossom planned on painting her—a tower of elegance, striding through acres ripe for harvest. She'd be barefooted with golden tassels braided into her dark hair.

Blossom didn't envy Lula, but she wished some of Lula's noble indifference would rub off on her. She was sore from the inside out, feeling all she did for her friends. Even her teachers' troubles touched chords in Blossom. Her strong feelings might be because of her mom and how she'd curled up within herself after the accident. Blossom hated to see the person she loved suffer, but she also hated feeling so alone and so helpless. Outside of bringing her dad back to life, there was nothing she could do to make her mom whole again. Nothing.

She glanced at Mr. Cochran. He'd stopped smiling or making jokes when he came back to school last week after spring break. The word was his wife had left and taken their son. How terrible for him. His wife and son hadn't died in a sudden accident the way her father had, but Mr. Cochran lost two people he loved, and all at once.

"Blossom," Mr. Cochran called to her, and motioned her to come up front.

"I just wanted to talk to you about this essay." He turned his laptop screen toward her.

She recognized the document as the short piece she'd written for a homework assignment. At the top of the page was a C-.

She blinked, not wanting to believe that grade. She'd worked hard on this paper. She'd re-written it twice and double-checked her sources the way she had always done. C- was the best she could get after all of that and in one of her favorite classes? Just once this year she'd like to have the feeling of doing something well for a change, something to ease the soreness in her chest, soreness that the low grades were partly responsible for.

"I wanted to give you a higher grade, but take a look at the typos and" —he pointed to the screen— "your citations aren't formatted correctly." He scrolled to the second page. "And here, you're off-topic."

He'd highlighted almost all of her citations and a lot of other places in the essay. There were at least twenty highlighted lines that streaked the two pages. How could she have so many errors? She closed her eyes and wished she could make all of what she'd done wrong vanish the way she did when she painted. If she stepped away from her easel and looked at one of her canvases, she instantly saw what needed to be changed, and she could go over it and fix it. Not so in English. Obviously. She swallowed, tamping down the urge to cry. Not so in science or math either.

She stared at the C- and imagined how an A would look there—the way it used to on those essays. How a B would look at the top of her biology paper—the way it used to on those tests. Her dad had wanted her to follow him into marine biology. At Christmases or birthdays, she'd hoped for a dog, but he brought home turtles and fish. He'd even started a special fund to save money for the family to visit a Caribbean marine park over summer break. Then he died. One day he was planning her life, and the next day he lay dead on Highway 85 next to his demolished Dodge.

At that thought, she blinked, her eyes stinging even more. With him gone, she felt some relief not to have to pretend she bought into his dream for her, but tucked inside that small bit of relief was some major guilt.

How could she even think it was better that her dad wasn't alive to watch her fail in the science class he loved, or see how dismal her grades were in any of the classes? He'd graduated valedictorian from high school, had straight As in college. She was absolutely stupid. But how? Her parents were brilliant.

She managed a glance up at her teacher. "I'm sorry, Mr. Cochran. I'll do better on the next one."

"I know you will. That's why I called you up here. You can do good work because I saw it at the beginning of the year." He took off his glasses and looked at her. "Blossom, I know you've had a terrible loss, so if you need help, ask."

Before she could answer him, he glanced over her head, looking out into the room where kids were still talking and making their way to their seats. "Okay, people," he said loudly above the chatter. "Lunch is over. Let's get to work."

As Blossom started toward her desk, Win, who stood in the aisle, stepped to the side and waited for her to go first. For a moment, she thought he might speak to her, but the teacher said something to him instead, and Win looked away without a word. And what would he say to her anyway? Probably nothing she wanted to hear. Probably something about how he wished she'd steer clear and let him eat lunch without bothering him.

She slipped into her seat and didn't look up when he walked past her desk.

Quickly, she opened her laptop and pulled up the outline for her paper: Watercolor Technique— determining the light source, sketching, brush selection for loose brushwork, color experimentation. She dove into her paper as thoroughly as she could ever dive into the warm waters of a Caribbean marine park—only in the world of art, she could swim very well.

Chapter Six

Lula

Cochran would give her an A whether or not she finished a term paper. Lula was positive about that. Almost. On her way into English, his eyes were all over her as usual.

"Afternoon, Mr. Cochran." She lowered her pitch so her voice came from the back of her throat. She'd always loved the way Lauren Bacall sounded in the vintage movies, and this was her best impression.

He nodded at her.

Such a dweeb.

She swung her tight-jean butt a little more from side to side as she passed him.

There's power in that tight butt, girlfriend.

At her desk, she gave him a different view by dropping her bag and leaning over to scoop it up. It never hurt to show a bit of cleavage just in case Cochran wasn't a butt man. He had to be one or the other. They all were.

Except for Marty.

Marty wanted all of her, not just certain angular or mounded bits. She hazarded a side glance in his direction, hoping he was riveted to his screen, so he didn't see her scoping him out. She didn't need to encourage him. Fortunately, he was already concentrating on doing his research, or at least trying to. Branch was leaning over his shoulder, and Marty kept pushing him back.

Why were boys so immature?

Marty had charm for sure, but absolutely no sex appeal.

At the bell, Win stepped into the room. Now, there was sex appeal. He'd had that since the grades, and since the grades, Lula had wanted him to notice her. But this year she'd hung a No Touching sign around his neck. Blossom, whether she admitted it to anyone or not, had developed one major crush on Mr. Knight and, if she was right, Mr. Knight had his eye on Blossom. Blossom was one girl Lula could not and would not hurt. To do that would be like hurting a kitten. *I do not hurt kittens.* Why couldn't Blossom be a big, grown-up hungry cat with claws—another Melinda Bailey—then the fight would be fair and fun.

Damn. Moral scruples were a drag, especially when they stopped her from getting what she wanted. And where had she gotten those scruples anyway? Her mother? She almost laughed out loud. *Please don't tell me The General had anything to do with passing on scruples to me!*

"Is there something wrong with your computer, Ms. Banes?"

She jerked her head up and stared at Mr. Cochran, who stood looking down at her.

"No, Mr. Cochran." She turned on her laptop, and as it whirred to life, she grinned at him. "It's just getting old and kind of slow."

His mouth tightened, and he bit down on his lower lip before he turned away. His shoulders drooped more than usual as he walked to his desk, so she'd made her message clear. Damn straight she had. But she couldn't stop the small twinge of regret when their eyes connected as he sat down. For a second, the gossip she'd heard about his break up with his wife was right there in that gaze. Well, *creeping-crap.* It wasn't her fault, and she didn't believe what Melinda Bailey was circulating about her mom and Cochran either. Everything that went south in this town couldn't be because of the Banes women.

Besides, her mother wouldn't waste time on a high school English teacher. Lucille might stoop to a pool boy once in a while for a diversion, but she set her eyes on men with trust funds and Maseratis for longer "commitments".

Lula scrolled down her document files, still not able to turn off Melinda Bailey's gossipy voice.

Cochran wasn't hard on the eyes, and he had a lot more going for him than the pool boy. *But would Lucille take a small detour between that boy and Mr. Millionaire?* No. Ten to one, her mother had never even met Mr. Cochran.

When she pulled up her term paper on Landscape Architecture, the tension between her shoulders eased, and the Lucille-Cochran debate slid off to a quiet corner of her brain. Landscape Architecture would be her life once she escaped from Las Animas and into college and the real world. She'd already done the outline and the introduction for the paper. Now she'd flesh out the body and finish it. This topic held her interest, so Mr. Cochran would have his assignment and probably on time.

Then, as she scrolled down the page to where she'd stopped work yesterday, she remembered the Open House before Spring Break, and her hand hovered over the keyboard. *Rats*. The one time her mother had come to an event for parents was this year. She'd been in this school. She could have met Cochran. All of Melinda's gossip could be true.

Creeping-crap!

Chapter Seven

Win

That bell, or one just like it, had chopped Win's days into forty-minute chunks of "prison" life since he could remember.

He made sure to step into Cochran's classroom just before it stopped busting his eardrums. It was a small mutiny, but Win knew it got to Cochran and every other teacher at Las Animas High. They'd talked to each other about his annoying little war against the bell in the teachers' room, and he knew that because last year, his biology teacher, Miss Crane, told him. She also told him that in her class being in his seat by the time that bell stopped meant being on time. The rest of his sophomore year, Win had stood with his arms crossed, facing the back of the room, then he'd sit just as the bell stopped ringing. He liked to smile up at Miss Crane while she watched him slide into his seat at the exact moment of silence.

Cochran hadn't tried the in-your-seat rule with him, so while almost everyone else, even Lula, had laptops open and fingers on the keys, he let Blossom brush past him before making his way to his seat at the back of the room. He thought about telling her he needed to ask a favor, but Cochran stopped him.

"Glad you could join us, Mr. Knight."

Win saluted with fingertips to his forehead. "It's always my pleasure," he muttered under his breath and made his way down the aisle where Dina sat a few seats ahead of him.

Last month, he'd given her one moment of attention, and now she was stalking him. He never should have stopped that day in the hall to see if she was all right. He should have ignored her leaning against the wall, her hands covering her face. It had been a trick. He knew she'd ambushed him the minute she took her hands away and looked up at him through those thickly mascaraed lashes.

Why had he even bothered to notice her at all? He was still in recovery from Melinda Bailey, the girl who believed gossip more than she believed him. No matter how many times he tried telling her he hadn't gone out with someone else behind her back, she thought he was lying.

Win shifted his gaze across the room and quickly away. Melinda leaned over her girlfriend's computer, pointing at something on the screen. Last month, between that girlfriend of hers and Melinda, they'd managed to turn him into a raving lunatic until he'd said screw it and broken up with her. And when he did, man did she set the wolves loose. She and her BFF spread every kind of story they could to get back at him. They even circulated a "Bad Boyfriend Checklist" online with his name next to each bad behavior.

By the time they were done, everybody in school believed he was the worst male on the planet. But he didn't care anymore what anyone thought. Melinda turned out to be just one more girl who'd set out to make him miserable.

He ran his fingers through his hair in frustration. Females. They were nothing more than a constant supply of trouble in eye makeup.

He was sick of all of them, and since Melinda, he'd made it as clear as he knew how that he wasn't interested in dating anyone. But now he had Dina who turned up wherever he was. She still called him on his cell and filled up his inbox. Or she texted again and again until it took a long time to clear his messages. He'd blocked her, but then she changed to a different cell, and last week she'd sent him a naked selfie.

On his way past her desk, she held out a hand, and he wasn't quick enough to avoid brushing against it with his leg.

She glanced up at him. "Did you like the picture?" she whispered, smiling.

He frowned down at her for a second. "What picture?"

She pouted and tapped her cell phone screen.

He walked away and swiped his hand over his jeans where she'd touched him as if he could rid himself of her that way. For a whole month, she'd been in his face, and for a whole month he'd been as rude as he could by dodging her, and still she wasn't giving up. He knew it was going to take a lot more than ignoring her. That's why he had to talk to Blossom. She was his best bet for warding off Dina.

Settling into his desk, he opened his laptop and typed in his password. The 1957 T-Bird wallpaper filled the screen, and he settled back against his seat, letting his jaw relax and pushing away thoughts about his messy girl trouble.

He already had two more classic cars tracked for purchase, and he was sure they'd be up for sale about the time he had the structure ready to showcase them. In his mind, he held his mother and thanked her for all she'd done for him. Eva Knight had known about his passion and had made sure he'd realize his dream.

The property she'd left him sat vacant upstate. An ancient barn waiting to be restored. Acres of land ready for him to create the perfect place for the vintage cars he'd always imagined owning. He had enough saved to get him started, and then he'd make money buying, restoring, and showing or selling his cars.

His paper for Cochran was already finished, so this period he'd scope out the classic car sites, and his life would be good for this one forty-minute chunk of time.

Chapter Eight

Dina

Dina kept her eye on the door. Win was always the last one to come in, and she liked to watch him enter, his head down, his hands usually stuffed inside his sweatshirt pockets, and his body language loud with protest. His defiant attitude stirred up so many strong feelings inside her that she'd never experienced before. It was as if he filled her with everything she lacked—confidence, excitement, mystery. He was exactly what she needed in her life. He was the perfect person to turn her dull existence into one that had purpose and meaning. She had to make him like her.

As he walked down the aisle toward his desk, she reached out and stopped him. She'd swapped phones with Brittany after he'd blocked hers, and she wanted to know his reaction to the picture she'd sent last week. But really she just needed to have him near her, even if only for a few seconds. And that was about all the time he gave her. Time enough to lie to her and say he hadn't gotten what she'd texted.

After he'd passed her, she fell back against her seat and pulled up the images on the phone. She scrolled until she found the naked selfie she'd sent him. There she stopped for a few seconds, and before scrolling through more of the pictures, she let her finger rest on the one showing off her narrow shoulders.

She was just the right height and weight to be a model, and she photographed well. The selfie was good, and it was satisfying to know that. She looked better in her photos than in real life, but she'd read how a lot of models did.

When she found the article in the library copy of *Style* magazine showing how models looked before they applied their make-up and did their hair, she'd torn it out. Now she opened her notebook to the page she'd pasted it on. She studied the glossy photos while holding the phone, so she could compare the way she photographed to the way they did. She'd done this so many times that she'd memorized the models and their names.

She imagined herself on that magazine page—on the one side looking like the famished girl with lank hair and deep-set eyes that she saw in the mirror each day, and then on the other, herself transformed by the magic make-up wand. With one quick click of the camera, she became a gamine-eyed model, her neck a graceful arc, her shoulders angled forward, seducing her audience into buying whatever the ad wanted to sell.

This article had given her the boost she needed to hold on to her dream. If some top models weren't pretty in real life, she'd have a chance to be one of them. For a moment the white noise of her life subsided, and she embraced the hunger roaming inside her body.

"Dina?" Mr. Cochran's voice brought her eyes up from her phone. He was walking toward her, his hand out. "Either get your cell put away or hand it over. You're here to write a paper, not catch up on your social media."

With one last glance at the phone, she clicked it off and quickly stowed it in her bag. She didn't want Cochran to see what she had on her screen. "Sorry. Small emergency." She smiled at him and turned on her computer, pulling up the outline for her assignment. That was as far as she'd gotten on writing the paper about high fashion modeling.

Chapter Nine

Two Days Before
After School
Clifford

Late that afternoon, Clifford parked across the street from the high school lot and slouched low in the seat, waiting. It wasn't long after the clang of the bell that the doors flew open and the swarm of students poured outside.

A head taller than anyone in the crowd, Win was easy to spot. Flanked by a bunch of guys, he crossed the asphalt to his car that was parked next to where Clifford waited. Unlike everyone else, he didn't get in to drive away immediately. Instead, he opened the trunk and pulled out a plastic kit. Then from inside that kit, he took out a large white cloth and set to polishing the hood. The boys stood together a few feet away, laughing and pointing at where Win was lightly dragging his cloth in long, even strokes.

Clifford rolled down his window and listened.

"Hey, you missed a spot. Right there in the center, man!"

Win swiped at the mid-line of the hood.

"No. More to the left." One boy waved his hand in the air as Win swiped again, then looked back at him. "You got it."

"Effin' rich brat," Clifford muttered, and he sat taller in his seat because he didn't want to miss seeing the one he'd come for.

As the cars streamed out of the lot and turned left toward the main street, Clifford didn't let his gaze wander. Marty's beat-up Toyota was one of the first to drive off. When the creep who'd called him Gramps earlier that day came out, Clifford opened the Notes app on his phone and typed the license number next to "Don't forget this guy". It would be easy to make that one very sorry. There were a few flat tires in his future … or worse.

Then Lula's black truck rolled over the curb with a thump. She laughed and the blonde girl in the passenger seat said something, and laughed, too. That's who he'd come to see. The girl he was sure was called Blossom. He waited for one more car to get into the line behind Lula, then pulled out to follow. When the car between Lula's and his turned, he kept a half a block between him and the Tundra for about a quarter mile. When the truck stopped in front of an overgrown lot, Clifford idled at the corner. The passenger door opened and the blonde girl climbed out.

She was crossing the street, waving over her shoulder when Lula leaned out the driver's window. "Hey, Blossom! Call me later, okay?"

The girl nodded and Lula drove away, her tires squealing as she turned at the next intersection.

He'd been right. That was Blossom. He waited until she started toward her house, then he drove down the street and pulled to the curb across from her driveway. He sat waiting as she walked slowly toward the back. She paused a few times along the way as if she didn't want to get to her destination, as if she'd rather be walking in the opposite direction. Sometimes she stared off into what must have once been a garden. After she rounded the curve, he could barely see her behind a tangled mess of bushes and trees.

It took a lot of will power, but Clifford didn't get out of his car to talk to her.

Too soon. Be patient.

He'd done what he wanted to do. He'd made sure of her name, and he'd found out where she lived. Quickly, he typed "Blossom, the Sunshine Girl" and then her street number into his phone contacts.

Chapter Ten

Blossom

Blossom usually walked home from school, but on Thursday she accepted Lula's offer of a ride. She felt drained, and a lot of that was due to Win Knight and how he'd treated her today. He hadn't stayed more than a few minutes at Best Burger when she came in. He barely acknowledged her afterward in Cochran's class when they'd been so close to each other. Why did he hate her? And why did that thought make her sick to her stomach?

She hopped out of Lula's truck. "Thanks for the lift," she said before closing the door and crossing the street.

"Hey, Blossom! Call me later, okay?" Lula yelled, then sped off.

Of course, she'd call her later. A long phone conversation would be something to look forward to before going to bed.

She waited until Lula wheeled around the corner, and thought, as she had so many times this year, how perfectly Lula Banes fit behind the wheel of a truck called Tundra. All Earth Goddess. That was Lula. Blossom imagined *Lula's Landscaping* painted on each of the two front doors and towering trees strapped in the truck bed, whipping in the wind. That *earthy* goddess made her happy and drove her crazy at the same time.

Smiling, she turned away from the street but came to a halt, her smile quickly fading as she faced the house. Far back on one of the oldest over-sized lots in Las Animas, only the pointy top of the Henley's roof was visible from the sidewalk. If anyone looked up, they'd see a chimney poking above the trees, but a passerby could only glimpse the red brick walls. Oaks and firs along with dense shrubs, and now weeds, had overgrown the front. Her dad had always made sure the yard was kept up. Either he hacked back the overgrowth or he hired a gardener, but after he died it seemed as if everything was growing twice as fast as normal. Sadly, her mom didn't notice. She didn't notice much of anything at all anymore.

As soon as Blossom reached the end of the long walkway to the house, the heavy weight of her dad's death slowed her steps. She dreaded seeing her mom's sad face. She dreaded not seeing her dad in his usual chair, a stack of books on the table next to him.

Even though it was only three, the TV light flickered in the living room window, so Blossom expected to find her mom in her usual place, dozing in front of her usual program. She grasped the door handle, turned, and pushed.

She took a deep breath, and then trying to sound as cheerful as possible, called out, "Hi, Mom."

Her mom turned her head and rested a dim gaze on her daughter's face. "Home already?"

"Yes." Blossom tried to keep lightness in her voice, but seeing her mother like this made light the last thing she thought of.

"That's nice." But her mother could have said, "Too bad" and the exhausted tone would have been the same.

At least she was speaking. When the police came to the door that night last November, Margaret Henley had collapsed, and when she came around, she didn't make a sound. She didn't even cry. When friends visited, she wouldn't see them. She stopped eating until her doctor threatened her with a feeding tube. Then, she only nibbled at the edges of toast or sipped a few times from cups of soup that Blossom offered up in the hope Margaret Henley would return to her body. Within two months, her mother's clothes hung loosely as if they'd been pinned to her shoulders. Some days she didn't dress at all, letting her robe flap at her legs when she shuffled down the hall, her hair as lifeless as her eyes.

Blossom became a watcher. She longed to see small signs—a few more bites of food, a shower, her mother's hair brushed and not snarled by sleep. Blossom's hope rose when two weeks ago Margaret Henley began walking from her bedroom to her chair in front of the TV. But that soon stopped and she returned to staying in her bedroom.

Discouraged by this setback, Blossom spent hours putting herself into her mother's position. What would keep her locked inside her room? And then it came to her, and one Saturday, Blossom moved the TV from the den into the front room. Now her mother didn't have to walk past her husband's empty office. It worked. But maybe too well, because her mother spent the entire day and most of the night in front of the TV, something she'd never done in her life.

Once a teacher at the local junior college and a hardy volunteer at Las Animas' fundraisers, her mom now telescoped her life to fit inside her house. Without Cal Henley, Margaret Henley didn't function, didn't care to.

The flickering of the light from the TV screen drew Blossom back to this moment, the moment she had to deal with now. She touched her mother's hand and waited, hoping for some kind of reaction. When there was none, she said, "I've got homework." The quicker Blossom escaped to her room, the better. There, she didn't have to watch her mother fade into the furniture.

She tried to understand why Margaret Henley

couldn't deal with her loss after so many months. Maybe it was because her parents had so looked forward to retirement together—more time just for themselves. That plan had been destroyed in one minute. He died instantly, the policeman had said that night. A young man with the eyes of an old man, Blossom recalled.

Once inside her bedroom, she leaned against the closed door. She wished she'd been born into the Henley household before her mother's fortieth birthday. Always so much older than the other mothers and so used to being in charge of a classroom, Margaret Henley either ran the Home and School Club or told other moms how to. Those moms didn't like Margaret very much, Blossom found out from her classmates.

"My mom says your mom always has to be the boss," one girl told her.

And it was hard going to school with kids who thought your mother might be your grandmother. Margaret's was the one gray head in any parent event, so even though the others resented her bossy nature, they easily gave way to whatever Margaret Henley proposed. Otherwise, it would be like defying their own mothers.

Her mother's take-charge nature was true at home, too. Cal Henley took care of the turtles and fish and anything outdoors. Margaret Henley used to run everything else. But not now.

So how had her mother unraveled and left Blossom more alone than if both her parents had been in the Dodge that night? How had she begun dying so fast that each time Blossom came into the house she feared what she'd find when she opened the front door?

Blossom sat at her desk and covered her face with her hands. She wasn't going to get any studying done this way, so she sat up and opened her biology text, then ran her finger down the page. She'd highlighted almost the whole book, so nothing stood out. It didn't matter. She wouldn't pass the test next week just the way she hadn't passed any test Jenson had given for the past few months. Her parents were both so smart, so was it possible she'd been adopted and that was why she was so dumb?

She shook her head. Not in the least. Blossom looked like both of them and neither of them at the same time. They were certainly her parents. She'd somehow managed to inherit a great-grandparent's artistic ability and barely any of her parents' academic brilliance. Still, she'd always managed to get Bs until this year, and that had been enough. Now Cs were starting to look like gold.

She laid one cheek on the open book and stared at the last drawing she'd done and tacked to her wall. It was of Win Knight, posed the way she often saw him in class, resting his chin on his hand. His dark jagged hair fell forward over one eye. After his break up with Melinda, he'd painted one thumbnail black, and on his index finger, he'd started wearing a ring the size of a walnut. In her drawing of him, that ring sent shards of light spiking to the edge of the paper. This was the sketch she was using as a guide for the portrait she'd paint. If she could put his soul into watercolors the same way she'd done in this pencil drawing, the judges would jury her into the county-wide art show.

It was the one thing she had to look forward to this year.

Her chest tightened, and she took a deep breath to ease the pressure she felt around her heart. And if she got into the show, then it didn't matter if everyone saw who she'd chosen as her subject. If she was in the show, she wouldn't even care if Win saw her picture and still rejected her. She would have done something and succeeded for a change. She was so tired of feeling like a failure all the time.

She only had until the end of the month to send in the entry fee and make an appointment to meet with the contest committee, so she set up her easel and started working. Her loneliness faded while she held her brush and made strokes across the blank paper. While she painted, she felt as if she were with the one she was capturing there. Mostly she painted him.

Chapter Eleven

Lula

Lula chalked up another day at Las Animas High, and after dropping Blossom at her house, she wanted to be home. Butter needed a run. She needed a run, too, so she sped off—a little too fast. The cop who pulled her over refused to believe she'd been doing the speed limit and gave her the gift of a ticket. Now she craved that run.

When she entered the house, Butter jumped up and wagged from his golden retriever head to his luscious, joyful tail just as he always did any time Lula came in the front door.

"Thank you, sweetness. I needed this."

Together, they started up the stairs to her room.

"Lucia." Her father stepped into the hall and called to her. "A word before you vanish into the upper regions of this house."

Lula dragged her foot from the bottom step and turned to face him.

General Banes crooked his finger at her.

Now what?

He disappeared back into his office, the snap of his shoes precise against the hardwood floor.

She set her backpack down and, as slowly as possible, made her way into his headquarters. At the door, she patted Butter's head. "Stay." Butter wasn't allowed in The General's office.

Her father was already seated behind his desk and tucking papers into a crisp manila folder when she stopped in the doorway.

"Sit down." He pointed at the chair she was all too familiar with. She'd first bumped into the curved legs as the five-year-old, trying to sneak into his office on hands and knees. She'd counted the brass tacks holding the oxblood leather in place as a curious eight-year-old. Now a teen, she frequently sat on the seat, facing her father, waiting for his orders.

He pulled out a drawer, filed the manila folder, then knitted his hands tightly together on his desk. This was not going to be good. Lula's experience in this room, in this chair, never was. He set his eyes on her, and she kept hers steady. No way was she flinching.

"Your mother tells me you've changed your major."

Lula threw her head back and stared at the vaulted ceiling. A few days ago, she'd had one of those encounters she'd vowed to avoid with her mother. *Double damn.* Whenever Lucille caught her off-guard like that, Lula always suffered in some way. Late one Monday night last week, her mother had slipped into her bedroom. In that moment, when Lucille sat on the edge of the bed and hugged her knees to her chest, she'd been like a girlfriend there for an overnight. Lula loved that side of her mom, goofy and giggly. It was a few moments of fun, kind of a slumber party. She hadn't had one of those since she'd been twelve and her father retired— never to leave Lula or her mother on their own again, unsupervised.

Besides, last week when her mother visited, Lula had already sipped her flask of vodka down to the not-wasted-but-happy mark, so it was easy to be taken in by her mother's youthful looks and sweet voice. The skin of Lucille's throat didn't drape under her chin, and her jaw was hugged tightly by pale, perfect skin. Lula was pretty sure her mother had had a nip and tuck, but never dared say so. When Mrs. Banes left on a cruise a few years ago, and then returned looking "refreshed", she'd played up that word for a month until everyone believed one cruise had taken off ten years.

"So what are your plans these days?" her mother had said that night.

"I'm thinking about changing direction." Lula's barriers weakened by vodka had collapsed, and the truth had jumped through. Now she was about to pay the price for her openness.

Lula brought her gaze down to meet her father's. "I'm not even in college. How could I change my major?"

"You've changed what you intend to major in. And remember who you're talking to."

And I could forget?

"Business is what you've decided."

"No, sir. You decided business."

He sat back in his chair and kept his eye steady on her. "You're forgetting who's footing the bill."

She didn't want to risk letting her feelings leap across the desk at him, so she looked down at her lap. She'd let him see how much she hated him before, and she'd suffered for it. He was the only human her stare couldn't intimidate, and when she turned it on him, it created all kinds of repercussions, including military discipline. He'd confined her to the house for two weeks one summer for one nasty sideways glance. He'd never hit her, but she knew he'd wanted to sometimes because he'd set his jaw tight and held his arms behind his back. Really big confrontations made him grip the arms of the chair as if he needed to keep his hands under control. He never held back the lash of words.

When she had the hate tucked inside her belly and hidden from view, she brought her eyes up to meet his again.

"So, you'd best rethink that plan of yours." He

glanced down and tapped a finger on the notepad under his hand. "Landscape architecture is not your career path. Are we clear?"

"Yes."

"Good." He opened his laptop. Just as she stood to leave, he said, "And give me the keys to the truck."

"What?"

He held out his hand. "You were speeding today, am I correct? I believe you also were issued a citation."

"I only—" She wished The General didn't know every cop on the force.

"Keys."

She dropped them into his outstretched palm and spun away. She liked to scuff over his hardwood floor anytime they had conversations like these. It made marks. He hated those marks. But today, she chose not to scuff. She'd hold back until the topic wasn't so important and until she was closer to graduating. Besides, she needed her truck back as soon as possible.

As she left, she considered revenge against Lucille. What if The General found out about the latest gossip Melinda Bailey was spreading about his wife and his daughter's English teacher? Lula didn't believe it, but Lula wondered what her father would think.

Even better … what if she stopped lying for her mother? Poor Lucille would have to give up Greg, the pool boy, if she did.

She'd be a traitor, yes. But after ratting on her to The General, Lucille deserved it.

Outside the door, she wound her arms around Butter, the golden retriever with at least two hearts, and buried her face in the thick, silky coat. Butter's warmth soothed the knots in her stomach and cooled her desire to get back at her mother.

It might be better to get Melinda by the throat and

stop her from talking. And now that Lula had taken a moment to calm down, of course, she'd continue lying for her mother. It was just easier in the end.

Chapter Twelve

Win

That afternoon Win was already well into his after-school routine, polishing smudges that didn't exist on the one thing he loved, his 1957 T-Bird. In the school parking lot, the regular gang of six teenage boys squatted around his green beauty—specifically, Sea Spray Green—a color that made the tan, white, and black cars on the road these days boring. He gently drew the white cloth across the side of the long, lean body. What a contrast to those lumpy boxes people paid good money for.

One of the guys yelled at him about a spot he'd miss, and everybody around him laughed.

Win glanced over his shoulder. "Just point!" he said and laughed too because he loved this time with them. These guys got him. They understood how he felt about his car—about vintage cars of any kind. There were only a few kids who did, but that was perfect. A perfect few.

No one dared touch Win's car, but they were allowed to admire it as long as they kept their distance. Win was polishing the grill when Dina and Brittany ignored the invisible line *past which no one should step.* The collective gasp of Win's male audience sucked the sound from the world around him as he faced the cousins and barred their progress.

"How about a ride?" Dina asked.

Brittany, almost more annoying than Dina, balanced her books on one hip and tossed her hair over her shoulder.

"Back away." Win flicked the towel in Dina's

direction. "I told you. I don't give rides."

Dina jumped out of reach with a shriek and laughter, and Win immediately regretted that towel flick. She never took any of his warnings seriously, and now from her grin, he knew he'd encouraged her even more. Once again, he'd given her the attention she wanted.

He turned away, reached inside the driver's door, and popped the hood. While he was concentrating on removing dust from the air cleaner, a T-Bird door clicked open, and one of the guys yelled, "Hey, Win! Heads up! You got a passenger."

When he ducked from under the hood, Dina sat staring out the windshield at him. "Just a short one around the block?"

"Hey! How about me?" Brittany grasped the door handle about the same time Win pulled her back.

"Get away," he growled. "And you, get out." He opened the passenger door to haul Dina from the seat by her arm.

She looked at where his hand gripped her, then stroked his fingers, looking up through her lashes like a coy cat.

He let her go and backed away. "Stay the hell away from me and my car." His voice came out low, and, he hoped, threatening.

But Dina didn't back away, and she fixed dark-rimmed eyes on him, willing him to stay pinned to this spot near her. "About that selfie—"

"I told you, I don't know what you're talking about." Win had deleted it the moment it came into his inbox.

Dina cocked her head to the side. "Liar."

"Send me another one, and I'm reporting it to the cops."

"I knew you lied."

Brittany tugged at her. "Come on, D. Leave the idiot alone with his car, and"— she nodded at the six guys sitting nearby— "them."

With Dina in tow, Brittany huffed her way across the parking lot, and before she reached the street, she flipped him off.

He had to make that deal with Blossom. She had to get these two out of his hair. Just until he graduated and could escape this place.

Even though it was only a little after four, he packed his cloths and his polishes into the kit he kept in the trunk and drove out of the parking lot. Dina and Brittany had ended the fun, but he glanced in his rearview mirror and smiled to himself. The "car nuts" were still watching as he turned onto the main street toward … home.

But Win never used that word. He called it the house his father lived in. It was a sprawling place that people had nicknamed Knight's Castle, and it was a twenty-minute drive from school, but Win made sure he didn't arrive there much before dinner.

It was a trip he'd made so many times, but it was never one he made without wishing he could go anyplace else. Anywhere his father wouldn't show up.

The year before his mother died, his father bought ten acres of rolling hills outside of town and built stables and a four-car garage before he put up the main house. His horses and cars needed protection. His wife and son … not so much. Win gripped the steering wheel until his knuckles turned white.

If his mother had lived, Win's life would have been different. That he was sure of. He even thought she might have left the bastard, taken her son with her, and moved upstate to the property she'd inherited from her dad.

Win slowed at the towering iron gate and pressed the remote. The gate swung in and he swept up the driveway and into the garage next to a black Jag sitting smug and shiny on the left. When he hovered his hand over the hood, it was still hot. His father had just driven in. He'd be in the bar having his first martini, so if Win hurried, he might be able to grab an early dinner that Kate would have ready and eat it before his father knew he was home.

He opened the door that connected the garage to the service porch and stepped inside. The aroma of Kate's cooking filled the air.

"The prodigy returneth!" Kate already had the kitchen table set for one, and before he'd finished washing his hands at the sink, she'd ladled a rich brown stew into a deep bowl.

"That smells amazing." Win smiled as he pulled out a chair and dipped his spoon into the rich chunks of meat and potatoes. He saved his smiles for people like Kate, who mattered. She'd been his nanny, his mother's housekeeper, and his friend. Without old Kate, the "family" would have disintegrated years before. He thought about the word disintegrate. It fit perfectly. He could almost see the crumbled fragments that were all that remained of his connection with his father. The only solid relationship inside these walls was between Kate and himself.

He knew she stayed because of him and because his mother had begged her to. He'd heard bits of those conversations the way he'd heard so many secrets in their house, late at night, voices floating in the darkness.

"I need you to take care of him, Kate," she'd said. His mother's voice always came to him with these words. "Take care of him. Take care of him."

He looked up as Kate sat across from him the way

she had since he'd been three. "I want news from the outside world, Win. Lay it on me."

He shook his head and spooned more stew into his mouth. After he'd swallowed, he said, "Just one more day done at Las Animas High." He made an invisible check mark in the air.

"Lovely, but I'd really like to hear how your term paper's coming or that you aced your last test."

"Right." He swiped his mouth with a napkin and pushed his bowl away. "I'm done with my term paper. So I spent time in Cochran's class doing some research into a couple of cars I want to buy."

She laughed. "Cars. Of course. But no research into colleges? I thought that was the plan. College, and then the great car collection."

"Yeah, that's still what I'm going to do, but I might do some traveling first. I'm looking at New York." He waited a moment, thinking he should expand his vision of the world. "Or London might be good for a real change. Maybe LA." That reminded him, he had to call his Uncle Marc. If he did get into UCLA and headed to Southern California, his uncle might put him up until he found a place of his own. And he liked the idea of being with his dad's younger brother. He was so unlike Kevin Knight. His uncle surfed a lot. He traveled. And he drove hot cars, not snobby ones.

"Hold it." Kate broke into his thoughts. "So tell me, where does college fit in?"

"Between traveling and moving onto the property Mom left me." Whenever he thought about the open land that had belonged to his grandfather, then to his mother, and now to him, he knew he'd fit there. He didn't fit in Las Animas. Las Animas was like a paper calendar. Outdated. Messy and crammed with too many memories.

"It seems we have some things to talk over. I

didn't know about all this traveling you had in mind."
Kate stood. "More?" She pointed to his bowl.

"You need to ask?" He held out the bowl and she refilled it.

When he left this place, he was sure Kate would, too. He wouldn't be surprised if all the while she stayed here she didn't plot poisoning Kevin Knight every time she cooked his dinner. It wouldn't surprise him if she had the perfect poison worked out by now along with a perfect alibi. She'd loved his mother like a sister. Eva had loved her back tenfold.

Chapter Thirteen

Marty

Marty couldn't remember when he started working at Skolinski's Hardware. He just always had. Every day after school and before he worked out, he put in two hours at his parents' store. For that, he received a paycheck. Mr. and Mrs. Skolinski didn't believe in allowances. Marty was an employee with a 401K that he contributed to every year.

"Hey, Marty." His dad greeted him as Marty came in the big glass door. "That sidewalk's a mess today. We had lots of wind."

"I'll take care of it."

"And the windows."

"I'm on it, Dad."

Marty took the push broom from the closet in the back and made his way out front to clean the sidewalk. When he'd finished, he set the step stool inside and, with paper towels and window cleaner, wiped the upper part of the glass, and then scrubbed the smudges customers had made coming and going all day. The dirtier the door windows, the better the sales had been. Today there were the usual few dozen fingerprints, but by the weekend, he'd have to wash away a lot more. Dad's sales were always a hit in Las Animas.

Everyone in town knew that if you wanted the right tool, you went to Dan Skolinski's store to find it. If you wanted to know how to use that tool, you went to Dan Skolinski's store and asked him. You also went to hear Dan's latest joke. His dad had the clown gene, and he'd passed it on to Marty. Dan Skolinski didn't do back flips like his son, but he made anyone he was with laugh.

While Marty cleaned the glass, his dad was at the counter, ringing up a sale. "So how's that boy of yours doing, Roger?" his dad asked the customer.

"Better. But I cut up his credit card. No more of those bills for stuff not school related."

His dad laughed. "Like I tell my kid 'You have to learn to save first and spend afterwards.'"

Marty rolled his eyes and then moved his stool to the next window. That was one of his dad's sayings, and Marty knew it by heart just like he knew hundreds of others.

Roger leaned on the counter, hanging around for a joke—one of his Dad's really bad and very old jokes.

After bagging the merchandise, his dad said, "So here's one you can take home to the Missus. The son says, 'Mom, can I get twenty bucks?' Then Mom says, 'Does it look like I am made of money?' And the son says, 'I thought that's what M.O.M stood for.'"

Roger slapped his dad on the shoulder and laughed. "She'll use that one on our Mr. Spendthrift tonight. Thanks, Dan."

Marty let the customer out, then did a final polish on the door. He stowed the cleaning supplies and grabbed his jacket. "Got to go, Dad. See you tonight."

"I'll be later than usual," his dad called from down one of the aisles. "I've got to set up for a sale this weekend."

****

At the gym, Marty dressed down and then started with easy standing stretches. He rolled his neck, worked his way down to a slow circling of his hips and into a full set of torso rotations. He did twenty straight-legged bends, hands crossed to opposite toes. Then a set of long shoulder stretches to loosen his biceps.

Slowly, his muscles warmed, then responded and

relaxed. His head cleared of everything except the feeling of control over his body, the way he moved smoothly from one warm-up exercise into the other. He set up a perfect rhythm and his body did exactly what he willed it to do. He hummed with satisfaction.

Soon, he was ready, and he set to work on his core strength routine. It didn't take long before his shirt stuck to his back and chest. He worked through plank, side plank, roll-over, repeat. Ten. Fifteen. Moving to the bars, he did shoulder rows. Ten. Ten more. Tonight, while he did his sets, with the football team out on the field and nobody shooting baskets, he had the entire gym to himself.

He wished there was somebody to coach him. Las Animas had a coach for football and basketball, but there wasn't one for gymnastics. After reading the Gladford information, he knew he had to push himself more. He had to go online and learn new sets, more demanding ones. He had to be the very best when he got to Gladford.

He finished his workout with twenty toes to the bar, and then grabbed the rings and did a couple of skin the cats. As he rolled his body up and over, then back again, while gripping those rings, his arms felt exactly like the name of the exercise. He'd have to ice his left shoulder tonight, but he never regretted the pain.

Hurrying to the showers, he peeled out of his sweaty clothes. He couldn't wait to talk to the Gladford coach on Saturday.

****

Just before dark, Marty pulled into the familiar driveway of the small stucco house on Grove Street where, like the rooms inside, the yard was spotless. The driveway clean, no leaves. The flowerbed without weeds. All compliments of Margie Skolinski.

In the last three years, the houses on either side

had become rentals, the driveways filled with Harleys, and the yard littered with bike parts and beer cans. His mom and dad needed to relocate, but would they? Not ever. He made sure to lock his Toyota. It was old, but he couldn't afford to lose it to the neighbors or one of their biker friends. He walked toward the front door, a door he'd come through since he could remember.

When he pushed it open and stepped inside, Margie Skolinski's voice boomed from the kitchen at the back of the house. "Is that you, Marty?"

"Yep!" He sniffed the air. Pot roast and something else. Cake was his guess, and he shook his head. *More cake.* He loved the smell of warm sugar, but he regretted the carbs he'd have to pack in so he didn't hurt his mom's feelings.

For most kids, having a mom who cooked real food and baked real cakes was more than unusual. Having two biological parents under the same roof constituted a miracle. He had both the food and that miracle right here, just inside the white stucco house, with biker gangs on either side.

Margie and Dan Skolinski didn't notice those gangs. They were too busy living their lives. Mom did the hardware store books and cooked, then cleaned the house to spotless. Dad chatted up his customers and made them happy enough to return regularly even if they didn't need anything in the nail, screw, or toilet plunging department.

If only his parents understood two very important things in his life, they'd be perfect. Getting out of this neighborhood was the one thing on his agenda. And most important, get over their fear of what he loved most. Why couldn't they support this one passion he had for becoming a member of the Cirque? But it didn't look as if that was ever going to happen because they threw up every road block they could think of. All he had to do was mention the Cirque, and both of them went silent before they launched into the same conversation they'd had with him since he'd said he dreamed of being a world-class *gymnast*.

"It's a career that can only last a few years. Then what, Marty?" Those were his father's lines whenever they talked about his dream future.

"Do you know how dangerous it is? I just read about a girl who fell fifty feet at the MGM Grand. Fifty feet, Marty! I worry enough with you practicing for half-time at the football games." Here's where his mom always shook her head and put her hands on his shoulders. "You're giving me gray hairs, Marty Skolinski."

The conversations pretty much always ended with his mom misty-eyed and him feeling like a heel, so he'd stopped bringing up gymnastics, and he never mentioned Gladford.

He dropped his books onto the coffee table and went to the kitchen, where his mom was frosting a cake. He'd been right. "Chocolate?"

"Is there another kind?" She always said that, and she always turned her cheek for a kiss. Round and firmly fitted into her flowered dress, Margie Skolinski formed a solid block of cheer.

He gave her a quick peck, and at the same time, swiped a finger into the frosting bowl, then licked the dark fudge. "Nope. I can't think of any." He'd have to double down on the push- ups this week and hand off huge chunks of this cake to friends. His mom wasn't helping his training regimen. But she never tried.

"So how was your day?" His mom looked up into his face, as always, waiting for the rundown on what happened, who it happened to, and, more important, how it affected Marty.

"I'm almost done with my term paper." He beamed, thinking of how much that research had already furthered his career. *Thank you, Mr. Cochran, for the "My Career" term paper assignment.*

"I'd expect that, Marty. What else?"

He wanted to say he'd contacted the head gymnastics coach at Gladford, and that he was driving there to see the practice and talk with him on Saturday. He wanted to tell his mom that, but he knew better. When he didn't answer her, she asked, "How's that girl, Lula?"

"Being Lula." There must have been a glum edge to his voice when he said that because his mom put down the spatula and hugged him.

"I've told you. There are other girls, you know. Much sweeter ones." She let him go and picked up the spatula again. She dipped it into a glass of water, then into the frosting and swept it into a perfect swirl across the top. "There!" She set the bowl in the sink, then, washing her hands, said, "Your dad's going to be a bit late. He's setting up for the sale this weekend."

"Yeah. He told me."

"Want a snack?"

How many times had Marty heard those words? He couldn't count them. "Sure. That's great."

Chapter Fourteen

Dina

The walk from Las Animas High to their house at the end of town took about ten minutes. Dina and Brittany didn't hurry. Instead, they lingered at Vicky's House of Style, deciding which of the sweaters they'd buy as soon as they had money. Then they moved down the sidewalk to read the posters inside the glass cases at the Grand Movie Theater—anything to postpone arriving at 101 Blackstone Street.

"We should go to see this one." Brittany pointed at the poster of a woman's naked back clutched in a pair of overly muscled arms.

"Right. Our moms are going to pony up cash for us to see that, all right!" Dina grabbed her cousin's arm and pulled her down the street.

"We need jobs," Brittany announced as if the idea had just occurred to her, when in fact, getting a job to help out at home had been a topic since her family arrived from LA. "Then we won't have to ask for money from anyone to do anything."

"You find work in this town, and I'll be your slave for a year," Dina said, knowing that if there was a job available, one of her family would be on it like a dog on a steak. Her father and uncle both commuted to work in Greenlee. After three months of looking, they'd found a company that needed night janitors and gave health benefits, but the pay was pathetic. Her mom and aunt had started cleaning rich people's houses, but it wasn't regular and their pay was worse than their husbands'.

At the corner, the two turned left and walked until they came to a row of small bungalow-style dwellings and commercial buildings that lined the east side of Blackstone. Number 101 was the smallest house in the cluster, squeezed between a storage facility and one of the older homes that had been built in the seventies. These still had some of that decade's turquoise trim around faded brown-framed windows and doors. Their rental was made of cement block and stucco with a small wooden porch tacked onto it. The front yard was cemented, but weeds—not to be denied their day in the sun—had poked their way through the cracks and bloomed with fat tassels of seeds that guaranteed a larger crop next year.

Dina stopped to stare past where they lived and in the direction Win lived. Only a few miles south of here was his house, if you could call it that. She'd seen the perfect green lawn that swept up the knoll, the fountain that spurted an arched rainfall into a wide basin. The front was mostly high windows and pillars, and upstairs, glass doors opened onto curved stone balconies. One half of the place was bigger than ten of where she lived.

She looked up at their flat roof, and then at the gray blocks that enclosed the two-bedroom, one-bath house that six people shared—sometimes not very well. She bit the side of her cheek. This could barely be called a house while Win's was a mansion.

She wondered how it would be to live in a place that had more rooms than people. She and her family hadn't always lived crammed together like this. Once, they had a nice place nearer Greenlee, and her dad and mom both held good jobs at the tool and die plant. Then the plant closed and her mom managed to find work waitressing. Her dad couldn't find anything. When they couldn't pay the mortgage for several months, they lost their home, and the only place they could afford was this.

They'd been here about a year when her aunt,

uncle, and Brittany arrived. Their apartment house had burned down, and they needed somewhere to stay, just for a while. That "just for a while" had turned into almost a year, and Dina was beginning to think it would turn into forever.

Brittany opened the door and looked over her shoulder at Dina. "You coming or not?"

"Not. It's nicer out here."

"And if you think that's true, you're going blind. Come on." Brittany held the door open and Dina followed her inside.

Everything in the living room was the way they'd left it that morning. The pull-out sofa bed that the two of them shared was still unmade, and the magazines they'd read before sleeping last night were stacked on the floor.

Neither of them needed to say anything about what they had to do. In silence, they straightened the sheets and blankets, slid the bed under the frame, and put the sofa cushions back. Then they tackled the kitchen. Since both of their moms cleaned other people's houses, Dina and Brittany cleaned this one.

Dina liked sharing the job with her cousin. She wasn't so keen on sharing a bed with her, and she couldn't help but resent not having her room anymore. That had gone to her aunt and uncle.

One good thing about having her cousin live with her was they understood each other. Dina didn't feel as lonely now that Brittany lived with her like a sister. She'd never had an ally before, so for now, her life was okay, just crowded and without any privacy. She hoped her aunt and uncle would get on their feet pretty soon and move, but she also hoped they wouldn't go too far away.

"Hungry?" Brittany asked as she took down a box of cereal.

"Sure." Dina handed her two bowls and pulled out

the milk from the fridge.

They stood at the counter and spooned cereal into their mouths. Dina finished first and rinsed out her bowl, then dried it and put it away. "Mom said for once she'd like to see the sink empty of dirty dishes when she came home."

Brittany gave her her bowl. "Wash away, cuz."

"Nope. That one's yours. I'm taking a shower before I have to compete for the hot water and there's a line to get into the bathroom." Dina started toward the door.

"D."

When Dina turned to face her cousin, Brittany was sitting at the table, her head cradled in her hands.

"What's wrong?" Dina hurried to sit next to her.

"I'm … sorry," Brittany said and her voice was teary.

"For what?"

"For what's happened to you." Brittany looked up, her eyes wet. "You don't even have your own room anymore, and it's my family's fault."

Dina went to Brittany and put her arm around her cousin's shoulders. "They didn't burn down your apartment house on purpose, did they?"

Brittany shook her head and swiped her eyes with the back of her hand.

"Then stop it. I'm grumpy about the bathroom and my room sometimes, but I like you being here. You help me out a lot."

"With Win, you mean."

Dina looked away. "Yeah. I like it when you have my back."

"You're not ever going to make him like you, D. He's full of himself and…" She hesitated.

"And what?"

"He hates you. He hates me, too. I get the feeling he hates just about everybody. You don't want to hook up with a guy like that."

Brittany was right about all the hate Win had inside him, but she wasn't right about the last part. She *did* want to hook up with *a guy like that*. He was everything Dina dreamed of. He was handsome in a dark and mysterious way. He had a style like no other guy she'd ever met, and he was rich. She had to admit she loved the idea of going with a guy with money.

"Don't worry. If he hates me, then there's no danger of me and him becoming a couple." Dina squeezed Brittany's arm. "Now seriously, I'm taking that shower."

She hurried into the bathroom and locked the door. She had to get rid of the cereal churning its way to her stomach. This part was never nice, but afterward the reward made up for the discomfort. She could almost float away. A feather. Exactly what she needed to be.

She peeled out of her jeans and t-shirt, then stood sideways to look into the full-length mirror hung on the back of the door. She slid a firm hand down her belly and pressed hard to flatten the tiny bulge at her navel.

Chapter Fifteen

Clifford

Clifford Mott drove from Blossom's to the apartment house on Highway 85. It had been a motel once, but the owners had knocked down some walls and made it into apartments, then sold it and retired to Florida. The ten units were on their way to crumbling into tiny beige stucco bits before the end of the decade.

He parked inside the faded white lines with the remains of a *3* painted on the curb and turned off the ignition before rolling down the window.

Harry Mott's car was gone, and there weren't any sounds coming from behind apartment number three, so that meant both his parents must be gone.

Because some idiot had T-boned him at an intersection a few months before, the driver's door was caved in. Clifford forced it open, then lifted and held it to catch in the lock. "Jackass," he muttered, remembering the old man who'd wanted to exchange insurance information. Clifford made sure that didn't happen. Who in the hell could afford insurance?

Before going inside, he put his ear against the chipped brown wood. Still silence, so he unlocked the door and slowly pushed his way inside. It always smelled of over-use, this place. Over the years, too many sweaty bodies had lived in the few hundred square feet, and the smell they left behind would never go away—no matter how many coats of paint and gallons of disinfectant were used.

He stopped at the door to his parents' room, again alert to any sound that might come from inside. Nothing, not even snores. They had to be gone. He should have driven by the Ridgeway Bar to see if his dad's car was outside. Harry'd been on the wagon for almost three months, and that was just about the man's record for staying sober. Harry was like a volcano. He gave signals when he was about to erupt, and last week the signals had been there. Lots of pacing. Doors slamming.

All of that made Clifford uneasy, and while what he needed most was a few hours of stress-free rest, that was never going to happen, not as long as he lived with Harry.

Maybe a hot shower and something to eat would help.

When he opened the refrigerator, it was stocked with three beers and one old Chinese takeout carton, but in the back, he'd stashed half a burrito. He turned on the toaster oven and shoved the burrito inside, then opened one of the beers and kicked back to wait for his dinner to warm.

He smiled, thinking that when he'd dropped out of school and landed a steady job, he'd become the most successful Mott on the planet. If he kept stashing most of his salary, he'd shake free of this place and his parents in about six months. He lied about how much he made, so his dad didn't know about his "savings". If he had, Clifford wouldn't be able to keep any of what he'd put aside. Now, all he needed was a good plan of escape, and with Blossom in the picture, he had a lot of motivation.

The timer chimed, and he was about to take a bite of the burrito when the sound of a car out front stopped him. Harry. The car doors slammed one after the other, and a few seconds later, there they stood—Harry, a bit bleary-eyed, and Marla, her cheeks flushed. Both Motts reeked of Ridgeway Bar air. The dry season was over.

His dad wasn't a tall man, but he was broad and beefy. Harry's belly rolled over his fist-sized belt buckle, and the lower buttons of his shirt strained to hold back years of beer and chili fries. Marla, like Clifford, had a small, angular body. She had a habit of cocking her head to one side, eyeing the world the way a sparrow does, and that was what she did now.

"You lose that job of yours?" Harry said, hooking his thumbs under the hidden belt loops and pulling up his jeans.

"Nope." Clifford kept his answers short and clear. He never knew what was going to set his dad off after he'd spent a few hours drinking. And his job was always a sore topic of conversation since his dad had lost just about every one of his own for either being drunk at work or not showing up. The exception being the tool and die plant where he'd drawn unemployment until it ran out.

"Then how come you're home this danged early?"

"It's four-thirty. I get off at four." This was Clifford's other lie. He worked the early shift, and that ended at two thirty. He just didn't arrive at the motel until much later.

Harry scratched his chin and belched. "So you got some cash on you?" He took one unsteady step forward.

Marla gave Harry a gentle poke in the arm. "Now, you know he don't get paid this early in the week. Come on. Let's us just go grab a burger. How's about that?"

Harry shoved her aside too hard, and she landed on the sofa with an "Oof!"

Clifford set down the burrito and stood. He'd grown taller than his dad over the past few years, but not beefier, so he couldn't take the man on with only his hands, whether he was drunk or not. The scar along Clifford's jaw was proof of that. Harry was a well-known Las Animas brawler, and he always gave out more than he took.

Clifford dug into his pocket and pulled out a

twenty. It was better to give Harry cash and calm him down when he was on one of his binges than tell him there wasn't any. If him and Marla were lucky tonight, a twenty would get Harry drunk enough that he wouldn't make it home until morning.

"Now, that's what I like to see. A son with some ready dough." Harry snatched the bill from Clifford's hand and walked in a semi-straight line to the door. "Marla!"

She looked up, her eyes blinking as if she needed to clear them to see.

"You coming with or not?"

Marla glanced at Clifford, the silent exchange they'd had for many years. "I'd... I—"

"Oh, for Chrissake." Harry yanked open the door and slammed it behind him.

Clifford slid the curtain aside and watched as his dad's car drove away.

His mom pushed herself up from the sofa and reached out to touch his arm. "Thank you."

"Sure." About the time he turned twelve, he'd given up trying to get his mother to run away someplace safe. He hated her for sticking it out with Harry, but he couldn't hate her for being afraid. He understood how that felt, only he was tired of it, so he was going to run away without her. He was going to get as far from Harry as he could. "Want something to eat?" he asked her.

She shook her head. "I'll just go to bed early tonight. You know, get some sleep before..."

She didn't have to finish the thought. They both understood what she'd say in the end. If they were lucky, Harry wouldn't come back to the apartment, but if he did, one of two things would happen. He'd pass out on the sofa—Clifford always hoped for that—or he'd turn into a raging animal. They'd given up calling the cops for every one of Harry's drunk nights. There were too many. These days they only called when he came armed with more than his fists.

Clifford had made sure Harry didn't have his gun after the time he shot holes in the ceiling and broke the table lamp in the living room, barely missing Marla. While Harry was in police custody, Clifford stole that gun, then staged a robbery in the apartment. Marla's rhinestone necklace went missing along with Clifford's pocketknife. He hid Harry's gun and the other things he'd taken in a box at the back of the janitor's closet at the convenience store.

When he discovered the robbery, Harry even called the cops himself, and both Clifford and the cops had a hard time keeping straight faces.

One cop took down a description of the missing items and asked to see the gun permit. His face registered surprise when Harry handed it over. "Sorry, Mr. Mott. We'll do our best to get your belongings back to you." So polite.

Right, Clifford thought. Harry without a gun was the answer to the Las Animas police force's prayers. He smiled.

"What you smiling at, Clifford?" Marla asked.

He looked at her as she stood ready to close her bedroom door.

"Nothing. Just remembering something kind of funny. You need anything?"

She shook her head. "No. Nothing."

After his mom had shut herself inside the bedroom, Clifford finished his burrito and took the last swig of beer. He shoved the wrappings and the empty bottle into the trash, then showered. The pelting water eased the tight muscles in his shoulders and washed away the stink of the convenience store as well as the stink of his dad. Relaxing that way made it easy to think about his plan. That plan was still not clear, but he had parts of it. A job. Money. And now, a girl. Not just any girl, a small blonde one with green eyes and a smile like sunshine.

He stepped out of the shower and swiped the mirror. One thing he knew was that a girl like Blossom wasn't going to take any interest in him unless he did something to get her attention. All he had to do was figure out what. He switched off the light and went to his room. Tomorrow would come early, so he pulled the covers over his shoulders and slept.

The dream took him to another place, one he'd often imagined. An ocean with big waves sweeping in and out, the sun warm on his face … and sand, a soft nest under his back. The air was clean and smelled like salt. He'd find a place like this to—

A sharp noise, then his mom's scream brought Clifford back from the beach and to his bed.

"Shut up!" Harry'd made it home. Twenty dollars hadn't bought enough beer to put the drunk's brain to sleep. "I said, shut up!"

Marla's voice was muffled through the thin walls, but the pleading, then the crying became clear. He'd heard those sounds for years.

A long time ago, maybe when he'd been four, there's been other times like this—but back then, his mom was always grabbing him into her arms and running. His dad yelling after them, "Get back in here, Marla. Damn it!"

The bus stop was a block away, and Marla, her chest heaving after her dash to catch the big white bus idling at the curb, climbed inside. Clifford loved the sound of her coins dropping into the glass box. She'd let him hold the ticket, saying, "Don't lose it. We need it to ride all the way to Grandma's." That made him feel like a grown-up, and he clutched that ticket tightly the whole trip.

He closed his eyes and looked back into the past, feeling himself pressed against his grandma's round belly and being rocked on her soft lap. As she'd shushed him to sleep, he'd wished his mom's belly weren't so flat and her lap not so bony.

Another crash came from his parent's bedroom, and just as he'd done when he'd been a little kid, he curled into a tight ball, pulling the covers over his head.

He'd hide.

He'd disappear.

Vanishing like this had been his only escape since his mom stopped running out the door with him, first in her arms, then pulling him behind her by the hand when he'd gotten older.

For a while, him and his mom would stay in that small white house of his grandmother's that had trees in front. But Harry always came, his face real sad, carrying flowers and a toy. Clifford liked those times. His mom and dad together, smiling. Him with a new car or ball or something.

"She died," he whispered to himself. "My grandmother died, so Mom didn't have any wheres to run to." After that, the two of them took Harry's beatings.

Harry's fist either pounded him or her. Him or her. Tonight, it was her, and Clifford felt guilty because since he'd gotten bigger and since that one night a year ago, it was mostly her. Harry didn't take Clifford on after Clifford put him in the hospital with a kitchen knife as his only weapon.

He cupped his hands over his ears, shaking with anger, but forcing himself to stay where he was. Gently, he ran a finger along the scar on his jaw. He'd vowed to kill that man the next time they faced off. That would change what Las Animas said behind his back. *He tried to kill his dad* would become *He killed his dad.*

But a knife didn't guarantee the results he wanted. A gun would be better, and he had one stashed safely away in case he needed it. It just wasn't handy tonight.

Chapter Sixteen

Friday, The Night Before
The Game
Lula

Seated in the bleachers, more or less paying attention to the football game on the field below, Lula pulled the flask from inside her parka. She gulped some vodka before passing it to Blossom.

"Not tonight." Blossom pushed aside Lula's hand.

"More for me then." Lula shrugged and took another long sip. "What's the score?" With her knee, she nudged Win, who sat in front of them, his knit cap pulled over his ears.

He twisted around to face her. "If you watched the damned game you'd know."

"Nice one, Win." She wiped the top of the flask and held it out to him. "Sip?"

He didn't exactly growl, but it was close, so she drew away and stuffed the flask back into her inside pocket.

"The kick's good!" Blossom clapped her hands and bounced up and down on the metal seat. "Right now, I love Branch Redford. He's one heck of a good quarterback. And look!" She pointed at Marty who was leading the other cheerleaders out for the victory routine.

Marty did his famous series of back flips while the fans in the small stadium shook their black and gold pompoms to the beat of the marching band's victory song.

Lula shook her head. "I swear his spine has to be made of elastic."

"He's so good," Blossom said with a huge smile.

She jumped to her feet and yelled, waving her arms. "Go, Branch! Go, Marty!"

Lula pulled her back onto the seat. "I say 'Go Party!'" She leaned forward to tap Win on the shoulder and shouted at him over the noise. "Hey, Sir Baldwin, are we partying tonight?"

When he looked at her this time, his eyes could have been lasers set to stun. She sat back. It was time to put some distance between him and her. Why did he always have to be so up-tight anyway? But she knew. He'd started being grumpy and withdrawn since his mom died. She wanted to tell him three years was long enough to be bitter about losing someone he loved, but she didn't know how to do that without stirring him up more than usual. And then there was Melinda Bailey and all the crap she'd pulled on him. That's what had finally turned him into the Dark Knight on campus.

"Hey, man, just want to know if you're coming to the party," she said. "Marty told me he finally convinced his mom and dad to turn over their house tonight."

"Later. Maybe." Without a glance back, he got up and clumped down from the bleachers and onto the field where the Las Animas players exchanged victory hugs, and the band blared the school song. He hunched into his sweatshirt and loped across to the opening in the chain link fence.

Lula stared after him, shaking her head. "Hopeless." She looked back at Blossom. "What about you? Are you coming to Marty's?"

"I can't."

"What's with you guys? We just won the biggest games of the season and nobody's celebrating?"

Blossom stretched and stood. As usual, her sweater was undone at the front so her lacy chemise peeked through.

Lula reached up and fastened the top button. "Your skivvies are showing, sweet thing."

But Blossom didn't pay any attention. She had her eyes set on Win's retreating back. "I've got tons of homework already and Jenson's nailing us with another science test on Monday."

"Blossom! You idiot! You'll have all day to study on Sunday." Lula stood and threw her arm around Blossom's shoulder. "Come on."

"No. I've got my eye on that A."

Lula smiled, but she hid her smile's meaning. Blossom Henley had zero chance of acing that science test. Just like she had zero chance of becoming a marine biologist the way she said her father had wanted. The girl was sweet and she loved her like a sister, but, honestly, Blossom would do better selling fish, not studying them. Only she either didn't know it or refused to accept it.

Lula had often considered telling her to stick with that little painting hobby of hers and stop worrying about numbers and formulas, but she wasn't going to. Blossom already had enough on her plate, and Lula couldn't add to her best friend's troubles. Sweet Blossom would have to figure it out all on her own.

"Well, I'll catch you later then. I'm going to Marty's for some R and R. So long! I have to snag a ride tonight before everyone's gone."

"No wheels of your own?"

"Nope."

"Where's the truck?" Blossom asked.

"It's in the … garage." Lula pushed into the milling crowd, without explaining her missing truck and found her way to the football field. Marty's Toyota ran most of the time and had gas to make it go, so she'd hitch a ride with him. She sure couldn't ask Win, not with his snarly attitude set to high tonight. Besides, he never gave lifts to female people. She'd only seen three girls in the passenger seat of his precious car. And each of them lasted about as long as milk with an old sell-by date. She'd worried that Melinda Bailey might be a keeper for a while, but enjoyed gloating when Win dumped her, too, just like all the others.

She grinned. Melinda spread the rumor that she'd broken it off with Win, but Lula knew the truth. She'd overheard that conversation and still loved the sound of Win's words replaying in her head. "Get away from me, and stay away from me. I've had it!"

"Yes," she whispered into the chilled air, thrilling to that memory. "Way to go, Win! And bye-bye, Melinda Bailey."

While she searched the area, she spied Dina a few feet away, looking thinner than a thread. Did that girl ever eat? When Dina caught Lula with her eyes fixed on her, Lula grinned and Dina turned away, then Brittany joined her cousin, and they hurried off the field.

"That's one weird twosome." Vodka made her talk to herself. She held the flask to her ear and shook it. "Sounds like I'm running low."

She spotted Marty on the sidelines and went to him. "Hey, Marty. Can I ride with you? The General's locked up the Tundra. He says I'm too wild on Friday nights. Imagine! Me!"

"Imagine!" Marty twirled his keys and grinned. "You can ride with me anytime, Lula."

She'd been in school with Marty since first grade, and she swore he'd never grown taller after fifth. They'd been eye-to-eye back then, but by the seventh grade, she could look over his head. Now that they were juniors— thanks to the General's tall genes—she'd soared to five-eight, and Marty barely reached her shoulder.

"Stop at the convenience store across from the

school. I need supplies." Lula patted the side of her parka, then pulled her coat apart to show Marty the flask.

"No alcohol, Lula. I told my mom—"

"Will you chill? I'm after some Dr. Pepper. It makes me burp."

"Sure, but I'm not going in there. That creep Mott's probably working tonight."

She ruffled his hair, and he ducked away to smooth it back into place.

"Don't fret. Mama Lula will take care of everything."

At the convenience store, Lula prowled the soft drink aisle. She examined the stack of Coke and Sprite, then picked up a large Dr. Pepper. On her way to the checkout, she walked along the liquor section and snatched a pint of vodka.

Just as Marty had said, Clifford Mott was at the counter, but next to him was Ryan Connell who'd graduated a few years before. They both eyed her, but Ryan's look was a straightforward, lust-filled leer. Clifford's unblinking gaze gave her the creeps.

"Working late, Clive?" She put the vodka and Dr. Pepper on the counter and dug into her pocket for money.

Clifford didn't answer, but his lips pressed together into a thinner line than before.

"Oops. I meant Clifford." She grinned, but she made sure there was a touch of evil in it.

Clifford flexed his fingers and looked up at her through his lashes. "No. I just came to check on the new clerk." He nodded his head toward Ryan at his side. "You're my first and last customer tonight. That must be special, right?" He rang up the Dr. Pepper and slid it across to her. "You got an I.D. for that?" He pointed at the vodka.

"Sure." Lula pulled out a license from her hip

pocket. "You know I always have my I.D."

"Hey, I don't think she's twenty-one, man," Ryan said. Clifford shot a side glance at him, and he backed away with his palms out. "Okay, man. Whatever you say."

Clifford bagged the vodka, then held it out to her until she pulled it from his hand.

Stepping back, she lifted the bag overhead like an explanation. "Marty Skolinski's having a celebration at his place. We won."

"I know. I was at the game," Clifford said. "Catch you later. Lula."

"Sure, Clive." And she was out the door and into Marty's car. As they pulled out of the parking space, she looked back at the store and into Clifford Mott's eyes. She couldn't stop the prickly feeling down the back of her neck. He had some weird stuff going on in his life, that was for sure. She waved, but he stared back at her without returning the wave. She shivered as if a piece of ice were sliding down her back.

"You cold?" Marty asked as she climbed into the car.

"No. Just *chillin'*. Mott's gone more creepy than usual."

"I didn't think he got to you."

"Not usually. Tonight, he's outdone his usual cobra stare."

Marty laughed. "Don't insult the cobras of this world."

Chapter Seventeen

Clifford

Clifford stared after Lula on her way out of the store and kept his gaze on her as she climbed into the car with Marty Skolinski at the wheel. She settled in next to him, and to Clifford, they looked like a cartoon couple with her towering over Marty even while sitting down. He shook his head. *Real weird.*

He'd watched Marty at the game tonight, his cheerleader's body flipping into the air and landing like he wasn't trying hard, just moving as if it was how everybody moved. When he glanced at the crowd, a lot of kids were locked onto the cheerleader, as many as were on Branch Redford. Blossom sure was. She jumped up, yelling his name, waving her arms.

Clifford didn't want her focused on Marty. He wanted her focused on him. Marty was a monkey, and Clifford hated him for the show-off he was.

When Lula spotted him staring at her through the window, she waved. Everything about her irritated him— almost as much as Marty did. She sneered at him with those eyes, and she tried to get a rise out of him, calling him Clive. He'd make sure to remember that. Somehow, he'd get back at her.

As Marty pulled away and into the street, the interior car lights came on, and Lula's long, dark hair shimmered like glass. Clifford would love to change the way she looked at him. If he had his way, she wouldn't sneer when their eyes met. He clenched his fists hard, cutting into his palms with his nails.

"Hot stuff," Ryan Connell said.

Clifford flinched. For a moment he'd forgotten he

wasn't alone, and he ducked his head so the guy couldn't see the look on his face. "Not my type," he said and finished counting the money in the register.

Ryan laughed. "She sure is mine."

Clifford found the checklist for closing the store and went over it with Ryan. "I'll have my cell if you have any problems or questions. Just double-check the door, and be sure you set the alarm."

Ryan nodded. "Got it."

"Good. Then I'm out of here." Clifford pushed open the door and started toward his car. He was glad he'd finished showing the new clerk how to close up the store and glad Lula Banes was out of his sight for now.

He pulled his parka closed against the cold night air and walked quickly back along the front of the stadium. And that's when he saw the girl crossing the street. It took a moment, but he recognized her when she glanced up before stepping off the curb.

Blossom.

Her head down, her hands in her pockets, she seemed so sad and lonely. That was exactly the way he felt most of the time, and that was something else that made him feel close to her. Blossom might be the one who understood how he felt. She might be the one who would listen and not cut him off, not look at him like something she'd stepped in and had to clean off her shoe.

He was so tired of ignoring the looks he got from those high school creeps. And he was tired of pretending he didn't notice. One of these days he'd change those looks they gave him.

He'd figure out how by the time he drove out of Las Animas forever, but for now, he'd follow Blossom. To be sure she got home safe.

Chapter Eighteen

Blossom

After Win disappeared across the football field and Lula left the bleachers to find Marty, Blossom sat back down on the bench, listening to the shuffling of feet and the last blasts of horns marking a victory for the Las Animas team. She folded her arms across her chest against the chill of the night and waited as the crowd slowly drained from the stadium. Soon, only a few kids remained, then finally, all of the seats were empty and the only victory shouts came from outside on the streets.

She didn't want to return home, but she didn't want to go to the party by herself either. She'd hoped Win would ask her. What a stupid girl she was. He'd never ask her to go anywhere with him.

Winding her scarf around her neck, she set off on the five-block walk from Las Animas High to her house. The main street was still jammed with kids piling into cars and leaving for different parties, but once Blossom started down one of the side streets, it became quiet with only one or two cars passing.

A truck slowed next to her and one of the Redford twins rolled down the driver's window and waved. She could never tell if she was talking to Branch or to Carter until one of them said something.

"Hey, Blossom. Want a ride to Marty's? Dina and Brittany can squeeze up and make room." He jerked his thumb to the back.

That was Carter. His voice had a higher pitch than Branch's. He sounded younger.

Dina looked out from the extended cab window, but her expression didn't seem to say she'd do anything to make space for another passenger, especially another female.

Blossom shook her head. "No. That's okay. I'm going home."

"I can give you a lift to your house, if you want," Carter said.

She shook her head. "I'd like the walk. But thanks anyway."

"Okay. You got your phone, right?"

"Yes."

"If you change your mind, give me a ring." He rolled up the window and drove off.

The air had turned even colder, so she shoved her hands into her pockets. Now that the truck had driven away, the empty street became even quieter. The sound of her boots against the pavement seemed loud and lonely. Otherwise, there was a stillness in this cold, a hush as if the night would curl around her, make her a part of it and she would vanish inside its dark fist. When she looked up, only a few white bloated clouds hung in the dark sky.

There'd be a storm soon. She was sure of it. And it would be a cold one because already her breath came like white puffs into the air. She should have taken the ride from Carter.

Shivering, she hunched inside her coat and pulled it closed at the neck. When she reached the end of the second block and was about to step off the curb into the street, the sound of footsteps came from behind. Slow and deliberate steps, not hurried, just keeping pace with her. She crossed the street and walked faster. Las Animas was a small, safe town. Nothing worse than petty thefts ever happened here, and those were done by kids who came from the bigger cities like Temple or Greenlee.

The footsteps quickened to match hers. Fear

pushed thoughts about how cold she was from her mind. Now she worried about the kids from other towns and what they might be up to on a big game night in Las Animas. She hadn't thought about that until now, and now was too late. She quickened her pace.

She came to the end of the next block where the golden glow of a streetlight poured over the intersection. From the sound, whoever was behind her was very close.

Feeling more confident in the bright light, she stopped and turned. It was Clifford Mott from the convenience store, and he was staring at her with eyes that she could only describe as haunted. She glanced around quickly, wishing the street wasn't empty.

"It's cold out tonight," he said. "I saw you at the game. That was one awesome conversion old Branch made, wasn't it?"

When he spoke, she relaxed. Her heart rate slowed. He sounded different than she'd expected. His voice was soft and almost sweet. If his face hadn't had such a dark look, he might even be nice looking—tall, a little skinny, but her artist's eye studied the angles, and she thought he'd be interesting to draw. He didn't seem to be the way Lula said he was. She always called him a *defective*.

"It was a great game," Blossom said.

"How come you're not at one of the parties? I hear there are a lot around town."

"I've got a biology test Monday. I have to study. And … and I better go or, you know, I won't do anything but face plant on my books." She turned away and crossed the street, but he stayed at her side until they came to her block.

"You live there, right?" He pointed ahead, toward where her house sat sheltered behind the tangle of dense trees.

"Yes." She swallowed. "I do." A trickle of cold ran through her at the thought that he knew where she lived. Lula's voice whispered in her head, *"He's warped. Steer clear of that Mott creep."*

But Lula never saw the good in anybody. She tolerated people, and not much more than that. Blossom still wondered how she'd been allowed into Lula's exclusive circle. She shook her hair back over her shoulder and kept her pace steady until she came to the long walkway that led to her front door.

"Nice talking to you," she said. "I've got to run. Biology." When Clifford remained quietly staring at her, the silence between them made her uncomfortable. "And I'm working on a painting. I have a deadline to finish it." Why she'd said that she'd never know.

"You're an artist." He smiled, looking surprised but pleased. That smile softened his face. He became a much younger, defenseless Clifford for a moment before the tightness around his eyes returned, and he once again looked like the convenience store clerk everyone avoided.

She nodded. "I'm trying to be one." Another silence fell between them. "Well, I have to go. My mom's waiting up." Which wasn't true, but she wanted him to know someone was inside.

He didn't say goodnight, and when she glanced back, he stood watching her. She waved to him, hoping to add a touch of friendliness, but even so, the tiny insect feet of apprehension crept up her back.

Chapter Nineteen

Clifford

He'd surprised her, and she'd been scared, but that would be normal. She was alone. It was dark. When Blossom turned and saw he was the one behind her, she only drew back a bit, but didn't blow him off the way everyone else in this freaking town did. She'd even kept her eyes on his face. He touched his cheek, wondering what she thought about how he looked. But it must have been good because she'd let him stay with her until they reached her driveway. And as he waited for her to go inside her house, she'd waved goodnight.

"Sunshine even after dark. Blossom Henley." Clifford said her name, then tapped his lips with his finger, thinking. She was an artist, like him. Next time he'd show her something he'd drawn. That would give them more to talk about. He walked down the street, lighter than he'd felt in years. He had the feeling she liked him. The thought of that spread warmth across his chest, and he opened his arms, leaning back to stare up into the cold, almost cloudless sky. "Yes. I think she does."

Since he'd followed her from the stadium to her street, he had about a quarter of a mile back to the center of town and his car. That was okay. He'd finally talked to Blossom. The walk across town had been worth his while.

He took his time and enjoyed the quiet streets. It was a perfect way to go over what had just happened and how she'd made him feel. Imagine feeling like this all the time. It'd be possible if she was his girl.

"My girl," he said, his words streaming cold and

white in the frosty air. And he repeated those two words again and again silently all the way to the converted motel.

The windows were dark, and when he opened the door, the tired refrigerator's hum and muffled snores from his parents' bedroom were the only sounds.

He sniffed the air. The room smelled like stale beer and cold pizza, dampening his hunger. In spite of the cold, he opened the windows in his room before stretching out on the bed to stare up into the darkness. For the first time in years, he felt a warmth in his chest, something he finally decided was hope. Hope for a better life with someone who cared for him.

He wrapped his arms around himself, imagining holding her to him, having her with him all night. But that couldn't happen as long as he lived in this place with Harry and Marla. How many more months would he have to save up to escape this crap apartment and his parents? If it was just him, he figured six months. With Blossom, he'd need more money and more time to earn it. He sat up, suddenly angry at the idea of another year like this one. He might make it through if Blossom was a part of his life. How was he going to be sure she was?

And sometime between undressing and slipping between the sheets, a vague shape of an idea fell into place.

He pulled back the covers and switched on his light. From the top shelf of his closet, he pulled out the box where he kept a few sketching supplies he'd splurged on—colored pencils and pens, a large sketchpad, and a roll of two-sided tape he used to put up some of his work at the back of his closet. Harry didn't usually come in his room, but Clifford didn't want to risk his dad seeing his art. That had only happened once a long time ago, and Clifford still shook with anger remembering his work being ripped and tossed on the floor.

Gripping the pad of paper, he gulped down the hate that rose like bile. *Bury that hate where Harry can't see it. Only a few more months, and then you won't ever have to see that man again.*

He flipped through the pad that was filled with a lot of drawings he'd never share with anyone. On them, Harry had died in as many ways as possible. Marla was always just a ghostly figure in the background. There were no self-portraits. Sketching his image was the last thing he thought of doing.

From the bottom of the box, he lifted out a small white book. A gift from Mrs. Stiles, his Freshman English teacher. Stiles had taught the one high school class he actually attended. One time she kept him after class and he slouched at his desk, arms crossed, waiting for the usual crap teachers laid on him. Lazy. Disrespectful. Sneaky. Those were the words he remembered they used while pointing at him.

Not Stiles. She'd sat at the desk next to him and asked him why he didn't think he could succeed in her class. Then she listened.

"I disagree," she'd said when he'd finished. "You're very capable of doing the work. Don't sell yourself short."

The next day she'd given him the white book, a journal she called it.

"Many great people have written down their daily experiences and thoughts in these. It might help you to sort out how you feel about yourself and the decisions you need to make in these last years of high school if you were to keep a journal of your own."

Since she'd listened to him, Clifford listened to her, and most important, he believed her. If he wanted a shot at being *great* at anything, he'd put down ideas in one of these books with empty pages. The problem was he never had anything to write, so finally he drew pictures of things that made him feel good. Harry and Marla weren't in his journal.

The smooth cover of the book had finger marks along the edges where he'd opened and closed it so many times. Now an idea was forming about how this journal might let him do more than just draw what he called his *feel-good* pictures. And it all centered on Blossom Henley.

He took last year's Las Animas yearbook from the bottom drawer of his dresser and placed it on the bed alongside the journal. He'd never had a yearbook before. His parents wouldn't buy him one, and he didn't care about it anyways. He'd never spend money on something filled with photos of people he didn't care about. But he'd found this one on a bench outside the convenience store at the end of last year and brought it here. When the idiot who'd left it behind came looking for it, Clifford shrugged. "Never saw it, man. Sorry."

He hadn't known the reason for keeping that yearbook until now. Excited by what he was about to create, he flipped through the pages, then stopped when he came to last year's sophomores. He drew a finger down the images until he found her. Gently, he stroked her cheek, and that feeling of warm calm came again, this time stronger.

Her shoulders were bare and her head tilted so her chin angled toward the camera. Even in this small picture, the green of her eyes glinted like jewels. He touched her hair, imagining the feel of it. Then from the same drawer, Clifford took the scissors and with slow, careful snips removed her picture. He pressed bits of the two-sided tape on the back of Blossom's image, then placed that onto the first page, which he'd left blank except for his name at the bottom.

When he closed the cover, it looked too plain. The way it was now wouldn't impress her enough to even open it. He had to make it better.

Taking up the utility knife, he bent over the white leather jacket, and with care, carved a heart in the center, being sure to have Blossom's image centered inside it. Then, with red ink, he drew tiny hearts pierced by arrows around her face. In one corner, he inked in a bright yellow sun with rays of light reaching to the edges.

He'd begun to make a present just for her. It would be a one-of-a-kind gift, and it was going to include … what? He tapped his fingers on her image. "My art but something more. Maybe … a letter."

Now, all he had to do was think of what to write, so it would be perfect. He had to show her how much he cared for her. If she understood his feelings, then he was sure she'd care for him, too. Maybe not right away, but with time.

Chapter Twenty

Win

After the game, Win ran down the bleacher steps, with one thought propelling him. Escape. Every guy he knew said Lula was good-looking, hot, a girl they stared after whenever she passed. To him, she was a pain in the ass and forever in his face. Why did she have to be at the center of any get-together, and loud about it?

And Blossom had a way of stirring him up that he didn't like either. Her damned lacy underwear—always just a glimpse, a tease. Her scent, not sweet exactly, but how the air smells after a first rain. Her hair a tangle of long honey-colored silk.

Damn.

He jogged across the football field toward the parking lot and all the way to the end. He always left his vintage T-Bird as far away from the tight spaces as possible. He never parked it where jerks could ding the sides with their cheap Volkswagen doors. He'd invested in special touch-up paint, but hated having to use it. It never looked right.

He stretched out his long legs and aimed for his car, his key already in his hand. He jammed that key at the lock but missed. "Damn it, Blossom." He ran his finger along the small scratch he'd made, then rubbed at it with the tip of his sweatshirt. He had to face the truth. She disturbed him even when she wasn't nearby. She might be more of a problem than that stalker Dina because there were times he didn't want her to leave him alone. Just thinking that made him angry, mostly at himself.

His breaths were deep and fast from his run, but

now he had to admit they were also from thinking about Blossom. He leaned against his car and stared into the night sky.

Knock it off, idiot! Remember what the plan is. Focus.

He steadied his hand and inserted the key carefully into the lock this time. Melinda Bailey had just burned him royally, reminding him about the meaning of love, and reminding him that he'd already seen what happened when people "fell" into it. His mom and dad were perfect examples of how it wasn't pretty and how that kind of "falling" broke a lot more than bones.

Opening the car door, he slid onto the carefully preserved pale green leather. He inhaled the smell of it, replacing the memory of Blossom's rainy day scent. For a moment, he sat in the darkness, emptying his senses of her, denying that she stirred him up the way she did. He wanted to make a business deal with her. That was all. And if he could get a few uninterrupted minutes alone with her, that's what he'd do. Since he never could manage a private conversation at school, he'd have to try something else, and he'd do that tonight.

He started the engine and drove out of the parking lot toward his father's house, taking his time as always, but still finding himself there before he wanted to be.

Before Win opened the connecting door between the garage and the kitchen, the aroma of Kate's Friday night special lasagna made his stomach gurgle. He didn't have to see inside to know that she'd be at the center of the kitchen, in command, and most of all, her solid, abundant self would be there to welcome him. Coming into Kate's kitchen was the only thing he'd miss once he quit Las Animas.

He pushed open the door. "Yo! How's the best chef in this state tonight?" He was often amazed at how different his voice sounded when he talked to Kate from when he talked with anyone else. It had warm light in it. And that was the best description he'd ever come up with.

"You must have won the game." Kate poured herself a shot of bourbon over ice and eased into the chair across from him. Taking a delicate sip, she closed her eyes and leaned back to savor her one and only alcoholic beverage. He'd never seen her drink anything else, and he'd never seen her drink more than one small glass at dinner time with him as company. The bottle in the cupboard seemed to last a year before it was replaced with a new one. She leveled her eyes on him, her dimples deepening with a smile she always welcomed him with. "I believe I heard victory in your voice just now."

"Yep. Branch Redford's the king tonight. He made three touchdowns, and every conversion was good."

"No celebrations?"

"There are a lot of them. I might go to Marty's later."

The air crackled with what they weren't saying. Fridays were his father's date nights, and he never missed dragging home an overnight guest that Win and Kate had to put up with at the breakfast table Saturday mornings. That's why Win had jumped at the offer of an early Saturday morning shift at Blendz and Moore, that and the need for the entrance fee at the Classic Car Show next summer. He never touched his trust-fund money. That, he was tapping into when he started building his car collection.

Kate finished the bourbon and thumped her glass on the table. "His company's already here tonight."

"Anyone I know?" His laugh was breathy and mocking.

"Nope." She pushed herself out of the chair and went to the oven to serve a large square of lasagna onto a plate. "New one." She didn't hide the anger on her face or in the way she scraped the spatula along the bottom of the serving dish.

He didn't react so she could see, but inside everything constricted.

He wolfed down the lasagna in a few bites and stood up. "Then I can't wait to shower and get to that party."

She took his plate to the sink. Then just as they did every night, Win wrapped his arms around her sturdy shoulders, and she hugged him like the three-year-old he used to be when she first came to work for Eva Knight.

****

Once he'd showered and dressed, Win picked up his cell and punched in Blossom's number. She answered on the third ring, and he spoke at the same time she was saying hello. "I'm going to Marty's. Want to come?"

The pause on the other end of the phone was only one heartbeat, but it was there. Was she about to say no?

Then he heard, "Sure. I guess."

"Meet me outside your house in ten."

He stuffed the phone into his pocket and bounded down the stairs, heavy-footed. He always gave his father and *the date* advance notice of his arrival. He didn't want to surprise them and maybe have to interrupt some too-cozy moment between the two.

Reaching the living room, he stopped and waited to be noticed. His father sat on the sofa with one arm slung behind a woman wearing a tight sweater, her hair streaked with blonde highlights. She tipped her head to the side, examining Win.

His father looked up. "Ah, Win. This is Gabby. Gabby, my son."

She smiled and extended her hand. "I've heard so much—"

"I'm going out. See you later."

The closest exit was the front door, so Win made for it and was gripping the large brass handle as his father said, "Teenagers!"

Win didn't have to see what his father did next. He'd witnessed it plenty of times over the years. Kevin Knight always shook his head and worked his face into something as close to "look how these kids act" and "I've done my best, but…" as possible.

He was almost outside when his father called to him. "Make sure you're home by midnight." He must have turned to his date. "Honestly, you can't get a word out of these kids anymore."

Win let the door slam, rattling the entry window. Giving himself a moment to let the anger subside, he stood with his back against the glass pane. He'd escaped the house again. Now he had one more escape to set up tonight.

He backed his T-Bird out of the garage and onto the driveway. He was pretty sure Blossom would take the deal he was going to offer if he ever had a chance to explain it. It was the way her eyes stayed on him that extra beat when she thought he didn't notice. It was when she hung back, slightly behind Lula, being Lula's shadow, but all the time, studying his face. Her eyes, cameras, storing his image to look at later. She was the only girl who could do that and not totally freak him out. That's why he'd chosen her to help him. He could stand to be with her.

He exhaled slowly between his teeth. He could lie to a lot of people, but he couldn't lie to himself. He couldn't only stand to be with her, he liked being with her, and that's what had him worried, but he wasn't going to let another girl into his life. All he had to do was keep to his plan and not think about anything else.

He made a right turn back toward town. Now he was looking forward to the party.

Chapter Twenty-One

Friday, The Night Before
The Party
Blossom

Blossom held the phone in her hand for a moment before putting it down on the nightstand. She hadn't imagined it. Win had called her. He'd asked her to go to Marty's.

The boy in the painting stared back at her. The expression in Win's eyes and the slightly off-centered, irritating—yet captivating—grin he aimed at the world were perfect. That grin had been the most challenging part of this piece, but she'd finally nailed it on paper. It was a touch surly and guarded, but it wasn't exactly the Win he showed to everyone. No. She'd hinted at the person she dreamed about in that half-moon curve of his lips. That kind of smile rarely crept across his mouth, but when it did, it was Baldwin Knight to the core, the core she wanted to tap into. And she would if only in the picture.

She knew there was passion in him, too. Mostly a passion for vintage cars, but at times she'd catch a look in his eyes, a look that said he had room for another kind. She wanted that to be true, and she still hadn't given up hope that there might be some of that for her.

Now that she'd finished his portrait in time to meet the deadline for the Water Media Showcase, she felt less stressed, but at the same time more. She'd never entered her work before, and for a couple of reasons. Even though she had dozens of paintings finished, she never had something she thought might be good enough, and she always had her dad at her back with his plans for her future—none of which included art. This time she knew her watercolor was good, and this time she was the one making the plans.

Plans! Oh no. She only had ten minutes to get ready, and she was a wreck. Her hair was bundled on top of her head like a messy bird's nest, tiny spores of ocher and blue spattered her blouse, and it would take a sturdy scrub brush to clean under her nails.

Quickly, she put away her paints and rinsed the brushes. Then she stepped back from Win's image and opened her closet. She'd wear the deep lavender dress. It set off her eyes. Emeralds, a boy told her once. That's what her eyes reminded him of.

The dress was a little over the top for the after-game party, and she'd be the only girl not in jeans. That was okay. Jeans weren't her. And she felt more comfortable wearing what was, even if she stood out as different. She'd gotten used to Lula's nickname. Retro Girl suited her—a lot. And who knew but that this dress might be sexy enough to catch Win's eye and keep him focused on her tonight.

She held it up against her and looked in the full-length mirror, letting a sigh filled with very little hope escape her lips. "I wish."

But she had to think he'd come around one day. She had to or she'd never make it through this year and the next. And thinking about how she'd be with that boy she'd just painted, the real one, not the one she'd created for the competition, made her stomach go into free fall. He'd be next to her, maybe touching her. She had to look special tonight. She closed her eyes, imagining his breath across her cheek.

Her hands and nails did take extra time, and the bathroom sink was ringed with a muddy mix of colors she'd scrubbed away. She brushed her hair, then daubed on lip gloss before stepping into the dress. The front had a dozen buttons from waist to neck, and she fastened them all, then laughing, carefully undid the top button. Now looking at her reflection again, she undid another.

Chapter Twenty-Two

Marty

It was only ten, but his party was at full rock-on-wild. Marty's big screen TV blared music, and if kids weren't dancing, they were in corners making out or in the kitchen scarfing the chips and dip. Others roamed the backyard, a drink in one hand, and an arm flung around a date. Despite the "Don't bring any dope or booze!" warnings he'd given, the air inside and out was flavored with a lot more than nicotine, and breaths reeked of spiked 7-Up and Coke.

Marty wrapped himself in his Mexican poncho, donned a wide-brimmed sombrero, and squeezed the arm of the first girl who passed him slowly enough for him to latch on.

She grinned but shrugged him off. Sometimes when he'd just done his cheerleading routine or, like now, played the fool, a girl found him irresistible. He planned to hook up with someone tonight, using his oversized hat as the lure.

Once he spied Lula, he made a straight line to where she leaned against the wall and sipped from her flask, bobbing her head in time to the tunes.

"*Hola, Senorita.*" He touched the wide straw brim of his sombrero.

"You look ridiculous."

"I'm so glad you came, Lula. Next time you need a ride, ask somebody else."

She grabbed his sleeve and hauled him beside her against the wall. "Here." She shoved her flask at him. "Chill, Pepe."

He took a quick swig and choked. "That is *not* Dr.

Pepper."

Lula grinned.

He handed the flask back. "You can't resist me much longer. It's only a matter of time."

"Grow up, Marty." She patted him on his sombrero and joined the dancers.

He wished he didn't have the hots for Lula. She inflicted great pain on him, but he couldn't stop fantasizing about the two of them together. His head nestled between her breasts, his lips on hers. Her arms around him and pulling him close to her. He stayed at the wall, his eyes closed with images of Lula scrolling across his lids.

A sound of shattering glass came from the kitchen and Marty's eyes flew open. "Crap!" He dashed down the hall. This party could be getting a little too wild. He didn't want any breakage that he'd have to explain to his parents. He'd had to do a lot of convincing for them to give him the house tonight and even more to get them out to dinner and a movie. He'd never be able to do that again if his mom's things were broken.

At the kitchen door, he sized up the damage. Not too bad. It was only a glass, and from the look of it, not one of Mrs. Skolinski's matched sets.

"Hey, sorry, man." Branch Redford, his tongue thick and his eyes slightly out of focus, held out a piece of jagged glass. "It slipped."

Marty grabbed the broom and mop. "Here, Mr. Quarterback hero." He shoved the mop at Branch. By the time Marty had swept away the broken glass and Branch had sopped up the sticky cola, the kitchen was filled with a whole new crew looking for food.

"Keep out of the cupboards, you hear?" He shoved a stack of plastic cups into the center of the counter. "Use these, okay? My mom's going to kill me if we break any of her good stuff."

Some of the kids looked as if they'd heard him. Others didn't.

"Only if you want to party here again, understand?" He shook his head and went in search of Lula.

He found her on the patio, the flask in one outstretched hand, twirling more or less to the beat of the music.

"Hey, Marty. Check me out! I'm flying." She swooped around once more and stopped, facing the lawn where someone was bent over barfing.

"Douchebag," she yelled at the guy's backside before falling onto the patio lounge chair and letting her flask tumble onto the flagstones. "Empty. Yep indeedy."

Marty tossed his sombrero over her stomach and squatted on the ground next to her. "I'm sober, Lula. Want me to prove it?" He grinned.

"Go away."

"Nope. I've got you now. You can't walk. All you can do is stay right here and kiss me." He leaned over her, but she pressed her hand against his chest.

"I'm not that drunk, 'kay?"

"I'll find more vodka. Be right back." Marty pushed himself up.

She grabbed his pant leg and tugged him down beside her. "I'm done. No more tonight." She blinked up at him, but he was sure she wasn't focusing.

"How many Martys do you see?"

"Some."

"You always say that about this time. Come on." He hauled her to her feet. "Let's go toss your cookies and make you all better."

"Not there." She pointed at the yard where the barfer was still at it.

"Bathroom it is." Marty pulled her arm over his shoulder. It hung limp like something newly dead as he dragged Lula into the hall bathroom.

When he thought she'd made herself spew enough vodka to stop the room from circling, he handed her a damp cloth and a glass of water.

"Why?" she asked.

She didn't have to explain her question to him.

"Because I love you."

She rolled her eyes.

"And because you have to help me clean up before my parents come home."

"That's more like it."

Chapter Twenty-Three

Blossom

Blossom snatched up her coat and walked to the door when she heard Win's car pull into the driveway. Her hand on the knob, she waited a few beats more, not wanting to seem too eager, but also not wanting to be one of those silly girls who played games to keep boys *guessing*.

He met her as she walked outside. "Thanks."

She stared up at him, puzzled about why he was thanking her.

"For coming with me tonight. Last minute and all."

It was the way he said it—she knew he was sincere. He understood how a last-minute date like this might make a girl feel. She liked his apology. She also liked when he opened the door of the T-Bird for her. She looked over her shoulder at him. "I'm glad you called. I wanted to celebrate. It was a great game."

For the rest of the drive, Win cranked up the radio and they didn't speak. She was grateful for that. They seldom ever had time alone, and she didn't trust herself to say the right thing. Not yet.

Win parked the T-Bird in front of Marty's but made no move to get out of the car.

Blossom gripped the handle but didn't open the door. She glanced back. "Are we going in?"

"I want to ask you something first."

Had she heard right? She looked out the passenger window, her reflection staring back at her, her heart racing. Her mind spun with possibilities, but she didn't dare hope he'd ask what she wanted him to. She didn't dare, but she couldn't stop herself.

When she faced him, he turned and stared ahead, avoiding her eyes. Then he said, "You know I'm not with Melinda anymore, right?"

Everyone at Las Animas High knew that. Their break-up hadn't been soft and quiet, but she didn't say what was in her mind which was "I'm not living on another planet, Win!" Instead, she said, "Yes. I know." And her voice sounded normal, not loud or sarcastic. There was no reason to be cruel.

"Well, ever since then"—he paused for a moment— "Dina's been coming on to me."

She waited, wondering where this was going. What did anything between Win and her have to do with Dina Strong?

He still wasn't looking at her. "I need your help to get her off my back. I wondered if... I hoped maybe...Well, will you pretend to be my girlfriend?"

She couldn't stop the sharp intake of breath. That was the worst thing he'd ever said to her. Avoiding her, being silent she could take, but not this. *Pretend* to be his girlfriend? If he'd punched her in the stomach, she wouldn't have been this breathless.

Her reaction registered because he jerked around in his seat. "Wait... I mean... I was serious about needing your help. I'm... I'm not..." The unflappable Baldwin Knight stumbled on words and ran them together. "That came out all wrong."

Blossom opened her door and closed it just a little harder than he'd like. She was up on what Mr. Knight didn't want done to his car, and while she wouldn't damage it, she wanted to inflict some doubt in this ... this... She searched for the word she wanted. "Ass," she said out loud. It didn't sit well on her lips. It wasn't a word she used about anyone, and not about Win, but that was what he was tonight. He wasn't just unfeeling and insensitive. He was a waste of heart.

Without waiting for him to get out from behind the steering wheel, she hurried to Marty's door and pushed her way inside.

As she stepped into the living room, the party noise blasted into the night. She glanced around, finding Lula sitting almost upright on the couch with one of the Redford twins next to her, his chin to his chest. Coming here had been a mistake, and getting home safely wasn't going to be easy. She pushed her way down the hall, hoping to find someone sober enough to give her a ride. If she was lucky there'd be at least one. She wanted out of here and far away from Win Knight.

Chapter Twenty-Four

Win

He'd blown it. Win rested his head on the steering wheel, tapping his fingers along the hard rim. The moment he saw the pain spread across Blossom's face, he regretted asking that question. Now what was he supposed to do?

Suck it up and apologize, that's what. Suck it up and tell her you didn't mean "pretend".

So what had he meant? That he wanted her to be his girlfriend?

He took in a gulp of air. Girlfriends hadn't worked in the past, so why did he even hope Blossom would be any different? He'd had three steadies, each one a disaster. He really didn't want to risk another of those complications in his life, and girls always were that—*complications*.

Every time he hooked up with someone, they made his life miserable. They got jealous. They got needy. They dragged him through long talk sessions about his feelings. Their feelings. Then he'd hear about the gossip that was going on behind his back. Every girlfriend came with at least one best friend out to shred him if he hurt her, even if she was the one who had hurt *him*. He still felt Melinda Bailey's dark eyes on him and heard her lies about their break-up that weren't true.

He looked at Marty's house where every light blazed inside and outside in the patio. But he couldn't have Blossom hating him. She was different from the others. He gripped his steering wheel. "Damn." She was... He searched for the word. *Sweet*. His mother would have liked her.

Why didn't he have Eva to ask for help about things as tricky as Blossom Henley? He covered his face with his hands, blocking out any light and wishing he could take back the last five minutes.

He waited a while, before stepping out of the car and locking the door. Taking his time to walk between the car and Marty's, he gave himself a few moments to come up with something he could say to Blossom. He needed a sure-fire apology coupled with an explanation, and he hoped he'd still find a way to get her help.

Win opened Marty's door and glanced around the living room in search of a lavender dress. Instead, he found Lula slouched crossed-legged on the couch. She held a glass of what could have been vodka or water, and when she took a sip, she missed her lips, so whatever she was drinking trickled down her chin. Her dark hair was pulled into a sloppy, sideways ponytail and small dark stains spattered her sweater.

Marty hovered over her like a guardian angel with a sombrero halo.

Blossom wasn't in the room, so he went on the hunt into the kitchen. That was where a lot of action happened. There and in the bedrooms, but Blossom wouldn't be in a bedroom. Rumors were she was a virgin of the highest order, and those rumors Win believed.

Poking his head inside the kitchen, he scanned the room filled with kids pressed together. They blocked the refrigerator, the sink, and the back door. Blossom wasn't there either, but Dina was. He ducked out before she spotted him.

Chapter Twenty-Five

Lula

"Did I just see *the* Baldwin Knight swoop through this room?" Lula said. Her head was clearer now, and the people around her weren't blurred along the edges.

"Yes, my little *paloma*, you did." Marty slipped between Lula and Branch Redford, who was still passed out on the couch.

"Cut the crap." Lula slapped his hand off her knee and stood. She was glad she'd sobered a bit after her purge because, with Win at the party, things would be far more interesting. And she was still high enough to be naughtier than usual.

She pushed her way through the bodies of tireless dancers who thrashed non-stop to the heavy rock beat. *"Tomorrow we're gone, our souls rising up to the sun."* She mouthed the words to the song, then stumbled a little, but put her hand out in time to catch herself and save the water in her glass from spilling over the top. Holding onto the wall, she found her way down the hall until she bumped into Win's back.

"I thought I saw you come in," she said to him.

"You can still see?"

"Ha. Ha. Ha." Lula took a sip of water.

"Where's Blossom?"

"She's here, too?" Lula did an unsteady three-sixty and then turned back to Win. "Haven't seen the girl. Are you together?"

"Yes. She came with me." He dodged around Lula and out toward the patio.

"Yes. She came with me." Lula mimicked him, wagging her head from side to side. She drained her water glass and went to the kitchen for a refill.

Melinda blocked the way to the sink and didn't move when Lula held out her glass and gestured for her to step aside.

"Are you blind or just stupid?"

Melinda glared at her. "Better watch it, Lula."

"And what happens if I don't, as you say, 'watch it'?"

"You and that mother of yours should both pack up and leave town. You cause more than your share of trouble."

"Shut the freakin-fuck up about my mother." Lula swept Melinda aside and stepped up to the counter.

The blow to her arm knocked the glass out of her hand and into the sink. It shattered and a piece of glass nicked Lula's finger. She pressed the spot where a small bubble of blood formed, then whirled to face Melinda, and with one quick jab to her middle, doubled her over.

"Girl fight!" someone yelled.

Lula was about to haul Melinda up and give her another good punch when Marty grabbed her arm and pulled her out of the kitchen.

"Let go, Marty!" Lula wrenched her arm free. "That bitch needs some straightening out, and I'm in the mood to do it."

"Stop. You're not doing any straightening out tonight." He guided her to the patio door. "Go outside and cool off."

She gave him a hard stare, but he crossed his arms, not budging. "Lula? I don't want a fight happening in my mom and dad's house, okay?" He pushed her gently outside. "I'm going to take care of Melinda. You go do something else."

Lula resisted, but only a little, and she didn't trail after him on his way back to the kitchen. "Tell her to put a plug in that big mouth of hers."

Without turning around, Marty nodded, his sombrero shuddering.

She'd had enough of this party, and she vowed that if she ever got Melinda Bailey alone again, she'd make sure to fix her mouth for good. She sucked at the small cut on her finger and walked out onto the patio.

Blossom sat on the same lounge chair Lula had occupied earlier. But unlike Lula, who'd been on her way to la la land, Blossom sat, talking with the sober Redford twin.

Win stood to the side, quiet and looking gloomier than usual.

"There you are," Lula said, taking a seat next to Blossom on the lounge. "Carter, your brother's on the couch and totally out of it, in case you want to know."

"Oh, man. He's not supposed to drink nothing. Coach is going to kick his butt if he finds out. I'd better get him home. Sorry, Blossom. See you." Carter stood up and went into the house.

"I didn't see you come in," Lula said to Blossom. "I thought you weren't coming."

Blossom shrugged and glanced up at Win, but only for a second. "I changed my mind."

When Lula was sober, she found Win's stormy face irresistible, but when she was drunk, she had a hard time holding back her natural instincts to conquer, so she tried ignoring him and kept her focus on Blossom.

Suddenly, Win was gripping Lula's hand and pulling her to her feet. "What the?" She had to grab the wall to keep her balance.

"Lula, make yourself, like, gone, okay?" He hauled her roughly toward the house.

"Jerk-off!" She wrenched her hand free and considered an end-run around him and back to Blossom, but his face was set to stun, and that stopped her. With a slow swing of her arms, she took long, angry steps as she returned inside. "With you here, this is one downer of a party," she shouted over her shoulder.

Chapter Twenty-Six

Blossom

When Lula finally made it into the house, Win sat next to Blossom, but not close enough for his leg to touch hers. He leaned forward, his arms across his thighs, and glanced at her sideways.

Even though there was space between them, she made it a point to shift away slightly and refused to look at him.

"She called me a jerk-off. What are you going to call me?" he asked her.

She clasped her hands together to keep from shaking, she was so angry. "Nothing. I'm not interested enough to think up names for you." Now she did want to be cruel. Now she wanted to insult him the way he'd insulted her.

"Ouch. That's harsh, Blossom." He rubbed his forehead as if it ached, then reached for her hand.

She yanked it away and folded her arms around her middle. She needed protection from being hurt by him again. "You have the feelings of a ... a"—she spotted one of Mrs. Skolinski's flower pots and pointed at it— "of that."

"I'm sorry. I just had this plan in my head, and when I asked you that in the car, I didn't think how it would come out. It was bad." He twisted to face her. "And I take it back."

Blossom never stooped to putting on an act about how she felt. She was hurt and she was mad, and she believed she deserved some time to stay that way. "I'll think about your apology, but right now I'm going to find something to drink, and I don't want to talk to you. I'll let you know when or if I do."

Before he could say anything else, she got up and walked inside. In the kitchen, she found a cold drink, popped the tab, and sipped. It had been a mistake to think Win would ever be the guy she imagined. She was sorry she'd said yes to coming with him tonight, but her painting and her dreams of him—of who she wanted him to be—that's why she'd come to this party. Then he'd ruined it. Although he'd hurt her a lot over the years, he'd never made her feel like a fool before. She'd never forget that moment in the car. She'd waited, expecting him to say something affectionate, and he'd insulted her. She drained the soda, suddenly needing to drench the heat in her throat and her belly with something cold.

Lula held on to the doorjamb and swung into the room like a pole dancer wearing too many clothes. "Yo, babe! What's with all the static between you and the Win tonight?"

Crumpling the empty soda can with more energy than she needed, Blossom looked away. Then she stooped to search under the sink for a garbage can.

"Come on. Spill." Lula pulled her around.

It was embarrassing to say out loud, but Lula had a firm grip on her arm and didn't look as if she would let go until Blossom answered her question. So she stammered out Win's "pretend" girlfriend plan.

"Whoa." Lula took a step back. "That's one cheap shot."

Blossom flinched. "Yes."

"What an ego that boy has, and he has no idea how the females of his species think. His having a girlfriend—pretend or not—won't sidetrack the chicks he fantasizes are after him. If anything, it's going to raise his status to unattainable again, and, therefore, even more desirable."

"I don't care. I'm not having any part of it."

"Do you want to do something to get back at him?" A slow grin tinged with just that touch of evil she loved to show the world curved Lula's lips upward, and her eyes became cunning slits.

"Stop looking like that." Blossom glanced away, then back.

Lula pointed at her own face. "This is the look of pure genius. You will love what I'm thinking because it's wicked."

"How wicked?"

Lula held up her hands, palms about two inches apart. "This much."

"And what is it?" Blossom didn't want to sound eager, but she couldn't stop sounding interested.

"Let's settle some scores with Mr. Knight right now. What do you think?"

"First, you have to tell me what you have in that treacherous mind of yours, Lula Banes, then I'll decide."

"Let's mess with his head." She held up her hand and stopped Blossom from interrupting. "Just a little. Just enough to show him he's not Mr. Everything to every girl in Las Animas, okay?"

"Not Mr. Everything," Blossom repeated. "I like that. Okay, tell me."

"Your job is to do a little snuggling and swipe the keys to his car."

Blossom's eyes went round and very large. "You are out of your mind!" She leaned against the counter and shook her head. "No way am I doing that."

"Are you talking about the snuggling or swiping his keys?"

"Just tell me what you're thinking about doing, Lula."

"Nothing illegal." Lula leaned closer. "While you

keep Win occupied, I'll move his precious car a few blocks down the street. Then when he leaves, we watch the fireworks."

Blossom knew that if anyone even thought about going near that car Win went ballistic. If someone so much as fogged its classic porthole windows, he turned into a raging maniac. There was no telling what he'd do if Lula got into it and drove it.

With the image of Lula behind the wheel of the T-Bird, Blossom shook her head. "No. First, I'm not a pickpocket. Second, I don't—"

"Fine. Then let him get away with his little male chauvinist tricks." Lula opened a couple of drawers before pulling out an apron. "This should fit."

"Oh, Lula, you're just plain awful sometimes."

"Only sometimes? I'll have to do better from now on." Lula yawned and started toward the door. "This party's turning into a bore."

"Wait."

Lula looked back at Blossom, who crumpled the apron and stuffed it back into the drawer. "I'm in."

"Okay. Now things will get interesting," Lula said. "I'll be in the living room. When you've got the keys, come find me."

Chapter Twenty-Seven

Win

After Blossom left him alone on the patio, Win ran through their conversation again. He'd hurt her a lot. Was that because she liked him more than he'd thought? Did she want to date, maybe have some kind of real relationship? She'd never said anything like that to him or texted or phoned. Most girls who were hot for him did all of that. Now he was confused about the next step. He'd apologized, but he might have to do more than that.

He stretched up from the lounge chair and made his way inside. As he stepped down the hall, he spotted Dina Strong coming in his direction and quickly ducked into the bathroom. He locked the door, taking as long as possible to pee, wash his hands, and smooth his hair. When he came out, Dina was waiting outside and Brittany had joined her. Dina always came with her cousin as reinforcement.

He searched over their heads and tried to avoid eye contact. He had to get out of here or he'd do something he knew would only cause him more misery in the long run.

"Want a taste?" Dina held out a glass filled with a dark liquid. "It's rum. I found it in the kitchen."

"What don't you get about *I'm not interested*?"

"What don't you get about *I don't give up*?" She stepped closer. "Check your phone. I sent you something new."

He'd forgotten to block Dina again. *Damn.* He shook his head and shoved his way between them into the clogged hallway where he shouldered through until he met Blossom, who was coming from the other direction.

She glanced behind him, then wrapped her arms around him. "I see you have your groupies nearby. You can *pretend* to kiss me if you want," she whispered.

"Look, I'm—"

"Sorry?" She pressed closer.

"Very."

Win based a lot of his romantic choices on first kisses. So many were huge fails. When a girl's lips didn't stir any heat inside him, he knew he was right in thinking that detailing his car was way better than steady dating. Now this kiss was a *pretend* one from a *pretend* girlfriend, so he didn't expect even the smallest stirring.

Mistake.

Once their lips touched, all the ones from before were gone from his memory. Soft. Sweet. Yet there was so much promise in this kiss. Blossom Henley's innocent exterior concealed a major planet of passion.

He forgot Dina and Brittany and that he stood in Marty's hall. He fell into Blossom the way he'd fall into a warm summer lake.

Chapter Twenty-Eight

Blossom

Dina and Brittany were a pushy pair. That Blossom knew from seeing them together at other parties and watching how they teamed up at school. For a moment, when she saw what was happening to Win in the hallway, she even felt a bit sorry for him. He might be a narcissistic jerk, but at the moment he looked like one of the hunted.

When she pulled him to her, the two predators fell back, and Dina radiated contempt.

Blossom held him close, her hand near his pocket, but as he tried to apologize again, Blossom hesitated. Taking his keys might be a joke for Lula, but Win would absolutely not laugh. Still, he'd humiliated her. He deserved a kick in the pants. Maybe if he found out how it felt to be the fool, he wouldn't do anything like that to her again.

As he pressed his lips against hers, she closed her eyes and tried not to feel the surge of excitement between them. But it was hard to think with his body so close to hers, a boy she'd had a crush on since eighth grade. She almost changed her mind about grabbing his keys, then the scene between them in the car replayed, and before she lost the chance, she slipped them from his pocket and hid them inside her fist. Done. There was no going back now.

She stepped away. "Your fans have left," she told him.

Win stared down at her, looking lost and confused. It was such a different expression than Blossom was used to seeing that she almost returned the keys and confessed her crime.

"Thanks for helping me out," he said. "And I meant what I told you about being sorry."

She glanced away. "I know." Then looking up at him, she said, "I'm still thinking about accepting your apology." Before she had second thoughts and didn't go through with the plan, she stepped out of his reach and went in search of Lula.

Lula was never hard to find, so in less than a minute, Blossom had handed over the keys to the T-Bird.

"Don't do anything to damage that car, Lula. Promise."

"Of course, darling girl. Back in a jif."

Lula walked away, her shoulders and hips moving in a sassy rhythm, until she was out the front door. Blossom felt the mistake balloon inside her before Lula had disappeared outside. She started to follow her, wanting to convince her not to move the T-Bird when Win caught her by the arm.

"We should dance at least once, right?" He drew her to him, and she held on, trying to steady herself and not hyperventilate. "Are you cold?" he asked.

"No. Well, a little." She had to have some explanation for why she was shaking.

He wrapped both arms around her and hugged her to his chest.

This was the moment she'd longed for, but now that it was happening, she wanted to run and hide. Swallowing several times in a row, she tamped down the urge to confess.

Chapter Twenty-Nine

Dina

Dina latched onto Brittany's arm and dragged her down the hall into the kitchen where she didn't have to watch Win and Blossom kissing. She dug out the rum bottle from the cupboard again and refilled her glass.

"No more, Dina." Brittany tried for the glass, but Dina yanked her hand away.

"I'm fine. Let's get something to eat." Dina split open a small bag of chips, dug out a handful, and shoved a few into her mouth. "Here." She leaned against the counter and held out the bag to Brittany.

Brittany shook her head. "I don't want any." She pointed to Dina's glass of rum. "Pour that stuff out, D."

"Are you kidding?"

"Let's find a ride and go home. Branch is out of it, so I'm bored," Brittany said.

"I'm not leaving yet."

"Look, Win's not worth the effort, and he's not worth getting drunk over either."

Melinda stepped in beside her and held out a paper cup. "I'll toast to that."

"Hi, Melinda. What are we toasting?" Brittany asked.

"To that jerk, Win Knight, not being worth getting drunk over," Melinda said.

"How come you went with *that jerk* for a while, then?" Dina bit into another chip and glared at her. She'd been the first one to celebrate the news of Win's break-up with Melinda. "And more to the point, how come he broke it off with you?"

Melinda ignored Dina. "He lies and he cheats. Then he thinks because he's got money, he can get away with it." She sipped from her cup and looked Dina in the eye. "And FYI, I did all the breaking up." She shoved herself away from the counter and left the kitchen.

"She's the liar," Dina said, taking another gulp of rum.

Brittany reached out for the glass in Dina's hand, and this time took it away.

"Hey! Do not throw that down the drain." Dina reached to retrieve her drink, but Brittany stepped back.

"Okay. Okay. Don't get all up in knots. I'm not going to pour this stuff out." She took a large sip. "Just remember, I'm saving your head by doing this, you know."

Dina popped more chips into her mouth and smiled. Brittany didn't really like to drink, but there she was, downing rum so her cousin wouldn't be sick in the morning.

"You're a good cousin, you know?" Dina felt the floor sway under her feet as she wrapped her arms around Brittany.

"I know." Brittany pulled away and grabbed the bag of chips. She reached inside and pulled out two. "You didn't leave many, did you?"

"No. I like chips." Dina smiled and walked to the bathroom.

Chapter Thirty

Lula

Lula unlocked the T-Bird and slid behind the wheel. It did feel special. The low profile, the heavy door, the hard crank of the steering wheel. The way it thrummed under the hood when she turned the key and pressed on the accelerator. She didn't flick on the lights as she rolled away from the curb and down the street. She'd only take it a few blocks, just far enough to give Win a tiny heart stoppage and a greater appreciation for the power of women.

Ahead was a single space, and she backed into it, taking her time. Pulling forward, she hit the rear end of Carter's pickup parked in front, but it was barely a tap. Then she straightened the wheel and rolled back until she'd nested Win's car between the pickup and someone's Bronco. It was a close fit, but he'd be able to get out with a little maneuvering.

She grinned. *Once he found his precious car.*

Climbing from the car and locking the door, she kissed the side-view mirror. "Poor Win. If you just weren't such a jerk."

Once back at the party, she hunted down Blossom who was now wearing Marty's sombrero. "New look?" Lula asked her.

"Marty wanted me to take care of it while he started cleaning up. His mom and dad are coming back in about an hour."

"Here." Lula tucked Win's keys into Blossom's hand and folded her fingers over them. "Best return the stolen goods."

"Where did you put it?"

Lula pointed in the direction she'd driven. "About two blocks from here."

"It's in a safe place, right? You know—"

"Very safe and easy to find. He'll only have a few minutes of sheer terror." Lula grinned and added a deep-throated chuckle.

"Look, Lula, maybe you should put it back where it was. I'm scared he'll strangle us."

"Stop with the worried look, Blossom. He's hot for you. I told you that." Lula reached over and plucked the sombrero from Blossom's head. "I'll guard this. Now toddle off and get those keys back into the Master's pocket."

"You're always trouble, Lula. Do you know that?"

"I do."

Chapter Thiry-One

Clifford

It was almost midnight, but Clifford was still excited about what he'd decided to do, and he couldn't sleep. His talk with Blossom had been exactly what he'd hoped for. Then the work on his gift for her turned out the way he'd wanted. He'd taped her picture into the journal and explained his feelings, so she'd know how much she'd come to mean to him, how he hoped she cared for him, too. All of that had made him more alive than he'd ever been.

He'd just replaced everything inside the box and set it back on the top shelf of his closet when the blare of the TV came from the living room.

Harry was awake.

No matter how hard he tried to bury the sounds from whatever Harry was watching, they came through the thin wall. Clifford needed to get out, maybe take one of his long walks. He didn't want the feeling of excitement and anticipation washed away by what Harry thought of as entertainment.

He cracked the door and peered into the living room. Harry's back was to him, the TV erupting in gun shots and screeching tires—all loud enough to keep everybody in the apartments awake. Harry wouldn't admit his hearing had gotten worse, so each month the TV got louder.

If Clifford was lucky, the chase scene would keep his dad locked onto the screen, and he wouldn't notice him slipping out the front door.

His hand was on the knob when Harry yelled,

"Where you going?"

"Out for a walk."

"Oh, yeah. A walk. What're you up to?"

"Nothing. I just can't sleep right now, and I thought—"

Harry aimed the remote at Clifford. "Don't bring no floozie to this home." He stood and took a beer from the refrigerator, popping the tab. "You hear?"

Home? Clifford hid the anger that rose like a tide inside him. He wouldn't bring one of the walking dead to this place, let alone a live woman. "Sure. Whatever you say." He ducked outside and got into his car. Harry wasn't only awake, he was drinking. There'd been four empty beer cans on the floor next to the couch. Clifford might just stay out all night. He didn't want a repeat of what had happened two years ago.

He put the key into the ignition but didn't start the car. Instead, he stared out the windshield and blinked at the sting of that memory.

That night, Marla did something besides cower and cry. She called 911 as soon as he took the knife out of the drawer. Clifford always wondered if it was to save Harry or to save him, but at least she made the call. Maybe she did it because Harry hit her harder than usual, and she lost a front tooth.

He blinked, once again seeing all that happened— how Marla leaned against the kitchen wall, cupping her hand over her bleeding and already swollen mouth—how he grabbed the kitchen knife from the counter and jabbed it at Harry.

By the time all three Las Animas cop cars screeched to a halt in front of the apartments, Harry was lying on the floor gripping his belly. Clifford opened his hand and dropped the knife to the floor, then backed up to the refrigerator.

The paramedics arrived shortly after. Two worked on Harry to stop his bleeding while a third one, a young woman with serious black-rimmed glasses, took care of Marla.

From what seemed like far away, Clifford watched as the men set Harry on a gurney and rolled him out. Clifford looked at the three men in uniform, trying to remember if he'd seen them before, but he was sure none of them had ever been to this apartment. They were new.

Once Harry was gone and Marla had stopped wailing, one of the cops pulled Clifford into a chair at the kitchen table and sat across from him. Clifford remembered thinking this guy was a lot older than he was—forty maybe. Another cop—his biceps beefed up by years in the gym—stood at the door, and a third, with a thin face and a nose that had been broken and set a few times, took Marla into the living room and spoke quietly to her. Clifford couldn't hear what he said, but Marla, who sank back into the couch, fixed glazed eyes on the wall across from her and managed to nod or shake her head.

"Want to tell me what happened here, son?" The cop pulled Clifford's attention away from what was going on in the other room.

Clifford lowered his head and stared at his lap. What had happened here? Most of tonight was a replay of a lot of nights, but two things were different. He'd fought back for the first time, and his mother had called for help.

"He … he hit my mom," Clifford said at last. "I stopped him."

"Is this the first time?"

Clifford looked up at the cop. "No, and yes."

"You'll have to explain that, okay?"

"It's not the first time he's beat her up, but it's the first time I stopped him."

"I see." The cop nodded that he understood.

Did he? Clifford still wasn't sure the man had truly understood what it was like being him. Fifteen. With Harry for a dad—Marla for a mom.

Clifford still remembered the peace, the silence, without his father in the apartment. While someone from Child Protective Services popped into the apartment to talk with the two of them, Harry did a year in jail. If that woman had kept coming, Marla and him might have made a go of life together. Marla even bought milk, and she made mac and cheese a couple of times. He remembered that once she heated a can of vegetable soup and served it in two bowls. They sat at the table.

But the year ended, the woman with the kind face and lots of paperwork stopped coming, and Harry sweet-talked his way back into the apartment. He'd only been there a few weeks before he somehow managed to buy a gun. He kept it in the cupboard above the refrigerator. It didn't take long before Marla returned to the ghostly figure that followed Harry out the door as if he had her on a leash.

Clifford shook his head, trying to clear the old memory. Then he started the car and backed out of the parking lot. He took the road that led to the highway, thinking he'd head over to Greenlee, but when he drew up to the stop sign, he spotted a familiar car. A unique one that he couldn't mistake.

It was the one he'd watched pulling out of the school parking lot and rolling past the convenience store a lot of times this year. A car with its privileged driver behind the wheel. It had to be Win Knight's. What was he doing on this side of Las Animas? He and his car didn't fit here.

He waited until the driver's door opened, then stuck his head out the window to be sure he wasn't mistaken in what he saw. He hadn't expected to see Lula Banes, but there she was.

She locked the door, kissed the side mirror, then strode off down the street.

Clifford waited, then drove slowly, following Lula until she went into a small stucco house with loud music coming from inside. The curtains were open, so Clifford watched as kids danced, drank, and laughed together.

For a moment, he imagined himself in there, but then shook off that idea. He'd found a party and something interesting to think about instead of Harry and the mess he lived in, so he'd stick around to see what happened. He drove down another block, parked, and walked back.

Chapter Thirty-Two

Win

After Win and Blossom finished dancing, he guided her to the side of the room, but before he had a chance to talk to her, Lula appeared next to them. She pulled Blossom out of the living room and into the kitchen with, "We have to talk."

Win didn't have time to stop Blossom from walking off, and as he watched them leave, he decided he hated Lula Banes just as much as he hated Dina Strong. He made his way out onto Marty's patio where he took his cell from his pocket and opened his text messages. The last one was from Dina, and just as she'd promised, she'd attached a picture of herself. This time she wasn't totally naked. She had on a see-through blouse and her message said, "I'm cold. Can you tell?"

He hit delete, blocked this new number, and crossed Marty's backyard lawn to where Marty held a hose, getting rid of guest barf.

"You give the best parties," Win said. He'd meant sarcasm, but Marty ignored it, nodding in agreement, and turned off the water.

"This is the last party if I don't have the mess gone before my mom and dad get home. Spread the word," Marty told him.

They returned to the house and Win picked up a black garbage bag already puffed out with party debris. He'd haul this to the cans as his contribution to the clean-up. He stepped inside at the same time Blossom started through the patio door.

"You're part of the clean-up crew?" she asked.

"I'm dumping this and leaving." He held up the

139

bag between them. "Are you coming with me?"

"I am. That's what I came to tell you." She looked away, then back. "So Dina and the cousin are gone?"

"The last I saw them they were in the kitchen looking for more rum, so I'm steering clear of there."

"Then you don't need me anymore tonight, but I'll help with that." She pointed at a second bag on the flagstones.

He decided against trying to say the word *sorry* again. "Be my guest." He shoved it across with his foot, and she grabbed the handles, but one slipped from her grasp and the top gaped, spewing plates and plastic cups onto the ground. "Damn." He passed her the sealed bag and started scooping up the litter.

"My fault. Let me help." She knelt next to him, reaching around him, her arm brushing against his side. Then again.

Blossom was feeling him up? Win caught her arm. "What are you doing?"

She looked up at him, then said, "Nothing. Just helping."

Her smile, usually warm and generous, failed to brighten her face, and after an uncomfortable moment, she shifted her gaze.

Win couldn't figure out exactly what Blossom was thinking, but if he didn't know her so well, he'd accuse her of hatching a plot. She just wasn't that kind of girl, so he let it slide.

Chapter Thirty-Three

Blossom

She and Win were both on their hands and knees, and Blossom still had the keys in her fist. But he held her arm, so she couldn't move. Her mouth had gone dry, and when she smiled, her upper lip stuck to her gums. Quickly she ran her tongue up there to unstick it. "If we both do this, we can get out of here quicker, right?"

He released her, but his look was deafening, full of suspicion. She was sorry she'd put him on alert. Now she'd have a devil of a time slipping the keys into his pocket.

Maybe she shouldn't try. Maybe... She waited until his back was to her, and then set the keys on the ground behind him. He'd think he dropped them while he was on the ground picking up trash.

She gathered a few more plates and a couple of cups and tossed them into the bag, then stood up and brushed her hands together. "Done." She reached out and took the bag. "I've got it." And this time she made sure she had a good grip on the top. "Ready?"

Win followed her through the kitchen where they were careful to skirt Dina and Brittany, who were sharing a bag of chips at the counter. Blossom and Win made it into the garage where they dumped the trash. When they returned to the house, they found Marty already busy tackling the mess in the living room.

He was pushing an overstuffed chair back where it belonged while Lula ran the vacuum over the carpet. A few others were carrying out more trash to the garage.

Lula shut down the vacuum and stared at Blossom. *Well?* she mouthed, silent and optimistic.

Blossom nodded but added a shrug because while she'd technically *returned* Win's keys, he hadn't found them yet. She glanced down the hall in hopes someone would be coming in from the patio soon. She counted on one of the clean-up crew to discover those keys.

She'd no sooner held that thought than Carter Redford, who hadn't dragged his brother off the couch yet, arrived.

"These belong to any of you?"

Win patted his jacket pocket. "Mine. Thanks. Where'd you find them?"

"By the door to the patio. Lucky, eh?"

Blossom, her eyes on the ceiling, said a silent thank you.

But the next part of the prank was not something Blossom looked forward to. Now that Win was at the door, she was sorry for what she'd done. He'd been terrible and rude to her, but now she felt as if hiding his car wasn't the way to show him how much he'd hurt her. Regret and a lot of misgiving prickled her skin. She never should have listened to Lula.

Chapter Thirty-Four

Lula

When Win opened the front door to leave, Lula leaped to follow him and Blossom outside. "I'm out of here, too," she said, and she yawned to stifle the near hysteria bubbling up from her stomach. She did not want to miss Win's reaction to his vanished T-Bird. She'd pay double for front-row seats to this little show.

They came to the sidewalk and Win stopped, the confusion spiraling out from his whole body. Then came the explosion, so much worse than Lula had imagined. Even she cringed in the path of his rage.

The cry came from deeper than his throat and clawed the night air. He stomped down the sidewalk, his hair gripped between his fingers. He ran into the street, making short dashes first one direction, then the other before setting out toward where Lula had parked the T-Bird. He'd only gone half a block before stopping and turning in circles as if he might have missed his car on the first pass.

Not far enough, she wanted to say. *One more block and your priceless baby is right there, Mr. Knight.*

Blossom's eyes suggested flight was on her mind, but Marty, who wasn't in on what she'd done, ran alongside Win, then took the other side of the street on the hunt for the car.

"Hey Win," Marty called. "We should call the cops." He pointed at his neighbor's house with a row of Harleys lined up at the curb. "The cops'll do a search."

His innocence was so sincere. It was so easy to fool him that Lula wanted to pat his head. She'd barely had that thought before she regretted it. That was mean, and she liked Marty too much to think about him that way. She just wished he'd accept his role in her life as a close friend or little brother and leave all the attempts at romance alone.

Win had reversed direction and was walking the wrong way. This drama was dragging out far longer than she'd planned, and now even she was getting nervous. She resisted shouting at him as he continued down the block.

"We should all look," Marty said, ready to set out down the street again.

Lula grabbed his arm. "Give it a minute. I'm sure he'll find it."

She was about to go after Win herself when he came back running. This time he was headed toward the car.

Everything was going to be all right, but she didn't want to miss the moment he spotted that car.

Lula pulled Marty with her. "Come on." They ran after Win and everyone followed.

Chapter Thirty-Five

Win

He'd kill whoever had stolen his car. He'd split them open from top to bottom and wrench out their miserable guts.

It couldn't be gone. He wouldn't let that be true. He ran. And he ran. Then he turned and ran in the opposite direction. Farther this time. Down the block. *Check both sides. It has to be…*

And there it was. He bent at the waist, panting with hot tears streaking his face. He hadn't felt tears since his mother left him forever.

On shaky feet, he approached his car and caressed the door handle, all the time swearing he'd get whoever had done this. He walked around it, examining the driver's side, the rear, the passenger side, the front—the front. Dead center, in the exact space the trailer hitch of Carter Redford's pick-up would fit, was a tiny ding. The perfect Sea Spray Green paint chipped. "Shit!" he screamed.

"Win?" It was Blossom.

He didn't answer her. He didn't acknowledge he'd heard her until she stood only inches away, looking up into his face. Then he fixed her with eyes still blurred. Sweat had turned to icy droplets beading up on his forehead.

"I'm … I'm so sorry."

Her words should make sense. So why didn't they? The message was simple. She was sorry. Why should *she* be sorry?

Then she touched him. She'd touched him that way tonight on the patio while they were on their knees.

They were on their knees because she'd dropped the bag and...

He grabbed her by both arms. "Who did this?"

"It was only meant to be a joke. No, it was meant to show you how humiliated you made me feel. I didn't—"

"Who drove my car and parked it here?" The veins in his neck bulged.

Anyone left at the party had finally followed the angry voices and stood watching from the sidewalk.

Lula, with Marty next to her, stepped off the curb and stood with feet apart and hands on her hips. "I did."

They faced each other squarely, and Win was only one blink away from lunging at her. He'd hated her for a long time—since grade school. And he'd hated himself for even letting something so juvenile continue to tick him off, but it did. In eighth grade P. E. and in front of all his friends, she'd pushed his knees from behind and made them buckle. Everyone on the field had laughed while he scrambled to his feet. Now, she was humiliating him again—in front of his junior class.

"Look, you jerk," Lula screeched. "It was a joke. I didn't hurt your stupid damned car."

"No? Then what's that? Right there in the front?" Spit flew from his lips and Win jabbed his finger toward the tiny ding in the front of the T-Bird.

He yelled louder, but the unmistakable thrum of Harleys drowned him out as two bikers roared down the driveway next to the Skolinski house and shot past them on the street.

Once the bikes had turned the corner, Marty wedged himself between Lula and Win and pushed them apart. "Hey! This is dumb. Lula, you tell him you'll pay to fix the car, okay?" He looked at Win. "Get a grip. You can get that ding touched up. I know because you've had other dings taken care of, remember?"

He remembered. It wasn't that he couldn't repair the car. It was because that bitch standing with her hands on her hips had dared to get behind the wheel and drive *his* car. He didn't allow anybody to do that, especially not Lula Banes.

Backing away, he unlocked the driver's door and got in.

Blossom stayed where she was and stared after him.

He leaned across and rolled down the passenger window. "Get in. I'll take you home," he said, his voice stripped of the anger that had been at the boil seconds before.

Without saying goodbye to Lula or Marty, Blossom slipped into the passenger seat.

Win drove in silence, and Blossom kept her eyes on the road. She didn't utter one word or look at him.

When he turned into her driveway, he shut off the lights and the engine, and they sat in the darkness until Blossom said, "I've already told you I know I shouldn't have gone along with Lula's idea, so there's not much more I can say." Blossom's voice was breathy.

"I hate Lula Banes."

She waited silently, not moving, then said, "And how about me? Do you hate me, too?"

Win shook his head. "I don't hate you."

"That's good," she said. "I don't hate you either, so I'll pretend to be your girlfriend."

"No. I'll take care of Dina and Brittany in another way. It was a stupid idea." He gripped the wheel without looking at her.

Blossom opened the car door and eased from the seat. "Okay." And then she was out of the car, walking toward the house.

He had his hand on the handle, ready to get out of the car and follow her. He should tell her he deserved what she'd done. He'd been an ass. He should tell her he was sorry again, but how many times did he have to say that before she believed him—before he felt he'd made it up to her?

He started the engine and backed out.

Chapter Thirty-Six

Friday, The Night Before
After The Party
Clifford

Clifford stayed in the shadows across from Marty's house, watching the argument between Win and Lula grow hot.

This was way better than any Telenovela his mom liked to watch. In a minute, Win was going to deck Lula. Then what would Lula do? She'd fight back for sure, and that was something worth seeing. A good fight, especially between his two least favorite people, would be fun to watch.

But the roar of bikers tore past and the tension lessened, then Marty stepped between Lula and Win, and they both backed away.

Clifford wasn't going to get his fight after all, so he switched his attention to Blossom.

It was clear she was really upset. He wished he could go to her and offer to take her away from there, but he couldn't do that in front of the others. Instead, he leaned against the tree trunk out of sight, watching.

Win put the car in gear, about to drive away, when he reached across and rolled down the passenger window. Was he going to tell Lula off again? Was there still a chance he'd get out of the car and...

Wait! Win was talking to Blossom. Clifford pushed away from the tree trunk, rigid with anger. She was getting into his car. "No. No. No." He spoke between his teeth, trying to hold back the panic in his chest.

He stood stunned as Blossom closed the passenger door. It took a moment for him to break free of the numbing disbelief as he watched Win's car vanish down the street, then he ran to his car.

He's not taking Blossom away from me. He's not!

In spite of the cold, sweat collected at Clifford's collar and he gripped the wheel, his hands shaking. From a distance, he followed the T-Bird to Blossom's and parked just past her driveway.

Time slowed while he sat waiting for her to get out of the car. He willed himself to stay where he was. *Just watch. Wait.* But all he wanted to do was yank open that passenger door, pull her from the seat, and run away with her.

Finally, she climbed out, and the T-Bird backed down the driveway, flashing past in a streak of turquoise, a color Clifford detested. He hated the stuck-up, smug kid behind the wheel a lot more than ever before.

Clifford gripped the steering wheel, releasing his anger in short, rapid breaths until his windows fogged. Once he'd calmed down enough to breathe normally, he walked up the long path to her house and knocked. She'd think it was the rich brat coming back for a last kiss, so he was sure she'd open the door for him.

The sound of footsteps came from inside, then the door swung in and Blossom looked up into Clifford's face. Her smile switched to surprise. She stepped back, but he pressed his hand against the door so she couldn't close it, all the time speaking quickly, forcing his voice to stay low and calm.

"I just want to tell you something." He didn't smile, but he smoothed his face into blankness and stepped back from the door. He'd show her he was safe to be near. "I didn't mean to scare you."

"You didn't. You just weren't who I expected."

It was great to hear her say she wasn't afraid of him. "Right. Well, sorry."

"What … uh, why are you here?" she asked.

The sound of her voice stirred the hollowed-out spaces in him and gave them a different shape. Those spaces were still dark and upset, but a bit more manageable now that he was with her. He released the pressure against the door and clasped his hands behind him. If he looked defenseless, he was doubly sure she'd want to hear what he had to say.

He wanted to tell her how much he cared about her. "I saw what happened at the party, and I wanted to know if you were okay."

She cocked her head as if she hadn't understood what he'd just said. "I didn't see you there." She frowned, looking puzzled.

"Oh, I was outside about ready to … you know … go in and say hi, but when I saw the fight, I didn't." He waited a moment, then added, "I'm not really welcome at the parties anyways, you know, but I get kind of lonely…" He let his voice trail off and hung his head. He'd let her see how those friends of hers hurt him.

He didn't look up until he felt her move closer. Then when she stood outside on the porch, he did bring his eyes up to meet hers, but with care. He didn't want her backing into the house just yet. He wanted her close. He wanted to take pleasure in being near her.

"You shouldn't feel that way, Clifford. I'm sure if you wanted to come to the party, kids wouldn't mind."

The tension eased from his neck and shoulders at the kindness in her voice. "You're sweet. Not like all the others at that school." He risked brushing her cheek with a finger. It was even softer and warmer than he'd imagined. He wished he could stay like this forever. Near her, feeling the warmth of her skin, seeing her face so close.

Her eyes tightened at the corners and her body

tensed, but she didn't pull away. He still scared her, but not as much. He wanted to stop scaring her at all. He wanted to make all that gossip he was sure she'd heard about him go away. And he would. He'd gain her full trust. Then he'd show her how really special he was. Not just a convenience store clerk. Someone with talent. Someone who was going to be a huge success one day, and she could share that with him.

He smiled and hoped she felt the tenderness he wanted her to.

"I'm sorry, Clifford, but I have to go." She stepped back to stand just inside the house. "I'm working on a project and I—"

"Project?" He wanted a few more minutes with her. "What kind?"

Looking off into the distance, she seemed to be searching for a way to explain what she meant before saying, "A painting. I'm almost finished and—"

"That's right, you're an artist." His heart sped up. It thrilled him that they had this in common. "I draw. I'm sure it's not as good as your stuff, but..." She stepped back again and put her hand on the door. "You have to go. I know."

"My mom's not well, and I have to check on her."

"Sure." He didn't wait for her to close the door before walking down the path toward the street, humming. Now she knew for sure that he was no threat. He saw that in her face before he left. He was certain she liked him. Next, he had to make her love him.

All he had to do was get Win Knight out of the picture.

Chapter Thirty-Seven

Marty

Once Win and Lula finished their face-off about the car and Win finally drove off with Blossom, Marty took Lula's hands in his and made her face him.

"You were very bad tonight, Lula Banes. Very, very bad."

"Yes. I was." She beamed.

"Come on. I've got to do a search and make sure no bodies are still on the property." He pulled her behind him, then opened the sliding door to the back. "Go check the patio and the backyard. I'm going to take a look at the bedrooms."

He was straightening the bed when Lula showed up and waited in the doorway of his parents' room, tapping her foot. He opened the closet and then knelt to look under the bed.

"What in the world are you looking for?" she asked.

Marty snatched up a black lace thong from the floor and swung it around his finger. "See?" He tucked the panties into his hip pocket.

"Okay, will you stop already?" Lula stifled a yawn. "Your place is cleaner than before the party and nobody's left but us." She pushed away from the doorjamb and stretched. "Now take me home."

"I didn't get the hall bathroom, Lula."

"Then do it later!"

She pulled him into the living room, and Marty was at the front door about to open it when it swung in and Mr. and Mrs. Skolinski stood on the stoop.

Marty stopped, his hand still outstretched. "Hey! I didn't hear you drive up."

His mom's face always radiated delight when she saw him.

The next moment, her smile vanished when she saw Lula behind her son. A blunt look of distaste took the place of all that happiness, and Marty stepped slightly in front of Lula as if she needed shielding.

Lula raised her hand in a tiny wave. "Evening, Mrs. Skolinski." She nodded at Marty's dad. "Mr. Skolinski."

"I'm taking Lula home. Be back in ten," Marty said, dodging around his parents and hauling Lula behind him.

"Just hold it right there, Marty." His mom sniffed the air. "Beer. I smell that and…" She sniffed again.

Marty shrugged, looking to his dad, but Mr. Skolinski said nothing.

"A few kids brought some stuff, Mom. Nothing happened."

"You're not driving, young man. End of discussion." Mrs. Skolinski marched into the room, inspecting it as she went.

"Hey, Dad. Lula came with me from the game. She needs a ride home."

Mr. Skolinski leaned in and whispered. "I think you'd best figure out how to get her there without being involved. Okay? It's already raining, and there's a storm coming in, so I agree with your mom on this one. Too dangerous, Marty." And he followed his wife to the back of the house.

"Mama Bear still does not like Lula Banes," Lula said. "Are you tattling on me, Marty Skolinski? Saying how bad this Banes girl is?"

"Not me, but Mom's got her sources." He poked

her arm with his finger. "Treat me better and she'll come around."

"So how do I get home? I'm in need of my bed." She folded her arms and perched on the sofa.

"At your service, M'lady." He pulled out his keys and dangled them in front of her. "I'll get my dad to drive me to your place tomorrow morning and pick up my car. Just don't crash it, okay?"

"Me?" She snatched the keys and stood. "I don't crash cars. I may move them around a bit, but I'm oh so careful."

"You know, Lula, I deserve a kiss."

"We've had this conversation before. You sound like a broken record, Skolinski, you know? What's the kiss for this time?"

"For giving one of the best parties of the year."

"Don't forget who wielded the vacuum cleaner. I'm the one who earned a kiss."

"I agree."

Before he could step closer, she opened the door and stepped into the rain. "See you."

Marty watched Lula drive off in his car and once again felt that emptiness he always did when she vanished from sight. One of these days she'd love him the way he loved her. He wasn't giving up. Not ever.

His parents were at the kitchen table when Marty walked back inside.

"Hey! You're still up," he said, bouncing in and taking a glass from the cabinet. He turned to the sink and filled his glass with water, then chugged it down. "Ah. Refreshing." He set the empty glass in the sink and backed toward the door. "I'm off to crash."

Mrs. Skolinski grabbed his arm on his way out of the room. "Just a minute." She reached around and tugged out the black lacy thong from his hip pocket.

Holding it on the tip of her finger, she said, "This isn't my size."

"You crack me up, Mom." Marty retrieved the thong and put it behind his back. "I found it. I don't have a clue whose it is." He held up Boy Scout fingers, feeling like he was ten again. His mom had a way of doing that to him. He glanced at his dad who had his hand over his mouth, stifling a laugh.

"So about the house? Looks good, right?" he said. "Lula and I did most of the cleanup." He needed to do more PR for the love of his life if she was ever going to win his mom over.

"She's not good for you, Marty," his mom said. "You tell him, Nick." She fixed a hard stare on her husband.

His dad took his time, before saying, "We're just worried, you know? That girl's got a reputation around town that's almost as bad as her mom's ever was. Two of a kind, Marty. You know it's true that 'The apple doesn't fall far from the tree'."

That was another of his dad's sayings Marty had heard hundreds of times, so he pulled out another one like it. "Don't judge a book by its cover, Dad. She's not bad. She just isn't as lucky as I am. She's got Lucille Banes and General Banes for parents." He grinned. "I've got you guys."

His dad held up his hands in surrender. "I don't have a comeback for that. Do you, Mrs. Skolinski?"

"You two!" His mom got up and kissed Marty's cheek. "I only want you to be careful," she said into his ear. "I don't want you hurt."

Chapter Thirty-Eight

Lula

After dodging Marty's kiss, Lula ran toward his car, covering her head with her coat. The rain was coming down hard. Mr. Skolinski was right. It was going to be a dangerous ride home, and neither of Marty's parents wanted their son to take any risks like driving in a major storm after a suspected few beers. While Lula didn't understand the whole parent-child-concern thing, it rankled a bit when she saw it in action. Lucille saved her concern for other people. The General saved it for himself. None of their concern was aimed at Lula.

Marty stood in the doorway watching, so she waved before backing into the street.

Even though it had been hours since she had anything to drink, she'd take her time, drive like a nun on the way to church. Everything would be all right, but even thinking it, she knew it wouldn't. Not between Win and her.

Payback. That was all she'd intended, but then it had gone so wrong.

"Stupid, stupid!" Lula gripped the wheel of Marty's car and kept her eyes on the road, her attention focused on steering between the lines and not weaving. All she needed to make the evening perfect was to catch some keen-eyed cop's attention and get pulled her over. Although she was alert, one whiff of her breath, and... She did not want to sleep in juvie. She did not want to call her parents to pick her up. If she had to do that, she'd either owe her mother another favor, or she'd have to deal with General Asshole again. He'd confiscate her truck for good this time.

Her options—be tangled in a web of motherly intrigue or ground to silt under military boots. She shuddered and doubled her focus on the road.

This late Friday night storm that was roaring through Las Animas came with jagged lightning and thunder that was guaranteed to send raccoons and feral cats scattering for shelter. She braked to dodge two critters. Her windshield wipers were at full speed and still not clearing the rain fast enough. One thing in her favor tonight was that she knew this road very well.

Lula slowed at a dip with the warning sign *Subject to Flooding*, but a little too late. Her tires sprayed a fan of water out both sides of the car. She yanked the wheel to keep it straight, fishtailing her way to the shoulder, clipping a lamppost before jolting to a stop.

Adrenalin shot through her like a flash flood and perspiration beaded on her forehead. She let herself fall back against the seat, exhausted. With her eyes closed, she took short gasps of air until her lungs steadied and she could inhale normally again. Tonight had turned into one vehicular disaster after another.

Telling Marty she was sorry about his car would be easy. It was Win who was going to be the challenge.

She didn't like the feeling that regret made while slogging its way through her conscience. It didn't come often, but when it did, she knew she'd stepped way over that invisible line of good behavior. She wasn't a good girl, didn't want to be, but she wasn't a total evil-doer either.

"Not until tonight," she whispered to herself before starting the car and easing it back onto the road. But it had been for a cause. For Blossom. No. That wasn't true. She'd wanted to "get" Win Knight back for years of indifference.

The house was dark when she rolled up to the

garage. The outdoor lights were timed to go out by midnight and had gone off over an hour ago. Before climbing from behind the wheel, she tucked the keys under the floor mat for Marty to find when he came. Then she made her way into the house.

Careful to close the door with the softest click, she fumbled with her shoes and was just slipping them off as a bundle of canine energy arrived. Lula petted and shushed Butter, then she climbed the stairs on tiptoe. Her dog bounded ahead, lighting the way with his golden coat. Her head was pounding, and her foot caught on the last step, sending her sprawling onto her stomach. She lay, listening, childishly crossing her fingers in hopes the thud on the floor hadn't alerted either of her parents.

When neither of their doors opened, she got to her feet and went to her room. She followed the tiny landing strip her nightlight cast across the floor, peeling off her jacket, then, not bothering to undress, she fell across the bed on her back. The ceiling was barely visible, but once she'd stopped moving, whatever alcohol was left in her bloodstream went straight to her brain, and everything overhead kept circling above her. She closed her eyes, willing that ceiling to stay still.

She'd read MacBeth a few weeks before in English class, so she had a passing thought about what the teacher called *the portent of storms*. But she was tired and grouchy over what had gone down between Win and her at the party, so the idea of deathly omens carried on the wind slipped like a silvery fish through her mind before the alcohol and exhaustion pulled her into sleep.

Chapter Thirty-Nine

Blossom

Once Clifford walked away and Blossom had closed the door, she locked it, then slid the deadbolt into place. She was glad Clifford had left. It was the way he looked at her. Yet, she felt sorry for him. Nobody in Las Animas liked him. They'd repeat snarky comments they'd heard from someone—they couldn't remember who—about his parents and why he'd dropped out of school, but they couldn't say anything more specific about him other than he gave them the creeps.

She shook her head. Well, he kind of creeped her out, too, but that wasn't enough to treat somebody like a criminal and shun him.

"Blossom?" Her mother's voice came from the back, startling her. It had been so long since her mother had called to her that at first, she doubted she'd heard right. Then panic hit. Something must be wrong.

She dashed to the back of the house, her heart set to rapid fire. In the kitchen, she found her mother seated at the table with a cup of steaming tea. "Mom," she gasped. "Are you all right?"

"Yes, dear. I couldn't sleep, so I thought some chamomile would help."

Blossom leaned against the jamb, catching her breath and letting her heart settle back into its normal rhythm.

"Didn't I hear you talking to someone?" Her mother stirred cream into her tea.

Blossom nodded. "A boy stopped by."

"So late?"

"We were at Marty's place and his party's just

over. That boy, the one who was here, is kind of strange, but I think he's lonely and sort of shy. He keeps wanting to talk to me."

"Be careful of the shy ones, sweetheart," her mother said, and she held up the teapot. "Would you like some?"

"Sure." Blossom hadn't seen her mother looking this alert in four months. Seeing her at the table, stirring tea, talking… It felt strange and yet very familiar, as if these months were slowly peeling away and leaving a clear picture of the woman she loved so much.

Blossom reached into the cabinet for another cup and set it on the table.

Once she'd poured the tea, her mother leaned back and sipped, keeping her eyes down. Then she looked up at Blossom. "Actually, I stayed up to tell you I'm sorry."

Blossom waited without speaking. What was her mother apologizing for?

"I'm sorry I've let you down," her mother said. "I'm not sure I can explain what happened to me, but it was as if every bit of energy was draining from me, and I couldn't find a way to stop it" —she reached out her hand and covered Blossom's— "until now."

"Oh, Mom." Blossom rose and wrapped her arms around her mother.

"You needed me and I wasn't here for you. I'm going to be here from now on." She cupped Blossom's chin in her hand. "I promise."

After her mother went to her room, Blossom stayed in the kitchen, feeling that finally her life had turned around—at home at least, and that was incredibly important. She'd missed her dad terribly, but until this moment she hadn't realized how really hard losing her mother had been.

It was almost one, but Lula was a night owl, so Blossom pulled out her cell and punched in Lula's number.

She picked up on the second ring.

"What's wrong?" Lula's voice sounded slightly boozy and thick with sleep.

"Nothing's wrong. Sorry for waking you up."

There was a moment that Blossom heard what must have been Lula settling against pillows, then she said, "So what happened with Win on the way home?"

"He said he didn't hate me." Blossom left out the first part about his hating Lula. There was no need to spread more hurt tonight.

"Generous to a fault, isn't he? What about the *pretend* girlfriend kaka-poop?" Lula asked.

"We're canceling all of that. He's on his own with Dina and her cousin." Blossom couldn't help but laugh. She kept seeing Win, sprinting to avoid Dina's outstretched hand and ducking behind corners whenever she and Brittany headed his direction.

"We got him good tonight, Blossom. You and me. But I'll grovel and pay for that itsy ding in his stupid car. All will be good. Promise."

"I hope so. We've got another year in the same classes. I don't want them to be miserable." Blossom waited while Lula rambled on about her plan to set everything to rights, then she said, "Lula, what's wrong with Clifford Mott?"

"Everything. Why?"

"He's been at my house twice tonight, and I'm not sure how to deal with him."

"You don't *deal* with that jerk! Tell him to get lost. He's a defective. Have you ever seen his parents? For heaven-to-hell sake, I've told you that, Blossom. Don't you listen?"

"I listen. I just thought you knew something—something first-hand, not gossip—that made you say that about him."

"Look, dear sweet person who I think is daft but I still kind of like, for starters people say he tried to kill his father. Isn't that defective enough?"

"But that's just gossip, and you know it. If he tried to kill anybody, he'd be in jail or counseling. He wouldn't be working at the convenience store."

"He'll wind up in jail," Lula said. "It's just a matter of time." There was a noise in the background, then Lula said, "Hey, gotta run. Lucille's here. Talk to you tomorrow. I'll be at Blendz and Moore bright and early."

"Tomorrow." Blossom shut down her phone and went to her room. How could anybody call their mother by her first name? She tested out her mother's name. "Denise." Then shook her head. That sounded so wrong coming from her.

Before she climbed into bed, she finished filling out the entry form for the Water Media Showcase and set it under the picture she'd painted of Win.

Chapter Forty

Win

After dropping Blossom at her house, Win drove slowly back to his father's. He'd made a mess of the whole night, and now his car had a ding smack in the middle of the front just above the grill. He'd get that fixed, then he'd steer clear of every damned person in that school. For the rest of his time in Las Animas, he'd pretend Lula Banes didn't exist. He'd dodge Dina and Brittany. And if that stupid Dina found another way to send him one more naked selfie, he *would* follow up on his threat and turn her in to the cops for sending out pornography.

He pulled into the garage and shut down the engine. The hard person to cut out of his life one hundred percent was going to be Blossom. She pulled at almost every part of him, even more after that kiss tonight.

He hit the steering wheel with the flat of his hand. "Damn her."

Inside, the house was dark except for the nightlight that Kate always left on for him. He found a plate with cold meat and cheese on the counter and pulled out a chair, wishing Kate was up and waiting for him in the kitchen. Tonight, he needed someone to talk to, someone he trusted.

He'd almost finished off the last bite of cheese when a door opened at the back of the house, and the soft sound of Kate's slippered steps came down the hall.

She walked into the kitchen, yawning and wrapped in her robe, but she looked as if she hadn't been asleep yet. "How was the party?" she asked.

"Not exactly perfect." He washed down the last of

the cheese with a long swig of water and wiped his lips before launching into what had happened at Marty's.

She waited until he'd finished, then folded her hands on the table and leaned forward. "Well, about the business deal with Blossom. You said you were sorry. And from what you've just told me, Blossom didn't leave still mad at you."

"True." But he knew she was really hurt by his stupid request. He'd seen it immediately in her face. He'd seen remnants of that hurt all night, and he'd heard it in her voice. "Even though you're right about Blossom, I'm still ticked. She knows how I feel about anybody even touching my car, let alone driving it off and wedging it between a truck" —he jabbed a finger at the image he had of Carter Redford's trailer hitch and the dent in his front end— "and a car so tight that..."

He rose fast and toppled his chair. He set it back up, and at the sink refilled his glass from the tap. No matter how he tried he couldn't stop seeing the tiny dimple in the Sea Foam Green paint. "She shouldn't have let it happen." He downed the water. "I know it's not her. It's Lula. It's always Lula!"

"How many times have I heard you say that?" She shook her head. "You're still carrying around that other prank Lula pulled on you in the eighth grade. Come on, Win. That was kid stuff, and it happened a long time ago. Some things you have to let go."

As upset as he still was, he had to smile. "How many times have I heard you say that?" But her advice had a settling effect on him. The tension between his eyes relaxed, and the back of his shoulders eased a bit.

"Well then, it's time you listened." She stood directly in front of him, so he had to look into her eyes. "Go make it good with Blossom. It seems she's important to you."

Win didn't answer, but she was right. Blossom was important to him, and once more he thought about how that idea scared him because he might actually want to include her in his life. That was something he'd vowed he wouldn't do with any girl—not ever again. He shook his head. "I don't trust relationships. They're doomed, and so are the people who get into them."

"Win, you're being impossible. Stop it."

"I'll think about it," he told her, leaning against the counter and staring at the floor.

Kate went to the cabinet and took down a glass. "Put some ice in this," she said, and handing it to Win, she winked. "Not too much. I don't like my drinks diluted." While he flicked on the ice dispenser, she reached to the top shelf and brought down her bottle of bourbon. After adding a shot to her glass, she sat at the table. "Join me. It's time we talked."

"Sure. Whatever you say. But it's kind of late for this tonight, isn't it?"

"Nope. This is the perfect time." She took a sip.

Once he sat down, she leaned across the table, rolling her drink between her hands. Then she said, "You were three when your mother fell in love with someone and left your father."

He hadn't heard that right, and his face must have registered the confusion he felt because Kate shook her head. "No. You heard what I said. And your mother wanted me to tell you when you were ready to understand." She toasted him. "Tonight, you're ready." She took a sip, then went on. "Eva always planned to come and get you, but she didn't have a chance. Your dad hired me—"

He jerked forward in his chair. "Wait. My dad hired you? I thought my mother did."

Kate shook her head. "No. Your father hired me

to look after you while he went to collect her. And he did. Like she said, she couldn't give you up, and that's what your father threatened to make her do. He had the money and the law on his side."

So this was what those whispers were about during the nights he huddled in bed listening to Kate and his mother around their kitchen table, probably sipping bourbon the same way Kate was right now.

"She could have divorced him, couldn't she?"

"Of course. But he would have kept you. You were his leverage."

"Mothers usually win custody. That much I know from the kids at school whose parents are divorced."

Kate tapped the sides of her glass lightly with her fingers. "Your mother loved someone named Anne O'Brian. Back then that made the difference, and as far as your father was concerned and as far as his lawyers were concerned, too, it made her unfit."

Win's chest tightened around his heart, and for a moment, he didn't feel the normal pulse of it. What Kate had just said shifted the way he understood his childhood. His mother and father. How they related to each other as well as to him. His world suddenly compressed into an unrecognizable knot and lodged where that vital heart should be beating.

He took a long drink, letting the cool water soothe his throat, the only part of his body he felt at the moment.

"Your mother and father figured out a marriage that let them live in the same house, and they both worked at being your parents." She drained her glass. "Then Eva took sick and died. Your dad filled his life with work and this," she said, waving her hand to indicate the house and the estate, "and later the *Friday Night Ladies*." She stared off into the distance for a while. "He's not my favorite person in this world right now."

She pointed toward the upstairs, and Win understood that his dad and his date had moved their party from the dining room to the bedroom. "But not all of what happened was his fault," Kate said.

Win felt numb. He tried to picture his mother the way he always had her in his head, but tonight her face came to him out of focus.

Kate carried the empty glasses to the sink. "She loved you, Win. That's the most important part of this story, but so did your father. He still does. He just can't get through to you, and you don't want him to." She walked behind his chair and hugged him, pressing her cheek against the back of his head. "Don't let what happened between your mother and father color your whole life. Relationships are complicated, and no one is a hundred percent wrong in them." She started down the hall, then looked back. "Keep in mind some people are good together."

He waited until the door to her room snapped closed, then when his legs stopped shaking, he walked upstairs to his bedroom. He had that early morning shift at Blendz and Moore, so he fell across the bed, kicked off his shoes, and let sleep pull him inside itself.

Chapter Forty-One

Clifford

After Clifford walked away from Blossom's house, he felt light and full of excitement. From the way she'd stepped outside and stood next to him, letting him touch her cheek—even if only for a brief moment—there was no doubt at all. Blossom Henley was the one. She was the girl he wanted, and he could make her want him. He was sure of it.

Clifford reached his car but stood with his hand clutching his key, not opening the door.

She was the only person in Las Animas who treated him like a human being. To everyone else, he was the one they spread lies about. They thought he didn't hear, but he did.

"His sophomore year he tried to kill his dad."

"Not true! He came at me. I … I had to. He was going to kill my mom. He was…" He stopped suddenly, aware he was talking and loudly. Even though it was well after midnight, he glanced around to be sure no one was nearby listening to things that should be locked away inside his head.

Once he was sure he was alone, he leaned against the car to calm down and stop the shaking that came whenever he remembered that night.

He might not be big like Harry, but he was fast, and over the years he'd learned how to get out of the way of those beefy fists. That night he'd learned how to attack. His dad had a scar across his stomach to prove it. When Clifford grabbed the knife, things changed between the two of them. He'd balanced the odds a little bit. From then on, even when Harry got drunk and looked like he was ready to take Clifford on, he held back. But the threat was still there. All it would take was one drink too many and Clifford was sure he'd have to save himself and maybe his mother again.

The night he'd taken Harry on changed the way Clifford thought about himself, too. Afterward, he knew exactly what he had to do to make his life work—quit school, get a job, get away. Afterward, he knew he'd never go for Harry with only a knife again. If there was a next time, he'd leave that man with more than a scar across his stomach.

Clifford gripped his car key so tightly it dug into his skin, and memories of that night in the converted motel room faded. He climbed into the car and drove to the convenience store parking lot. He'd sleep there tonight and not take a chance that Harry would still be awake, mean, and chugging beer.

Chapter Forty-Two

Saturday, The Day Of
Win

On Saturdays, Win always rose before Kate. And that Saturday morning he rose even earlier. He'd dreamed of his mother. He'd tried to remember the time when she wasn't there in the house, when only Kate answered his frightened baby cries. He couldn't. Maybe it was that he didn't want to. When he'd been a toddler, his mom left him for someone else she loved. Ann O'Brien. That was going to take some getting used to. That and what Kate had said about his father forcing his mother to stay.

He showered, dressed, grabbed an apple from the basket on the counter, and was out the door before Kate or his father came into the kitchen. He'd eat at Blendz and Moore.

He was still angry about Lula and her crappy stunt that had put a ding in the front of his car. And Blossom... Damn her anyway. He didn't hate her, but he hated that she'd agreed to be a part of that prank Lula'd hatched.

When he entered the garage, he stopped to run his finger over the front of his car. He could fix it so nobody would see it, but he had to admit there was damage of the humankind he couldn't repair. He'd been a jerk and hurt Blossom.

I want you to pretend to be my girlfriend.

He gripped the door handle until his knuckles turned white. Why had he said that?

He got into the car and started the engine, letting it warm up before slipping it into gear. As he backed out of the garage, it purred like a giant cat. If only his life ran as smoothly as his T-Bird. He wished he didn't have these conflicting feelings about Blossom because they were driving him nuts. At least he could look forward to his job at Blendz and Moore this morning. That was something he had control over and could do well. He planned to be there even before his shift started, so he'd have a good hour before he had to take care of customers. One customer he didn't want to see would be there by ten if she wasn't still in bed nursing a well-deserved hangover. Lula never missed a Saturday morning with her favorite caffeinated beverage.

Last night's storm had brought down a lot of tree limbs and the street gutters were still rushing with runoff. He guided his T-Bird around the street clutter and safely into the parking lot until he found a space at the end next to a hedge.

Before going inside the coffee shop, he wiped his hand across that ding in the front of the car again. It could have been a lot worse with Lula behind the wheel. He clenched his jaw at the thought of her sitting in the driver's seat. She'd made him furious since grade school, and nowadays, she pushed every anger button he had. He punched the air, thinking how it would feel to land his knuckles on Lula Banes' jaw just once and get away with it. He pushed open the glass door to Blendz and Moore and stepped into the warm air tinged with the lingering scent of years of darkly brewed caffeine-laden coffee.

Chapter Forty-Three

Lula

By early Saturday, the California rainstorm had tapered off. Lula climbed out of bed still wearing the clothes she'd put on the night before. She blinked up through the skylight at the drizzle pattering onto the Plexiglas and squinted as a watery sun seeped through her drawn curtains. They didn't glow the usual cheery yellow but were a drab beige. Yawning, she swept them open and looked out the window at the swimming pool below. The last raindrops from heaven spattered over the blue water, making thousands of tiny dimples across the surface, and a warmed chlorine mist spiraled into the chilled air.

Lyrics from a song they'd played at the party last night popped into her head. *"Tomorrow we're gone, our souls rising to the sun."* That's what the mist reminded her of—souls on their way somewhere—but she was tense and still totally whupped after last night's vodka, so no wonder she was gloomy.

The scratching sound at her door meant Butter had collected his leash and was demanding a run. When she opened it, he poked his nose through and wriggled his eager furry body into her room and into Lula's arms.

Lula only had to see her dog and the world brightened. With Butter she smiled easily and laughed, loving nothing more than to hold his silky warmth close to her.

"Have I told you how much those morning kisses make a hangover so much better?" She shed her clothes from last night and pulled on her sweats while Butter did impatient circles around her ankles, dragging his leash.

"Give me a minute, okay?"

She ran her tongue over her teeth. They felt mossy, and she could only imagine what her breath must smell like. The toothpaste and mouthwash made her feel marginally better. "Come on, you." She opened the bedroom door and Butter darted into the hall. "Just don't expect a full loop out of me this morning."

But once she was outside, she managed to do the whole trail to the lake and back. It gave her time to sort out how she'd talk to Win. Apologizing wasn't in her vocabulary, but this morning it would have to be, if for nobody else but Blossom.

Back at the house at last, she and Butter loped down the long driveway, both panting and with feet soaked. The storm had left puddles ankle-deep along the trail. She'd missed most of them. Butter missed none and now wore mud socks.

At the door, Lula knelt and pulled her dog to her. "Come here. You're a mess," she said, taking a rag from her pocket. She gently wiped Butter's paws, and then took off her shoes and socks and left them outside.

When they entered, the only sound in the house was the hum of the refrigerator. Early mornings were the times when this space felt at peace. She could even sit at the kitchen counter, nibble on dry toast, and enjoy orange juice without her stomach flinching.

She'd poured a second glass of juice and was taking a sip when Lucille came in. For a moment, Lula stood in shock at her mother's unexpected appearance at that early hour. Lucille never showed up in the kitchen or anywhere else before eleven, so this morning she had to really need that favor.

"Good morning. You've already run your dog?"

"Best time of day to do it."

"For very few of us, sweetheart." Her dark hair

fanned around her face—wild and sexy. She wore a black silk robe with a feathery collar fluttering around her neck like an excited feather boa. Even without makeup, Lucille was beautiful—a Hollywood version of a *real* woman just out of bed. She reached out and tucked Lula's hair behind her ears. "You set such a high bar in the exercise department." Yawning, she turned on the coffee maker, then as she reached for a cup, she asked, "How was your run? Where did you go?"

Uh oh. Whenever her mother asked a question about what she was doing, there was a reason for it.

"It was good. I just went to the lake and back." Lula took another bit of toast and swallowed more juice.

"Nice."

Lula popped the last of her toast into her mouth, then sat back in her chair. "What do you want?" She might as well get this over with.

One thing about Lucille, she appreciated a direct question. Her lips parted in a genuine smile, and she leaned toward Lula, lowering her voice to a whisper. "It's about that favor."

"I told you I'd think about it."

"Well, I'm ready to up my offer from twenty to thirty on your allowance, but I'd like you to say the two of us took some girl time away for a weekend, not just a night. Some shopping, a show, dinner. We stayed in the city."

Carlos, the pool boy must have more charisma than Lula had detected during his chlorine sessions in their patio. She silently thanked him for that. The extra thirty each month would help with the repairs for Win's car, and she'd be able to pay for that traffic ticket. There might be some left over for an extravagance of some kind. She shrugged. "I'll check with Blossom today." Lula hoped her friend would jump at a chance to have her stay for a couple of nights. It might ease some of the strain her father's death had caused between her and Mrs. Henley.

Lucille poured herself a coffee and leaned against the counter. "You're such a good girl. I don't know where I got you."

It was very strange that to everyone else she was the bad girl of Las Animas. To her mother, she was good. That said a lot about where Lucille Banes was on the goodness scale of life.

"I'll figure something out, but I need a few weeks advance. I have some unexpected expenses coming up."

"Hmm. Okay." Lucille held out a hundred-dollar bill. "I knew I could—" The sound of the General's footsteps stopped Lucille from finishing. "Later."

Lula pushed away from the table as the General arrived, and Lucille saluted him with her cup on her way through the door. Lula's so-called family interacted like the tiny mechanical people living in a cuckoo clock—circling in and out of rooms, barely glimpsing each other.

Lula stayed long enough to take back the keys to her truck and listen to the short lecture from her father about obeying the traffic laws of Las Animas and not wasting money on tickets for moving violations.

"Which" —he raised a firm index finger and directed it at her— "increase insurance costs."

She'd only been going a *few* miles over the speed limit, but the cop had been unsympathetic. She'd have to pay for the ticket, which she'd thought was punishment enough. The General—not surprisingly—disagreed and had taken her Tundra hostage all of Friday night. Now that was excessive in the penalty department. She didn't say any of this. Instead, she chewed the inside of her cheek and nodded.

Once she'd been dismissed, she downed the last

of her orange juice and went up to her room for a shower, dressed quickly, and after feeding Butter, climbed into her truck. "Let's get this over with," she said to herself.

It was time to face Win.

Chapter Forty-Four

Blossom

Blossom sat with her mom in the kitchen, eating breakfast and picking up where they'd left off in their conversation the night before. The sound of their voices brought warmth back into the room, and when Blossom glanced around, the room was brighter than it had been in months. Having her mom back was wonderful.

"And so I've hired someone to come in a couple of times a month to clean this place," her mother said. "Mrs. Strong starts Monday."

Blossom looked up quickly. "Strong?" That had to be Dina's mom. Blossom didn't know of any other Strongs in Las Animas.

"Very nice girl. She's had a run of bad luck. Guess she and her husband lost their jobs when that plant over near Greenlee closed, and then they lost their home." Mrs. Henley sipped from her mug of tea. "We're so lucky to have all that we do."

Blossom hadn't known that about Dina. No wonder the girl always seemed so uptight. "I know her daughter. She's kind of a weird girl, and I don't think she likes me very much." Blossom closed her eyes, remembering Dina's stricken face in Marty's hallway last night, then for a moment she remembered Win's lips against hers. She put her fingers against those lips and wondered if she'd ever kiss him again.

"Blossom?"

Blossom felt the touch of her mother's hand on hers and opened her eyes.

"Are you all right?" Concern drew her mother's forehead into tiny crevices.

Blossom had longed to see her mom like this again, the way she used to be, and now that it was happening, she relished that feeling of being loved, of being cared about by her mother.

"I'm good. I was just thinking that you make judgments about how people behave, and then find out there are reasons they act the way they do."

"So true. So you say this Dina's a weird girl? How so?"

Blossom didn't want to bring up what happened at the party, so she voiced something she'd always been puzzled by. "Dina always looks hungry." A new thought suddenly stopped her from taking another bite of toast. "Oh, no. Do you think the Strongs don't have enough food?"

"Mrs. Strong seemed very healthy when she was here. She told me she has steady jobs around town and that her husband has a good job in Greenlee now. I don't think they're without food, Blossom." She went to the sink and rinsed out her mug. "Anyway, all of the people she gave as references said she was good. So that's one thing off my list for the week."

Blossom grinned and slathered extra jam on her toast before taking the last bite. This was turning into a very good day, with her mom making a list and checking things off the way she used to when she ran everything so well.

Mrs. Henley leaned over the sink and pulled the curtain aside. "Oh my goodness! Just look…" She stopped, staring out into the garden.

Blossom tensed and sat up straight. "What's wrong?"

"Would you look at your father's roses! I have to find a gardener before there's nothing left of them."

Blossom collapsed gently in her chair. This was

going to be an absolutely perfect day.

Her mom came back to the table and sat down again. "I know you're off to see your friends at the coffee shop, but" —she covered Blossom's hand with her own— "can you come home early?"

"Uh. Sure. Do you want me to do something?"

"I hoped we'd go somewhere. Maybe downtown for a late lunch or a movie." Her mother reached across and gently brushed a curl back from Blossom's forehead. "It's time we got out of here. I mean it's time I did, and I'd like it to be with you."

"That would be great, Mom." She squeezed her mother's hand, taking a moment to cherish the anticipation of an outing like the ones they used to share. It would be like before. "I'll just see if I can talk to Win and make sure things are good between us."

"Win Knight? What happened?"

"I played a trick on him, and he didn't think it was funny. I have to apologize."

"A trick? On Win?" Her mom laughed and hearing that laughter after months of it being silenced, Blossom was even more sure everything was going to be much better at the Henley house from now on.

"That boy was always so moody but adorable when he was little. I used to call him Mr. Storm Cloud, but never to his face, of course. I haven't seen him since Eva died."

"He hasn't changed, but you can add infuriating."

Her mom tipped her head, looking more playful than she had in years. "You've always liked him, haven't you?"

"It's my curse I guess." Blossom stood. "He's not easy to have in my life."

Her mother pulled Blossom to her feet and wrapped her in her arms. "None of the boys are, sweetheart. As much as I loved your father, we had our times of trouble. Why don't you go work it out and make yourself and him happy."

"Thanks, Mom. I'll try." Blossom grabbed her car keys and her sweater. "See you this afternoon."

Chapter Forty-Five

Marty

Marty sopped the last of his pancakes with more syrup and closed his eyes. Nobody made pancakes like Mom Skolinski. For years he'd held back on thirds. Gymnasts burned a ton of calories, but not even his routines were a match for his mom's triple egg, melted butter, and buttermilk pancakes.

She poured him more milk, then sat across the table from him and his dad. "So what's the plan for tonight, then?" she asked.

He'd mentioned not being home for dinner that night, but he hadn't explained the reason. Now he'd have to tell her the lie. "Lula needs some help with her term paper, and—"

"Lula? I didn't think that one needed help with anything." Any time his mom said Lula's name her voice grew spines.

"Well, she does this time, and I've got my paper finished, so I said I'd…" He picked up his glass and took a long swig of milk. Lying always made him nervous. Lying to his mom made his stomach jump and do more flips than he did during half-time. He swiped his mouth with the back of his hand. "…said I'd stay through dinner, so we could work on her, uh, her citations."

His mom stared across at him, but he was sure it was a stare about Lula, not his lie. "How late will her citations make you?"

His dad chuckled and patted her shoulder. "Better the devil you know than the one you don't."

"Dad!"

"Just saying."

Marty stood up. "I should be home by eleven. Not later than that." He'd stop at Blendz and Moore to check again that his alibi was set, then he'd drive to Glenford and see the university coach. He was all nerves about this meeting today. He had to make a good impression, get the coach's attention, and make sure he remembered Marty Skolinski when he finally showed up at college for a place on the gymnastics team.

His hands shook as he carried his plate to the sink, and then he ran to find the car keys. The faster he got out of the house, the fewer lies he'd have to tell. There was only one thing worse than being a liar, and that was being a serial liar.

Chapter Forty-Six

Dina

Dina pulled the covers aside and got out of the sofa bed. Yawning and stretching her arms overhead, she looked down at Brittany who was still curled under the blankets but not asleep. "How much money do you have?" Dina asked her cousin.

Brittany pushed herself up and sat on the edge of the sofa, rubbing her eyes. "Enough for coffee and doughnuts, if that's why you're asking."

"Then let's escape from here before our parents get up. I'm feeling *sardine-ish*."

Brittany frowned, then stared at the floor. "I'm—"

Dina grabbed her arms and made her look up. "I didn't mean you were making me feel that way. I just meant…" She shook her head. "I need some away time from parents and this house, not from you."

"And Win's at Blendz and Moore working this morning." Brittany eyed her. "Am I close?"

"You hit the bullseye." Dina touched her lips and grinned with a look she hoped was adorably charming and playful. That's what she practiced in her selfies. One day it was going to get her into the top modeling slot. One day it was going to make Win stop and finally see her. "My turn to be first in the bathroom this morning, right?"

Brittany nodded and fell back onto the bed. "Take your time."

There was no such thing as taking time in the Strong's bathroom, so Dina—out of habit—was quick to finish. On her way out, she pulled on her coat and checked her makeup in the hall mirror. She looked back at Brittany who was pulling up her jeans. "He'll come around if I keep at him. I know it."

"I hope so. I'm getting tired of the chase."

"Ready to get out of here?"

"Let me brush my teeth," Brittany said, and she went into the bathroom, which would soon have four people standing in line.

While she waited in the hall, Dina straightened the mirror, pulled her hair back into a tight ponytail, and turned her head to the right. She dipped her chin, then turned left and elevated it enough to deepen the shadow along her nose. Sliding her gaze to the side so she appeared to be flirting with the mirror, she tucked her face into a coy smile. She might need to add a touch of mystery to that doe-eyed look.

For years, she'd studied photographs of the top models and mimicked them in this hall mirror when she was alone. She'd made it a point to remember the sensations across her forehead and on her lips, the way her neck felt when she wanted to be shy, or how it felt to look bold when she thrust her head forward just so. One day, she'd have to duplicate those emotions in front of a camera, and she wanted to have all her poses down. A lot of online articles explained just how important all of that was.

But that was in the future. First, she had to get enough money together to hire a photographer and have a topnotch portfolio made.

She looked around the house. She could sell every piece of crappy furniture in this place and she'd still never have the money for even one photograph. She had to graduate and find a job. If only she could skip her senior year and get started on what she wanted to do with her life.

Wishing took up a lot of her time, but it also kept

her thinking about her future and distracted her from the present, which was not where she wanted to be.

She banged on the bathroom door. "Hey, Brittany. Come on."

"I'm enjoying the privacy, okay? Give me a minute."

"Whatever." Dina pulled out her phone, and taking a moment to make sure she had exactly the inviting look she wanted, she took a picture of herself in the mirror. In the email to Win, she typed, "Good morning. I'm coming for some of your super coffee." Hesitating only a few seconds, she attached the photo and hit Send.

Chapter Forty-Seven

Lula

Lula drove down the main street of town to Blendz and Moore, looking forward to her favorite coffee but dreading that bit of groveling she had in store. She parked in her spot, the one smack in front of the glass door with the giant steaming mug painted on it. But once there, she didn't pile out of her truck the way she usually did. Before going inside, she had to work up some courage, and that was a real first for her.

Creeping crap, Lula Banes, get your sorry butt out of this truck and into that place.

Lula checked her hair in the rearview mirror and tugged it into a tighter ponytail. "Euu." Her post-party head still wasn't ready for any tugging.

There were two reasons she might have to give up vodka forever—the revenge it took on her the next day and how it led her to do the unthinkable.

But seriously, Win had made a big deal out of practically nothing. He'd gone ballistic in front of everyone, and for what? Still… She confronted her eyes in that narrow mirror and said, "What happened was your fault, so go fix it." For a moment, she waited with her hand on the latch. "Now." She pushed open the driver's door and climbed out.

Growling under her breath, and with her jaw clenched, she stomped inside the coffee shop.

Dina Strong, the short, thin-faced junior, who was more bones than flesh, huddled with her cousin, Brittany, at one of the tall tables by the window. She shouldn't be surprised to see them. They always turned up when Win was in a room. They'd become Sir Baldwin's most recent groupies.

Lula couldn't remember if they'd seen her fight with him last night, but they broke their huddle when she walked inside and kept their eyes on her. Dina flashed some attitude and grinned. Of course they'd seen the fight. Hadn't everybody who was there seen it? Now these two didn't want to miss what might happen when she faced Win this morning. She glared back, but they didn't look away. She should charge for those kinds of stares.

Both of them were a waste of her attention, so she turned away and sniffed the concentrated coffee smells. She wished she could be anywhere but here, facing the wrath of Win Knight. And she didn't dare yank his chain by calling him Sir Baldwin to his face this morning either. She had to wear her good-girl pants and apologize. Last night she'd been very bad, even for her.

Win stood at the espresso machine—a tall, darkly disheveled wizard pulling levers. He frothed milk, then pressed finely ground coffee into the holder and fastened it into the machine. A hot black stream dribbled into the cappuccino cup.

He didn't see her at first, but when he did, he drew his eyes into missiles. *Majorly pissed* sprang all over his face.

Ordinarily, Lula would counter with a hostile comeback of her own, but today was different. She held up her hands and mouthed, "I'm sorry. Shoot me."

He ignored her and helped the next customer. When her turn came, she ordered a double latte, then leaned across the counter. "I'll beg forgiveness right here. Now. On my knees."

Win knocked the used coffee grounds into a bin, refilled the holder, and set a clean paper cup under the spout.

"Well?" She turned her palms up in supplication.

He shoved the latte at her. "Four dollars and twenty-five cents."

"You can't stay mad at me forever, Win. And I plan to fix that *itsy* ding in your car. I do."

He dropped her change on the counter, shoved it at her, and growled close to her ear. "I've already forgotten it, so stay the hell out of my life." He glanced up. "Go away. You're holding up the line."

He hadn't forgotten a single bad, or even slightly bad, thing she'd said or done since kindergarten, and Lula knew it. But there were five grumpy, caffeine-deprived people behind her, so instead of pushing her point, she took her coffee to a table in the corner, sat down with a bump, and drew herself up into a sulk.

She hated groveling for anybody, in particular the almighty Baldwin Knight. But she did have something of a conscience, so if for no other reason than she didn't want it making her feel guilty forever, she'd repair Win's car. Fortunately, her funds were at an all-time high with Lucille's contributions. That was a relief because last month her father, General Asshole, had cut off the stingy allowance he doled out like a Dickens character. One month without an income and a hefty traffic fine had set her back a lot.

She sipped her latte and stared out the window at Blossom Henley who'd just pulled up in her mom's car and was on her way inside.

This was going to be interesting—Blossom, Win, and her all together again. What a way to start a weekend. But this might be the chance to sort out some of her mess with everyone at the same time.

Chapter Forty-Eight

Dina

Brittany elbowed her cousin as soon as she spotted Lula's truck pulling up to the front of the coffee shop. "Hey, D, look! It's the junior class witch we love to hate."

Dina spun around in her chair and watched Lula check herself out in the rearview mirror before climbing down from the shiny new Tundra. Every time Dina had a chance to spy on that one, her head filled with imagined things she'd like to see happen to Lula. A terrible accident that ruined her perfect, conceited face. A super embarrassing moment that exposed her to the whole school's ridicule. She longed for anything that would bring Lula Banes off that tall pedestal, anything that would wipe away all that queenly indifference.

Over the past year, Dina knew envy too well, and she'd learned how to carefully cultivate it so it grew as wild as the weeds around the house she lived in.

She glanced at the counter where Win was serving coffee to a line of customers. "This is going to be fun," she said to Brittany. "It looks like the fight last night wasn't enough for her Highness. She's back for more."

What Dina really meant was she'd give anything to be the one fighting with Win. At least that way he'd notice her instead of looking through her as if she didn't exist.

Brittany stretched up from her chair and yawned. "Let's get out of here and do something fun. I'm tired of Blendz and Moore and" —she jutted her chin in Win's direction— "him."

"And miss the fireworks?" Dina shook her head.

"No way. Besides, what can we do that's fun in Las Animas this time of day?"

One thing Dina didn't want to do was return to the place she and her cousin lived.

"We're staying until the blood flows." Dina sipped her coffee, swallowed the last of her doughnut, and pointed to Brittany's chair. "Sit down. We have front-row seats."

Brittany rolled her eyes and slid back into her chair. "Whatever."

"I'm back in a sec. Don't take your eyes off that counter. You have to tell me anything I miss." Dina hurried to the bathroom.

Once inside, she checked to see if anyone else was in the room. It was empty. She shut herself in one of the stalls and poked her finger at the back of her throat. A few seconds later, she'd gotten rid of the doughnut and flushed the toilet. Then she rinsed her mouth and freshened it with breath spray.

Patting her cheeks, she smiled into the mirror. "That's better." The restroom door opened and she edged past a girl on her way in, relieved her timing had been perfect. Conversations were still at a low buzz in the coffee shop, so she'd either missed the explosion or it hadn't happened yet. She slipped onto the chair across from Brittany again. "So what happened while I was gone, anything?"

"No. You're just in time. Look." Brittany pointed out the window.

"Wow! Even Blossom Henley's here. Did we pick the right day to be at Blendz and Moore or what, Cuz?" Dina's insides burned when she thought about Win kissing Blossom in front of her at the party last night. If her stomach weren't already empty, she'd hurl again. Instead, she kept her eyes on the blonde girl she now hated almost more than Lula. But what roamed inside her was more complicated than hate. There was a longing tucked inside it.

Chapter Forty-Nine

Blossom

Blossom turned into the coffee shop parking lot, and when she spotted Lula's truck she almost didn't stop, but as she rolled past the plate glass windows, it looked as if everyone sat calmly sipping coffee. Nobody was yelling. Either Lula and Win had had it out with each other in there, and everyone had recovered from the explosion between them, or Lula had done what she'd promised last night—she'd apologized and Win had accepted.

Blossom took in a deep breath and parked. She might as well go inside and face the carnage or, if she was lucky, find out all was good between her best friend and Win.

When Blossom stepped into the shop, Lula sat in the corner, her feet propped on the chair with her arms wrapping her knees. She couldn't pull herself up any tighter. Blossom saw her as a spring ready to uncoil. And the moment the door closed behind her, that's what Lula did. She jumped to her feet and strode straight across to where Blossom stood.

"Before you say anything, I'm sorry. I shouldn't have pulled that stunt on Win, and I apologize for getting you involved." Lula nodded her head toward Win. "I told him, too. But he's being a pain in the butt."

"That's hard to believe," Blossom said and ducked her head to hide the smile she couldn't stop.

"What? That I apologized or that he's being a pain?"

Now Blossom looked at Lula and let the lopsided grin turn up the corner of her mouth. Lula Banes was one of a kind. Bitchy most of the time, snooty a lot of the time, but someone Blossom couldn't help liking. Inside that bitchy girl was someone very special, and the artist in Blossom saw it. Lula's eyes might shoot bullets at everyone around her, but there was a softness in them, too. A little-girl softness. Someone who took the time to plant seeds and pet dogs. You only had to look carefully to notice it.

Blossom glanced across the shop at Win, who shifted his gaze, but not before she caught him watching her.

She hoped they'd be all right after some time passed, that they'd at least hang out together once in a while. After last night, she should give up trying to make him love her. Win didn't let himself love anybody. She was very sure the only way she might capture his heart was to transform herself into his vintage car. That was all Win lavished affection on.

"I'll grab a coffee, and we can talk." Blossom walked to the counter and ordered as if Win was just another barista and not the guy she craved more than life or had finally kissed last night. He didn't meet her gaze as he set her coffee in front of her and took her money, but she put her hand over his when he held out the change to her. When he didn't pull away, a small spurt of hope gave her the courage to say what she'd rehearsed this morning.

"Look, I'm so sorry I got involved in the prank, and I'm going to tell Lula I forgive her. I know Lula's really sorry about what she did, too." Blossom glanced back at Lula, who'd returned to her seat and drawn her long legs close to her chest again. "Please accept our apologies."

"Do whatever you want about her. I'm not interested in how sorry she is." He slipped his hand from under hers and walked toward the employee's door at the rear of the building.

"What if she pays for the damages to…" She didn't get to finish before he disappeared into the back room, but she said it to the closed door. "…your car." She shook her head, giving up any hope he'd come back and let her finish her apology. "Okay, maybe not."

On her way to sit with Lula, she spotted Dina and Brittany on the opposite side of the room.

Dina stabbed her with a look that screamed, "I hate you!"

Blossom winced and gripped her cup.

Dina wasn't forgetting their run-in at the party any time soon any more than Win was. Blossom wished she could explain the "pretend girlfriend" deal she'd had in her mind when she kissed Win, but she doubted Dina or her cousin would give her a chance to do that. So now Blossom not only had Win angry at her, but a new enemy to face in class every day. She glanced at Brittany. Probably two enemies. All because of last night. Why hadn't she just stayed home after the game and skipped the party?

She pulled out the chair and sat across from Lula. When she glanced up, Marty, Lula's shadow, stood in the doorway.

Chapter Fifty

Marty

Marty didn't drink coffee, but everyone he knew did, so he showed up at Blendz and Moore on Saturday mornings to check out who was there and what was on for the weekend. Then he'd head for the gym and a couple of hours of training. Today he had another reason for being here. He had to be sure Lula was going to lie for him. If she tried to back down, he had some leverage because, while that dent in the Toyota's fender wasn't major, it had Lula written all over it.

Seeing Blossom and Lula together after last night's major blow-up brought him to a quick stop, but then he hurried to their table and sat before either of them could tell him to get lost.

"So is this the kiss and make-up I see happening?" he asked.

"Go away." Lula pointed at the door.

"Come on, Lula. Be nice. For once. You kind of should be, you know." He grinned. "My car's a classic, too, and now it's got a new Lula signature 'dent' in the right fender."

Lula rolled her eyes. "I don't think that Toyota qualifies for classic except in the clunker category."

"I'll remind you of that the next time you need a ride."

"Okay, you can stay if you're silent. Understand?"

Marty shoved his chair a few inches away and pretended to cringe, then mimed zipping his lips. With a quick nod, he sat back, silent. Then because being quiet wasn't part of his nature, he said, "Totally not saying anything." He pointed at himself. "That's me. Silent."

One thing about being the guy who made everybody laugh, he was highly visible, yet nobody took him seriously. He'd wait and listen while Lula and Blossom worked out the kinks in their relationship. He was positive they'd launch into how to make Win gather them back into his circle—meaning he'd growl at them and maybe let them be near him at parties, so while all of this happened, Marty feasted on Lula. His Lula. The tall, lanky girl with ebony hair he longed to stroke, and lips that he'd always fantasized about kissing.

He licked his own lips at the thought.

"Will you stop staring?" Lula scooted her chair around so her back was more to him and she faced Blossom. "I need to crash at your house tonight," she told Blossom.

Now he gazed at the way her spine rounded and her sleek hair shimmered like a dark mirror under the lights. He loved her fingers, too. They were long and tapered at the tips. She kept her nails blunt cut and always shiny, like little stars. He gazed, mesmerized by the way she used those fingers to punctuate her sentences. Beautiful.

Over Lula's shoulder, Blossom stared at him. He was sure his face was all about longing because it usually was when he thought about Lula while looking at his reflection. Quickly, he crossed his eyes, hoping she'd only see the clown in him. It was better to be the fool. That way everybody, but most importantly Lula, let him hang out near her.

Blossom shifted her attention to Lula again. "You can sleep over, but are you telling me why?"

Lula pointed at Marty. "Don't you remember him asking me to cover for him?"

Blossom shook her head. "No."

Lula pulled the silver rabbit's foot from under her sweater and dangled it on one finger. "His bribe?" She sighed, then slowly, as if reminding Blossom of what she should have remembered was a huge chore, she said, "He wants to go somewhere and do something his parents do not approve of." She glanced at Marty. "Am I right?"

As Lula explained his plot to deceive his parents, regret wormed its way through Marty and doubt followed on its heels. He'd never lied to his mom or dad. But then he'd never craved something as much as he craved a shot at being on Gladford's gymnastic team. His conscience shrugged. They'd understand once they saw him at the events. He was sure of that.

Lula nudged him. "I asked you if I had your story straight."

He nodded agreement, and Blossom said, "Oh yes. I do remember, but I'm not clear on my part in this."

"Look, I can't tell Mrs. Skolinski he came to my house and not have him actually be there. You've met The General, the cross-my-heart-and-hope-to-die soldier. If anyone can ferret out a lie it's that man, and he'd narc to Marty's dad in a heartbeat. Las Animas is not big enough to keep anything secret from him. L.A. isn't big enough. The universe—"

"I think I've got it. So you want to say you and Marty were both at *my* house?" Blossom still looked slightly confused.

"Exactly. We say we were working on our career papers for English together, and Marty and I had dinner with you. He can go home late from wherever he really goes without his parents getting all uptight, and I'll sleep over." She glanced away, then back. "There's more. My mom needs a favor tonight and tomorrow night. If I stay with you, I can tell The General I went somewhere with her after we finished our homework. Look, I'm doing two acts of kindness for two people, Blossom. It's complicated."

"You're right about it being complicated, but I'm okay with it. Just don't ask me to keep it straight." Blossom sighed. "I guess I'll see you later. I've got to go. My mom asked me to come home early so we could do something together today. She's even up for us going to a movie later."

"Your mom's talking about seeing a movie? Wow! That's huge."

"I know. I'm really excited. She was the way she used to be about making plans this morning. Maybe you better text me before you come over tonight, in case we're out. But I can leave a key."

"Will do. And I'll work on Win. Promise." Lula drained her cup and, without glancing at Marty, passed it to him.

He took it with an exaggerated bow, then tossed it into the recycling bin.

Lula leaned across the table and put one hand over Blossom's. "It's good about your mom. I'm happy for you, and I'm glad you're not mad at me."

"Thanks. I'm so relieved to have her back." She gave Lula a quick hug. "And I'll stay not mad as long as you promise me you'll never pull any more of those jokes, especially on Win, okay? I don't like them any more than he does."

Lula heaved another exaggerated sigh but managed to get out a tight-lipped, "Promise."

Marty turned away from their hug-fest in time to see Clifford Mott open the door of the coffee shop and walk to one of the back tables.

Chapter Fifty-One

Win

In the back room of the coffee shop, Win leaned against one of the storage cabinets, Blossom's voice playing over in his head.

"Look, I'm truly sorry and Lula is, too. I'm going to tell her I forgive her," she'd said.

She'd said more, but he'd stormed off and slammed the door before she finished. He hadn't heard whatever it was she had to tell him. That wasn't fair. He'd hurt her feelings, and she had every right to get even. If he'd tell her he accepted her apology she'd accept his. He hoped.

It was Lula he was really ticked at, so he shouldn't take it out on Blossom.

He'd go out there and pull her away from that She-Devil. He chuckled at that name, which was perfect for Lula. He imagined her with horns, standing with her feet braced wide and holding a three-pronged spear. She'd be dressed top to toe in flaming red.

He shoved open the "employees only" door and started straight to where Blossom sat with Lula and Marty.

Clifford Mott stood in the far corner and tracked him across the room.

He'd never seen Mott here before, and Win was almost as surprised as if a zebra had wandered in and taken a table. Dina was at the window and her eyes were fixed on him, too. All of the undesirables were in Blendz and Moore this morning. Well, screw them. He had a mission, and they weren't important enough to keep him from completing it.

"I have to talk to you," Win said, reaching down to take Blossom's hand and pulling her to her feet.

He stood facing her, and the chatter in the coffee shop faded into the background.

Her forehead creased into a puzzled look as if she wanted to ask a question, but she remained silent.

"Look, I've said this before, but you didn't seem to believe me." He stepped closer to her, ignoring the hostile stares he knew would be coming from Lula and Dina. "I would take back everything I said in the car that night if I could. Since I can't, I'm asking ... begging you to forgive me."

"Oh." Her voice was whispery, but her expression changed from confused to happy, and she reached up to touch the side of his jaw. "Of course I forgive you. Now it's your turn to forgive me, and then we'll be even."

He nodded and, smiling, said, "Yes. Absolutely. I'm over it."

"And you're over what Lula did, too?"

Win glanced down at Lula's upturned face—calm as glass and just as cold. Between very tight lips, he said, "If she'll come up with the money to fix my car, I'll *forget* what happened." He couldn't say the word forgive whenever he was talking about Lula's misdeeds.

Blossom hugged him close to her. "Thank you, Win. You've made everything good again."

The footsteps came fast and hard, and in the next moment, Clifford Mott grabbed Win's arm and yanked him back.

"No! Don't touch her!"

Chapter Fifty-Two

Clifford

Clifford chose his best jeans and polished his black boots to a high shine. He smoothed back his hair and used extra mouthwash. When he was satisfied that he looked his best, he tucked the journal inside his duffle bag and drove into Las Animas.

He stopped at the convenience store on his way to Blendz and Moore. There was one more thing to add to his gift for Blossom. Something sweet. Chocolate. She'd like that. He was sure.

Ryan Connell looked up when the buzzer sounded. "Hey! It's your day off, man. What're you doing here?"

"Just need a couple of things. How's it going?"

"It's not busy yet." Ryan held out a copy of a car magazine. "I'm catching up on my reading."

Clifford nodded as if he understood, but he didn't. There was always something to do in this place, and a quick glance at the racks out front said so. "Better see those are stocked." He pointed to where there should have been magazines and free newspapers.

"I'm on it!"

"Right." Damn, Connell was a lazy jerk, but that wasn't Clifford's problem. Let the manager figure out who was doing the job and who wasn't.

Clifford picked out a small heart-shaped box of chocolates he hoped she'd like. Then he went to the back of the store and his locker. He'd made up his mind that he'd have that gun with him when he got back to the apartment just in case. Harry was as unpredictable as a swamp alligator, and since he'd started drinking hard again, Clifford wanted to be ready.

Taking the gun from his locker and stuffing it into his sweatshirt pocket, he went to the cash register and rang up the chocolates. Last Valentine's Day, the manager did a special gift promotion with free wrapping for purchases over ten dollars. It was a bust, so they had a lot of red ribbon left under the counter. Clifford snipped a length of that, and then left with a quick wave to Ryan who was still reading his car magazine.

The Blendz and Moore parking lot only had one space available next to the Tundra Clifford recognized as Lula's. The T-Bird was at the far end.

So they're both here.

He didn't know Blossom's car, but he recognized Marty's beat-up Toyota parked a few spaces down.

Clifford dug inside his duffle bag and took out the journal. Using the red ribbon, he tied the journal and the heart-shaped box of chocolates together, then zipped them inside the bag again. He'd planned his meeting with Blossom so carefully, but as sure as he was that she'd be happy with his gifts, his hand was sweaty when he took hold of the handle and opened the car door.

Inside the coffee shop, he spotted her right away. So bright and beautiful.

Good morning, Sunshine.

He swallowed and gripped the bag handle tightly. No one stood behind the counter, so he took a seat at the back of the shop and waited. He didn't plan on ordering anything until after he'd talked to Blossom. Then he'd buy her a coffee. They'd sit together. Talk. She'd tell him how much she liked the journal with his art. He'd be nervous when she read his letter, but if he was patient and let her get to the end, she'd have to see how much he really meant all he'd written. Maybe she'd share some chocolates with him while they had coffee together.

"A little early for dessert, but these are so good, Clifford. Thank you."

"I'm glad you like them. They're my favorite. Next time I'll bring you something more special."

"This is perfect, and so is the journal. You're really thoughtful, you know?"

That's when he'd lower his gaze and say something like, *"I can't afford to buy you expensive presents yet, but I will soon. I'll make it up to you other ways."* He was sure she'd let him take her hand. He wouldn't try to kiss her, not in public. He'd show her the respect she deserved.

He leaned back in his chair, closing his eyes, imagining how it was going to feel—that first kiss. It would be warm and sweet. He'd be gentle and kind because that's what he was sure Blossom wanted.

He unzipped the duffle bag, took out the journal and the chocolates, and set them on the table, his hand shaking with excitement and a serious attack of nerves. He was ready to go over to where Blossom sat and ask her to come to the back with him. He stood and took a deep breath. This was one of the most important moments of his life.

The slamming of a door brought Clifford to a stop. Win Knight walked with long, serious steps across the shop straight to the table with Blossom, Lula, and Marty.

He couldn't hear what they were saying to each other, but Blossom nodded and then smiled. Win took her hand and pulled her out of the chair. She stepped closer and…

Inside his head, an avalanche of shattering glass stopped Clifford's hearing. A blast of cold stopped his heart. His vision of the room narrowed to two people, *her* arms around *him*. It was not supposed to be this way. He had to make it different. He *would* make it different. He rushed toward them and grabbed Win by the arm.

"No! Don't touch her!"

Chapter Fifty-Three

Marty

Marty scrambled out of Clifford's way. The guy looked desperate.

"What's wrong with you, jerk?" Win's voice was loud enough to silence the conversations at the nearby tables.

Clifford shoved Win aside. "Get away from her."

"Clifford, what … what are you doing?" Blossom fell back against the table.

Clifford didn't answer, but he caught her by the hand and drew her close. "You can't be with him. Do you hear me?"

"Go away. Leave me alone!" Her high and frantic pitch stopped the last few conversations in the coffee shop.

"What the freaking hell?" Lula jumped to her feet. "Let's get out of here." She brushed past Clifford in Lula fashion—fast, with eyes aimed over his head.

Marty switched his attention between Clifford and Win, then between Clifford and Blossom and Lula. "Hold on," he shouted. He had to calm them down, but the exchanges were coming too fast. When Marty looked at Blossom, her face had drained of color. She seemed frozen in fear as she stared up at Clifford Mott who still gripped her hand.

Lula stood at the door, ready to pull it open. "Blossom," Lula shouted. "Get over here. Now!"

Clifford held out a small book and a heart-shaped box tied together with a red ribbon, but Blossom shook her head and pulled her hand free. She backed away, still shaking her head no.

"It's for you, Blossom. Please take it." Now the desperation Marty had seen in Clifford's face was in his voice, and he shoved the package into Blossoms' unwilling hands. "You have to take these."

"No. Let me go, Clifford." Blossom tried pulling away again, but he tightened his grip.

"She said, let her go," Win said.

Blossom yanked free of Clifford and fled after Lula.

Win pushed Clifford aside. "Get out of here. Now!"

Marty made for the door but stopped short when Clifford brought his head up and gazed around him as if he'd lost sight of someone and was desperate to find them. Then he fixed his stare on Win with such hatred that Marty broke into a sweat.

Before Blossom had taken three steps, Clifford had a gun out of his jacket and aimed at her. When Marty understood what was happening, his one thought was to reach Lula. He bolted toward her at the same time she yanked open the door.

Dina and Brittany were a blur on either side of his vision. Seconds later their screams mingled with three gunshots that echoed like canon fire around the coffee shop. One more shot. Then another.

In the seconds after, people dived for the floor. They scrambled behind tables and piled together. The explosions kept coming from the gun in Clifford's hand. Sugar containers shattered. The door where Marty and Lula stood crumbled into glass bits. Cups rained down in a white flurry of pottery.

Marty's back exploded in a sensation of white heat, then everything fell into a black silence.

Chapter Fifty-Four

Win

Frame by frame the images flickered past Win—a carousel of stills.

The shattering of cups, the screams.

The wall with the giant poster of the Blendz and Moore logo erupting with splintered pockmarks.

The steady flow of white crystals sifting from the sugar canister on the counter. He stared first at the holes in the wall, then at the small sugary mountain mounding on the floor. He didn't understand how the two were connected, but it was very important that he figure it out.

Dreams made odd demands like this, but he wasn't dreaming. He'd just come to work, just fought with Lula, just accepted Blossom's apology. They were all right here at this table, talking a minute ago.

Marty. Where did he go?

His mind had to be playing tricks on him. Kids he'd just served coffee lay sprawled on the floor. Most of the tables had overturned. An earthquake must have rumbled through and he'd missed it, but that made no sense. He would have felt an earthquake. Why couldn't he think straight?

Maybe if he moved. He took a step into a slurry of water, coffee, and a sticky substance that sucked at the soles of his tennis shoes when he lifted his foot to go around it. Pieces of cups and plates were scattered across the floor. Where the main door used to be, Lula lay face down and very still. Marty, his hand outstretched toward her, was on his side and whimpering, making the sound of a hurt pup.

Dina sat propped against the counter, her legs

stretched out in front of her. She stared without seeing anything, but her eyes streamed tears. Next to her was Brittany. She was on her back. Her eyes were open wide and turned toward the ceiling.

Then he saw her—Blossom facing away, lying on her side, one knee drawn to her chest, the other leg stretched long. Her hair fanned out behind her as if she'd just brushed it and then decided to rest. Standing over her with his back to Win was someone wearing polished black boots.

Win's every step felt as if he were pushing through thick crude oil, not air. It took what seemed like a very long time before he raised his eyes from Blossom and those boots. When he did, he was staring into Clifford Mott's face, a face twisted into terrible pain.

In one hand, Clifford held a gun pointed at him. In the other, he gripped a small book and a heart-shaped box tied together with red ribbon. His gun hand fluttered like a bird in distress.

Clifford yelled. "She ruined everything! I had a plan. She was supposed to go with me." He waved the gun at Win. "You. You're the one to blame."

Win reached his hand out the way he'd calm a snarling dog. "Put the gun down, Clifford. I didn't do anything. Let me help—"

A sharp heat burned Win's left arm, and in seconds, that same heat surged through one of his thighs.

Win went to his knees. He held down the bile forcing its way up from his stomach and burning at the back of his throat. Time stretched even longer, drawing out the moment, distorting the images and the sounds, freezing everything in place until Clifford stepped away from in front of him and moved to stand over Blossom.

Win swallowed and swiped at his forehead with the back of his hand. Now, he couldn't move no matter how much he willed himself to, and dark edges formed around everything he tried focusing on.

"You're like all the others," Clifford shouted at Blossom. "I thought you were different. I…" His arms hanging at his sides, he walked toward the shattered glass door. With great care, he stepped around Lula and Marty and over the dark pools that spread at their edges.

Moments later, the loud crack of two more shots ended the numbness inside Win's head and freed him to move. He pulled out his cell, but even as he did that, sirens were shrieking in the distance, so he dropped the phone and crawled to where Blossom lay so still. He gathered her to him. Her back was warm and damp, and that dampness spread thickly between his fingers and seeped into his pant legs.

"Blossom," he whispered down at her, and for a moment, her eyes fluttered open. "Nothing's going to take you from me. Do you hear?"

Win tightened his arms around her as police pounded through the door and ambulances swarmed into the parking lot with sirens screeching and red lights flashing.

Customers who'd been shielded behind tables rose and ran outside where they fell into the arms of onlookers in the parking lot and sobbed. Shortly, the news cameras arrived and two men with microphones pushed their way toward the front of the crowd.

Win heard but didn't see the man who knelt next to him. "Let us take her, son," the man said. "You come with me."

A sea of hands—reaching, pulling, checking for pulses—appeared around him. A pair of these hands took Blossom from his arms and laid her on a gurney. More hands put wide collars around Marty's and Lula's necks, then lifted them onto gurneys as well. People in dark blue uniforms placed oxygen masks over his friends' faces, inserted needles into their arms, then rolled them off into the backs of ambulances.

Win felt a hand grip his arm. "Let's get you to the hospital." It was the same voice he'd heard earlier, and now Win focused on the man who knelt talking to him.

About thirty, he had steady dark eyes that locked onto Win. Small bits of gray already threaded through his hair at the temples, and he looked as if he worked out. His chest filled the blue uniform shirt and lean muscles ran the length of his arms.

It was important to focus on him. Somehow this man was Win's connection to reality. Nothing else around him made sense. Only this man kneeling in front of him, holding him by the arm was keeping him in the world.

"I'm not hurt," Win said finally.

"Just let me do my job, okay?"

"Help me up. That's all you need to do. Or go away!"

The paramedic wrapped Win's arm over his shoulder and helped him to his feet. The pain shot up through Win's left leg, and he sank into a well of ink.

Chapter Fifty-Five

Two Weeks After
Lula

Lula wheeled herself to the nurses' station. "I'm looking for Marty Skolinski's room."

The duty nurse rose from her seat. She leaned over the counter and peered down at Lula. "And who are you?"

"His friend."

The nurse sat back down. "Family only."

Lula pushed out of the wheelchair, and levered herself up, with her forearms on the high counter. "I'm his sister, then."

The nurse clicked her ballpoint. "No."

"No? I'm not his sister? How do you know that?"

"Yes. You are not his sister, and no, you can't visit him."

Lula flipped the nurse the bird.

"Very sweet," the nurse said. She turned her back and busied herself searching through a file drawer.

Lula sank into her wheelchair and rolled herself down the hall toward her room. At the corner, she did a U-Turn and slid low in her seat. Building up speed, she rolled silently past the nurses' station. She was on the hunt for Marty's room, and from the gossip she'd overheard, he was on this floor along with the other shooting victims from Blendz and Moore.

Once she was out of sight of Nurse Nasty, she sat tall and read the nameplates along the hospital corridor. But it wasn't the nameplate that told her where to stop. It was Mrs. Skolinski.

Marty's mom came out of a room just a few doors

down from where Lula sat, so Lula waited until the small bundle of a woman walked away. Her back was hunched, and that made her seem an even more compressed ball of determination than usual.

As soon as Mrs. Skolinski stepped into the elevator, Lula wheeled herself into Marty's room, where unlike hers, three beds lined up side by side. She found Marty by the window.

His eyes were open, and he was on his back staring at the ceiling. The TV overhead was silenced, but the pictures of dancers and acrobats filled the screen.

"Yo! You awake or what?" she asked.

He acted as if he hadn't heard her, so she moved closer and tapped his shoulder. "I'm talking to you, my man."

Marty didn't look at her, but he raised his hand and pointed at the door. "Go away, Lula."

She sat back. *What? Go away?* This was not the Marty she knew. And if she did leave, it wouldn't be the Lula she knew either. "Not until you look at me and say something stupid."

The rattle of meal carts and the beeping of doctor calls over the intercom came from the hallway and made the room even more like a square cave. It was a year of waiting until Marty rolled his head toward the window and away from her.

"The cops came to see me." She wheeled closer to his bed and wished he'd say something, but when he didn't, she said, "They asked a lot of stupid questions." Again, he didn't move or acknowledge she was in the room. "Okay, then. Be a butt. Just remember I came to see you, so you owe me a visit. Four-fifteen. And when you come, bring that ridiculous sombrero, or don't bother." She pushed away from his bed. "By the way, tell that witch of a nurse out there that I'm your sister. I need backup."

　　She didn't leave right away. She hoped he'd turn toward her and they could talk, but he didn't.

Chapter Fifty-Six

Win

Win lay in bed staring at the ceiling of his room, relieved to be out of the hospital. For the first time since he'd been little, he was glad to be in his bedroom. The cops had been to see him in the hospital, then detectives came, asking and re-asking questions about Clifford Mott and what had happened that Saturday morning.

He felt stupid telling how his shoes had stuck in coffee and sugar. But that's what he remembered most, that and Blossom, how he'd gone to her and held her. But he hadn't told the cops about Blossom. He'd only told them about Mott's eyes and how he'd stood with a gun in one hand and a book with a heart-shaped box tied to it with red ribbon. And he told them about the pain of being shot, only he hadn't known he'd been shot. Not until later.

Pushing himself up, Win grabbed his crutches, then swung between them to the toilet, peed, and dropped back onto his bed just as his door opened.

Kate stuck her head inside. "You up for breakfast this morning?"

"Pancakes?"

"Of course. I'm bringing them in."

He sat up. "No. I'm coming to the table. I've had enough room service, and you look like you've had enough time playing nursemaid."

Kate winked at him. "How'd you guess?"

"I know you, Kate. There's only so much pampering you'll agree to." He smiled at her and grabbed his crutches again. "Besides, my butt's sore from all the bedtime. I'm there in three minutes."

When Win came into the kitchen, his father was already sitting at the end of the table, freshly shaved and smiling. "Good morning. Glad to see you up and about."

Win had stopped in the doorway, assessing the scene, but now made his way to the other end of the table and the stack of hot cakes that waited for him.

He slathered butter and syrup over the top and cut into the sweet dough.

"You can't beat Kate's pancakes," his father said. "Real comfort food."

Kate busied herself at the sink and kept her back to the two of them.

Win chewed and nodded, then took another bite. He didn't want to talk to his father, and keeping his mouth full was one way to avoid it. He cut a large chunk from the stack, chewed, and swallowed. Again. Too fast. His plate would soon be empty at this pace, and the excuse eating gave him for remaining silent would be gone. He slowed his jaw, slowed cutting the pancakes, and took more time lifting the fork to his lips.

Still, his father stayed across from him. Usually, he left within minutes of Win's entering any room, so what was up with the old man today?

"Kate's making her stuffed trout for dinner. I'm coming home early, so you don't have a chance to eat it all." His father stood and carried his plate to the sink, then he came to stand by Win. "I'm picking up your favorite dessert from Kimble's. We're celebrating tonight."

Win's fork clattered onto his plate and he stared up into his father's face. "What are we celebrating?"

Kate turned off the faucet. She glanced back at him and shook her head. Since his father had his back to her, he didn't see that, so Win kept his eyes on her and tried to understand what she meant.

"You. We're celebrating you being home and safe," his father said. There was a catch at the back of his throat, and he covered his mouth to cough. He squeezed Win's arm, then left the kitchen.

Once his father had gone, Win opened his hands to Kate in a wordless question.

She dried her hands and sat at the table. "Let him celebrate with you, Win. He's earned that much."

Was he hearing right?

"When the police came that Saturday, he was out the door and on his way to the hospital before I could pull on my pants. He was there with you after the surgery and until you came to. All night. And when the doctors gave you the all-clear, he collapsed."

Win glanced up.

"Yes. Heart attack. Not a killer one, but a warning for sure. He asked me not to say anything. But" —she put her hand on his shoulder— "this is as good a time as any to knit up some of those holes between the two of you. You're family. And besides your uncle, you two are the only family left, so help him make it work."

He took his time before standing on his good leg and picking up his crutches. "Are you going to be here for this celebration?" he asked her.

"Wouldn't miss it for anything. I love your favorite dessert."

He looked over his shoulder at her. "What *is* my favorite dessert?"

"Oh, Win. You're nearly impossible sometimes. Make that most of the time."

He waited until she said, "It's Burnt Almond Cake. That's your favorite dessert."

"Hmm. You're right." He swung between his crutches down the hall to his room. On the way, he said, "I'd forgotten."

Chapter Fifty-Seven

Dina

The house echoed with emptiness and silence. Dina turned on the TV to fill it with sounds, but even with the daytime soaps, the quiet wrapped around her, too tightly, too confining. Her parents had left for work, but not before checking to see if she was okay. They'd been in her bedroom each morning and night since she'd come home from the hospital, asking what they could do, or if she needed something.

She only managed to shake her head no. She didn't need anything. After all, she had her bedroom back. The house no longer was noisy or crammed with three additional people. She had the quiet and the space she'd craved for a year. But since she'd reoccupied her own room, that quiet and that space had crept into her, and now she was as silent and empty inside as this place that surrounded her.

Her cell phone chimed, and she jumped at the shock of it. When she looked at the screen, it was the social worker's name that flashed white.

Dina hesitated. What did that woman want from her now? While she'd been in the hospital for observation, Brigit had already fished around in her head until she'd discovered her secret. Now she had therapy scheduled every week. Wasn't that enough?

Dina tapped the Accept on the screen. "Hello?"

"Hi. Just checking in with you. How's it going?" Brigit sounded too cheerful. She always sounded that way.

"I'm okay. Good really." Dina squeezed her eyes

shut to stop the burning that meant she was going to cry again. Would she ever run out of tears?

"We're scheduled to see each other tomorrow at ten. You remembered, right?"

Dina took a moment, then said, "My mom's taking off work to drive me." What Dina hoped she'd implied was that Brigit had better not be a waste of time, and in this family's case, gas money.

"That's wonderful. See you tomorrow then."

After she clicked End, Dina shut down the TV. She hadn't eaten since sometime yesterday, so she trailed into the kitchen, and when she reached the hall, what she saw in the mirror brought her to a halt. Her face was no longer pale and thin—it was a terrible white and skeletal. When she tilted her head, the shadow along her nose only added to the ugliness that reflected back. She could be a hundred years old and not look so dreadful.

The eyes that gazed out at her had death in them, and that frightened her so much she had to look away. She'd seen eyes filled with death before, but those had been Brittany's. Dina needed the support of the wall for a moment. The memory of that Saturday morning in Blendz and Moore never failed to buckle her at the knees. She saw everything as it happened—how she'd reached across and grabbed her cousin's hand, how she'd tugged at her. Shaking her. Shouting. But Brittany would never feel anything again. She'd never hear anything again.

Dina pressed her hand to her chest. She had a heartbeat. She was alive. But when she looked up at her reflection again, her eyes said otherwise.

She pulled her gaze away from the mirror and went into the kitchen to yank open the refrigerator. From inside, she took out a hard-boiled egg, cracked it, and after dashing salt over it, nibbled at the rubbery white exterior. Adding more salt on the yolk, she bit it in half, taking her time to chew. Still, it stuck in her throat and she choked.

With the half-eaten egg yolk in her hand, she dropped onto one of the kitchen chairs. If she ate the whole egg, could she keep it down? Would her stomach—would her head—let her keep this food inside and maybe fill in some of the emptiness she felt? She didn't know. But she had to find out.

Carefully and even more slowly, she chewed the last of the yolk and waited, willing that egg to stay where she desperately needed it to.

Chapter Fifty-Eight

Two Months After
Marty

Marty woke up to another day just like the one he'd lived the day before and the day before that, except he was home and not in a hospital or rehab facility. Until he could perform certain tasks on his own, each day would now be the same—a day he didn't want to face.

A caregiver would be at his side, watching him lift himself into his wheelchair and following him as he rolled himself into the specially modified bathroom. They'd wait while he made it onto the toilet. They'd wait close by while he showered. Then they'd follow him as he rolled back to the bedroom where he'd dress.

In a couple of months, he'd learned a lot about how to do everything differently. He'd learned just how much longer everything took.

Physical therapy would occupy the morning. He'd be an expert on afternoon TV. He was already an expert on misery and loneliness, and he'd only been a student at that for two months.

He couldn't stop the stab of pain, the sudden twist of the knife in his center that he recognized as fear.

"Yahoo, Marty." His caregiver swept into the room, his toothy smile a brilliant white in contrast to his deep cocoa skin. "I see those baby blues wide open and ready to go."

Marty didn't answer, just as he hadn't answered yesterday or the day before right back to day one when he'd discovered his toes didn't move when he willed them to. His legs wouldn't swing to the side of the bed when he wanted to walk outside. Everything from his butt down ignored him. He'd always associated the word paraplegic with guys coming home from wars or people in car accidents. Now he associated it with Marty Skolinski.

"So, Marty, what shall we wear this bright and beautiful day?" Akoni said.

Marty looked away as the caregiver's two powerful arms tugged the covers from his grasp and propped him up to sitting. In another practiced move, Akoni slid the transfer board onto the bed and rolled the wheelchair within reach.

"You are allowed to say, 'Thank you, Akoni. You are very strong and gentle with me.'"

Marty said nothing in response to that. He was focused on transferring from the bed to the wheelchair. He still had good upper body strength, so shifting between the two went fairly smoothly.

"A very good job," Akoni said. "Now let's get you into the bathroom, shall we?"

He went ahead of Marty and waited until Marty had come inside before closing the door behind them.

The humiliation of having to sit on a toilet with someone watching curdled Marty's stomach, but Akoni busied himself with setting up the shower, and Marty had a small moment of privacy before the man turned his attention on him again.

"The water is a perfect temperature. Again, Akoni does the best job. Don't you think?" Akoni waited a moment. "I do not hear anything, and I expect someone to tell me I do the best job for you."

When Marty still didn't answer, he laughed. "Well, another day then, but you must give me a recommendation soon, or I will have to give this job to someone more suitable."

"It's not a recommendation. It's a compliment," Marty muttered.

Akoni hesitated one moment, then said, "Ah, yes. Compliment. I appreciate a compliment." He grinned. "And the correction to my English." He stood by until Marty negotiated himself into the special shower chair and sat under a fine, warm spray. Then Akoni held out a plastic tube. "Shampoo." He put a bar of fresh soap in the tray. "Soap."

Marty blinked up at the tower of a man.

"I do not do everything. You must now wash yourself. The doctors say it is time for *indepenénce*."

"It's not *indepenénce*," Marty snapped. "It's indepéndence."

"But, yes. Of course." Akoni closed the shower door and stood outside, a blurred image on the other side of the fogged glass.

Akoni was the new caregiver. He'd only come last week after the first one rushed to manage a family emergency in the Philippines. Marshall Ocampo hadn't been a giant like Akoni, but he had a hidden strength that surprised Marty. He also did everything Marty needed, including brushing his teeth. It had been easy to turn over his life to Marshall. That way Marty could curl up inside himself and pretend nothing was happening in the outside world—all was imagined there, while his life went on exactly as before in his head.

He stared first at the shampoo, then at the soap. Foreign objects. *What do I do with these?*

The door opened and Akoni peered through the steam. "I do not see sudsing now, do I? Best get on with it. You have an appointment in only half an hour with the stretch and bend people." He opened the tube of shampoo and handed it back to Marty. "Hop to it."

Marty stared up at him and barely managed to

stop the grin. "I can't hop, you know."

"Well, one never knows what is in the future now, does one?"

Marty was the first to agree with that. He leaned his head back and squeezed the tube, working up a lather. He rinsed his hair, then soaped his body. When he stroked the bar of soap across his thighs, he pressed hard, hoping he'd feel something, anything. He sank back against the shower chair, pounding on his legs, but he might as well have been pounding on the tile wall. His legs were numb.

Chapter Fifty-Nine

Lula

The path from the street to the Skolinskis' front door hadn't gotten longer, but with crutches and a heavy boot encasing her left foot, it took Lula one heck of a long time to travel it. She had the taxi wait at the curb because the other two times she'd come to talk to Marty, he'd turned her down. She probably wouldn't be here long.

Mrs. Skolinski opened the door.

"I came to see Marty. Again."

"I'll ask. Again." Mrs. Skolinski left the door only slightly ajar and walked down the hall.

They had a pattern now that was a little different since before the morning at Blendz and Moore. Mrs. Skolinski didn't scowl at Lula. She didn't slam the door. Lula didn't pretend to be sweet.

Lula slouched on her crutches and looked around the neighborhood.

Two bikers waved and wooted at her.

"Lovely. I have admirers." She waved back. *Who knew when you might need a biker to haul your butt off the sidewalk?* She'd already planted her best side on the ground twice since she started swinging between these armpit killers. She adjusted the crutches so they fit in a different painful spot.

When she heard the quick steps coming from inside, she peered into the Skolinski house at the determined little figure of Marty's mom headed her way.

"Still no." Mrs. Skolinski shook her head.

"You told him it was me, right?"

Mrs. Skolinski pulled her lips up like a drawstring bag.

"Okay. Fine. Don't pucker on me." Lula hopped back and swung down from the porch. "Tell him I'll call."

"I wouldn't bother."

"Then I'll come back."

"He's not interested in seeing you," Mrs. Skolinski said. "So don't waste your money on taxis anymore."

Lula went a few hops down the path. "I don't give up on my friends, Mrs. Skolinski. You must know that by now. So I'll be back to see that little twit."

The door closed sharply behind her.

The bikers wooted again and toasted her with their beer.

"Bye, guys. See you around." She waved one crutch in the air.

More wooting as she opened the taxi door and hauled herself inside.

****

When the taxi stopped at her house, it had to pull in front of a dark sedan. Behind that was a local police car.

As she paid the fare, the driver turned to look at her. "What's up with the cop? You rob a bank or something?"

"Not today."

He shook his head and drove off.

Lula swung her way into the house and maneuvered around Butter, giving him a small pat on the head to calm him down.

Several male voices came from the living room, so she made her way there and stood in the doorway.

Her father waved her in. "They want to ask you

some questions again."

She set aside her crutches and plopped onto the couch next to her father, pushing the ottoman under her left foot to keep it elevated. "What are the questions?"

The local Las Animas cop stood to the side while two guys in suits sat in armchairs facing her.

"Are you Watchtower people?" Lula asked. "You look like Watchtower people."

Her father reached across and patted her knee. "Lucia."

"No, Miss. We're FBI." The taller one adjusted his tie. "I'm Agent Stanley. This is Agent Conners." They both held out an ID.

"Okay. Just as long as you're not peddling that rag, I'm good."

Agent Stanley cleared his throat. "All we need is to go over your description of what happened that morning at Blendz and Moore. And anything you know about Clifford Mott that you might have left out when we talked before." He took the seat across from her. "We've noticed some conflicting eye-witness accounts, so to close this investigation, we're revisiting everyone there that day."

She didn't want to talk to anyone about that morning. Not again. She'd blocked out Clifford Mott's name, and until this moment she hadn't heard it spoken out loud since that day at the coffee shop. She'd even muted any news coverage and quickly switched channels when his picture flashed on the screen.

"Ms. Banes?" Agent Stanley's voice nudged her to look up at him.

"I told the cops what I knew when they came to the hospital."

"Yes. We've read the reports, but we'd like to hear your account ourselves."

Lula sat back and crossed her arms. "He'd never come to the coffee shop on Saturday mornings before. At least that was the first time I'd ever seen him there."

"You went there regularly?" he asked.

"More or less." Closing her eyes made it easier to talk about Blossom and Marty and how she'd sat with them hashing over Friday night. How she planned to pay for the damage to Win's car. The apology she'd gone there to make. Swallowing, she skipped over the details of their conversation, about the lie she was preparing to tell her father so her mother could have a fling. "And then when I was on my way out…" She swallowed again, her throat suddenly dry. "He came after us."

"Clifford Mott."

"Yes." She told them how he'd yelled at Blossom, how he'd grabbed her and wouldn't let her go. The image of that moment stopped the flow of words as effectively as a red light, creating a traffic jam in her head. Then the fear in Blossom's eyes scrolled across Lula's memory. Fear followed by revulsion—a foreign expression for that girl. Mott's face twisted in pain and anger, as if he couldn't choose what feeling to give himself up to.

Instinctively, Lula placed her hand in the center of her chest. She remembered the feeling of being struck hard, then the explosion of pain in her foot, the nausea, and sinking to her knees. Anger rushed into her like heat, and she brought her head up, eyes set hard on the agent. She was once again Lula Banes, ready to confront. "You guys should have put him away years ago."

"And that would be why?" Agent Stanley asked.

"He tried to kill his father, for one."

"We've read the reports."

She ignored condescension in both of their faces. "And he was a creep, always giving kids a bad time when they came into the convenience store. Put it together for freakin' cripe's sake. He quits school and starts clerking at the store across the street where he keeps an eye on anyone from the high school. Ask any kid who ever went in to buy a Coke. Believe me, that guy was a creep, like, major *creepola*. No lie."

"Thanks, Ms. Banes." Agent Stanley and his partner stood up together, as if they'd exchanged a silent *time-to-go* message.

"That's it?"

"That's it. And we appreciate your cooperation."

"Are you talking to everyone else who was there that day again?"

"Yes. We've talked to all of the witnesses a few of times now."

"So what are they telling you?" Lula pushed herself up from the couch and balanced on her crutches.

"Thanks for your help." Agent Stanley motioned the Las Animas cop to leave along with them.

When they'd gone, she eased back onto the couch. "Jerks. I give them all I know and they clam up."

Her father shook his head, his breath audible with fatigue. "You can see it in on the news, Lucia." He left her with Butter snuggled against her bad leg, and Lula let the tears sting her eyes a while before she swiped them away.

Chapter Sixty

Three Months After
Lula

Lula hobbled into first period. She was down to using a single crutch, and she could put some weight on her foot again, so it was easier to manage books and classes these days. For the whole month since she'd returned to school, student voices dimmed to murmurs when she entered a room, but it wasn't the kind of dimming she was used to before that morning at Blendz and Moore. It was pity.

She'd searched for the best way to describe her new status in school, and *pitiful* was the only word she'd come up with. Nobody envied her now. Nobody was in awe of her or feared her either. All envy, all fear and awe, had been blasted away by Clifford Mott and his twenty-two caliber bullets. That was the caliber the police said had ripped through her boot, shredding the tendons and splintering bones in her right foot. A second one hit her in the breastbone. She'd be among the dead right now if Marty's lucky rabbit charm hadn't deflected the bullet that critical inch in her chest.

No longer recognizable as a rabbit's foot, the mangled piece of silver still dangled from its chain between her breasts. It stayed there when she bathed, when she slept, when she did anything. She'd never take it off again.

And damn. Why wouldn't Marty see her? Why wouldn't he take her calls? It used to be she couldn't empty her phone from Marty's messages fast enough. She was going over to his house again, and no matter what Mrs. Skolinski said, she was seeing that son of hers. Then she'd trounce that boy.

She started across the front of the classroom when Melinda Bailey came at her. Lula's first thought was to use her one crutch as a weapon, but Melinda only stood in her way with her arms crossed.

"I'm sorry," she said. "I'm sorry for everything I said about you and your mother." She looked at the floor, and then she walked to her desk. Once she sat down, she kept her eyes on her computer screen.

She's sorry? Melinda Bailey apologized to me? It took a moment before Lula was sure she'd heard those words from the girl she'd put on her forever hate list. So how was she going to deal with this new Melinda? Lula stood like a boulder in a stream while other students flowed around her on their way to their desks.

More to the point, how was she going to deal with this new Lula? It seemed Melinda had put her at a crossroads here. She had to make some kind of decision. And at this moment. Waiting and thinking about who she was going to be from now on wasn't an option.

She glanced around the room.

Branch caught her eye and gave her a thumbs up before going back to work.

She turned her head to face front and watched the teacher leaning in close to his computer screen, intent. Then she set her eyes on Melinda, and in the space of a single breath, Lula made her decision. She hobbled over to the girl she'd labeled the Rumor Queen, and rapped knuckles on her desk.

Melinda glanced up.

For a while they locked eyes, neither of them speaking.

"Apology accepted," Lula finally said, and with her one crutch under her arm, she started toward her desk.

On her way, she scanned the room for Win.

He was there, already in his seat with his hands folded as if in prayer. He didn't look up at her. Since he'd returned to school, he didn't look at anybody, but he was in every class and seated before the last bell. A big part of who Win was had gone missing, the defiant part. Clifford had blown that completely out of Baldwin Knight.

Dina—little, skinny, annoying, and obnoxious Dina—sat hunched over her notebook. She'd returned to Las Animas High like a ghost she thought no one could see. It was true that any of those annoying and obnoxious parts of Dina were invisible, but Brittany, who'd died that day, was very visible.

All who'd died that day were. Five. Two juniors, two seniors, and a freshman. It was the empty spaces that everyone noticed. On their way to classes, students slowed while walking past the unused lockers. They'd sweep fingertips over the unoccupied desks or leave small tokens. A flower. A note. It was their way of saying how much they missed the teens who used to walk these halls, attend classes, eat with them in the cafeteria. They suffered the loss of them every day.

Lula didn't leave tokens of any kind, but she never missed noticing the vacancies. And today, she eased into her seat again, but not before feeling the pain that spread like a bruise inside her belly when she looked at the three empty seats behind her.

I'll feel better when Marty comes back.

Chapter Sixty-One

Win

Win felt Lula come into the classroom and chose not to glance up. She used to push earth's atmosphere aside in long, leggy strides, but now on crutches, she disturbed it in jerks and bumps like a badly tuned car. He missed the old Lula, and that was a huge difference in his life.

Rubbing his eyes, he thought how strange that idea was because, while he missed the Lula of those other times, he didn't miss the Win he used to be. Not even one bit. He despised that other self almost as much as he despised his father.

He tuned into the noisy stir of students still making their way to desks, dropping into seats, and shuffling their devices out of backpacks. When someone brushed against his arm, he jerked away and looked up.

"Hey, sorry, Win," Branch Redford said.

Win waved him off, but didn't say anything because he'd caught Dina staring over her shoulder at him. He kept eye contact, not feeling the repulsion he used to, not feeling much of anything he used to. The classroom noise faded to a dull hum under the silent grief they exchanged in that moment before she turned back to face the front of the room.

When the teacher flicked on the overhead with the assignment, he might as well have flashed an empty computer screen on the wall. Win didn't care about assignments or due dates. He cared less about Las Animas than ever before.

He was in his seat because Kate told him he had to be. She'd played the Eva card with, "Your mother would give you the same advice. Get back to a routine. Finish school, then move ahead with your dreams for the property your mother left you."

The problem was his dreams didn't mean what they had a few months ago. He'd parked his T-Bird in the garage and taken the bus, then walked as soon as he could move without hurting. He told Kate he needed to get his strength back, and walking was how he planned to do it. The truth was driving his car stirred too many memories of his life before.

The doctors told him he'd been lucky because his had been small wounds. One of Clifford's bullets had pierced the fleshy part of his left arm. Another had gone in and out of his thigh, missing bone. His worst wound was dead center in his heart. It was the one that would never heal because any time he thought about that day, it opened his chest—raw and bleeding—and the pain was unstoppable as if a real bullet had lodged there. He pressed the heels of his hands against his eyes and tried to block out the empty seat where Blossom should be.

Chapter Sixty-Two

Five Months After
Lula

Lula was about to leave her bedroom when her cell chimed with the Ragtime-Jazz melody that was special for Blossom. She'd felt heartache before, but she'd never felt her heart blunder until perspiration broke out on her forehead, not until now. She pulled the phone from her pocket and stared at the caller ID. Her hand shaking, Lula hovered her finger over the keypad, then tapped Accept.

"Yes?" she said, her voice barely a whisper.

"Lula, this is Mrs. Henley. I'm so sorry to call you like this, but I don't have your number anywhere else."

Lula cleared her throat. "That's … okay."

"I was hoping you'd put the word out to Blossom's friends for me."

Lula waited a moment, then asked, "About what?"

"Blossom's work was juried into the county watercolor show, and this Saturday it's going to be at Greenlee's art gallery on Forest. I thought her friends would like to see it. She won First…" —Mrs. Henley's voice faltered— "First prize."

Blossom Henley won a prize for a painting? Lula tried to put that idea together so it made sense. She never knew Blossom painted well enough to enter a show, let alone win a prize. A first prize. And why hadn't she known that? She'd known a lot about her, and Blossom had known a lot about Lula. They were best friends, but

Blossom never said a word about a watercolor show or planning to enter it.

"Lula? Are you there?"

"Uh, sure. Yes. I'm here, Mrs. Henley." Lula sank onto her bed and closed her eyes. "I'll tell her friends. We'll all go."

"Thank you so much."

Long after her conversation with Mrs. Henley, Lula hadn't left her room. She hadn't moved from the bed or opened her eyes. Blossom did her best to hide her F's on her science and math homework and her tests, but Lula had always known about them. It didn't matter that the girl wasn't going to be a scientist. It didn't matter that she wasn't smart when it came to numbers. What did matter? *Being friends. So why didn't Blossom tell me she was a serious painter?*

She let the hurt filter through her. *Friends shared secrets.*

And then it came to her. Blossom didn't tell her about entering the watercolor contest for the same reason she tried to hide those failing grades. She didn't want to risk being humiliated if her work didn't get into the show. Blossom hadn't trusted her.

Lula fell across the bed on her back. "I'm so sorry, Blossom. I should have shown you that you could trust me. I should have been a better friend and told you I knew … I knew you were failing those classes. I should have offered to help."

She covered her face.

But I didn't.

****

The next day at school, Lula went into the office, and on the secretary's desk, she dropped a note about Blossom's painting being exhibited at the Greenlee Art Gallery. "Can you have this read on morning announcements?"

The secretary read the note. "Yes, of course." She smiled at Lula. "This is wonderful…"

But Lula didn't wait to hear what the woman had to say. She was already out the door and heading down the hall.

During the announcements, Lula kept her eyes forward. She didn't want to connect with Win until he'd had time to process the news. She wondered if he knew Blossom painted well enough to enter a county-wide contest and win the blue ribbon. She'd ask later when she talked to him about picking up Marty and going to the gallery together.

The rest of the day, each class hummed with kids making plans to see Blossom's painting in Greenlee's on Saturday. The art teacher offered rides to students who needed one.

When the last class ended Friday afternoon and before Win got up from his desk, Lula hurried to stand over him. "I'm picking up Marty on Saturday about ten. I need you to come with us."

He didn't look up or acknowledge he'd heard her.

She touched his shoulder. "I need your help."

Now, he did look at her, and her breath caught in her chest when she saw the suffering in his face. She considered walking away, but she couldn't do that. She had to convince him to be at Marty's with her on Saturday, so she stood her ground. "I need help with getting Marty out of his house. He probably won't go with me, but he might if you're along."

She gazed across the room for a moment, "Then there's Mrs. Skolinski. You know how popular I am with her." She waited one beat. "Please." That foreign word slipped through her lips before she could stop it.

He stood and put his book into his backpack. "I'll

meet you at Marty's." And he was out the door.

Lula waited in the classroom until the banging of lockers closing stopped. She waited until the loud, excited end-of-week hallway noise quieted.

"Lula?" Mr. Cochran stuck his head inside the door. "Are you all right?"

She shook her head. "Not really."

"Come on." He waited for her to walk out of the room. "I'm sure you're going on Saturday."

"Yes."

"I'm glad. This will be good for helping all of us get over this tragedy."

The school had brought in counselors for everyone to talk about the shooting, but Lula refused to go.

She looked up at her teacher. "That's bullshit, Mr. Cochran. Nobody's getting over what happened."

She expected him to tell her to watch her mouth. Instead, he said. "You're right. That was bullshit. The best we can hope for is we'll live with greater awareness for the value of life."

She didn't say what was in her head. *I'm living with greater awareness of what it's like to fail a friend and never be able to tell her how sorry I am.*

"Come on." He motioned for her to walk with him.

At the main entrance to the school, she stopped and without looking at him, said, "Do you know my mom?"

She felt his hand on her shoulder and stared up at his face. It had been stripped of everything except bitter pain.

"Yes."

She stepped back as if he'd struck her, but he reached out and grabbed her arm before she could get away. "Lula, it's not true what people are saying. I met your mother at the Back-to-School Open House. That was it." He released his grip on her. "My wife left me for someone else, not because of what the gossip mill is churning out."

She believed him. It was the bare honesty of the way he looked and the way his words were stripped of any deceit. Lucille hadn't broken up the Cochran marriage. For once, Lula could squash the talk about her mother and be sure she was doing the right thing, not simply trying to cover over what really happened. And if Melinda lived up to her promise, this would be the last rotten story about Lucille or Lula Banes to come out of her mouth.

"Thanks." She left her teacher on the school steps and headed for her truck.

Chapter Sixty-Three

Marty

Akoni answered Marty's cell after it rang five times. "Akoni, here. Mr. Marty Pants's secretary." He shot a hard look at Marty, who turned away. "Yes, of course, he is here. Let me connect you. One moment, please."

He held the phone out to Marty. "That lovely girl is calling again. I suggest you speak with her this time."

Marty snatched the phone and held it to his ear. "What?"

"Nice, Marty," Lula said. "Are you always too busy now to answer my calls?"

Marty used his hands to push himself straighter in the bed and punched an extra pillow behind him. "Talk."

"Not unless you're nicer." Lula stopped, silent on the other end.

"That's my line," Marty finally said.

She cleared her throat. "Not anymore." And in two words she'd summed up their new relationship. "Okay, so here's the deal. I'm picking you up Saturday morning. Ten o'clock. Be out front so I don't have to go any rounds with your mom."

"No. I have—"

She cut in before he could make an excuse. "Marty, just shut the freakin' fuck up. Every time I call or ask to see you, you're not *available*. Who do you think you are?"

"Listen, Lula. I can't—"

"Walk. But you're breathing, aren't you? Your hands still work. They did in the hospital. How about your big dumb head? Does that work?"

"You don't—"

"Oh, yes, I do. I understand. Now, we're going to see Blossom's painting at Greenlee's gallery. She won first prize. Dress nice. Win's coming with us."

The phone went dark and Marty let it fall on top of the sheet. *Blossom has a painting at Greenlee's?*

"So what is it this beauty wants?" Akoni picked up the phone and clicked End.

"How do you know she's a beauty? You've never seen her."

"Akoni knows such things. I just don't know why she is calling. That you must tell me."

"It doesn't matter. I'm not going." Marty slid lower against the pillows and closed his eyes.

"What time is this event that you will not attend?"

Marty cracked one eye. "Go away."

"Not until I know what I want to." Akoni hovered over Marty. "Speak."

"You're the most annoying—"

"Indeed. And I return the recommendation."

"Compliment! I told you. It's not a recommendation. That's what you get when you go for a job interview. Which I'm hoping you're going to do soon."

Akoni picked up the phone, and before punching the call back, circled his index finger like a small target-seeking missile.

Marty groaned. "Not funny."

"Hello again. This is Akoni. You are Lula?" His mouth opened in a generous smile. "Wonderful. What time should Mr. Marty Pants be ready?" Nodding, he said, "He will be at the curb."

At dinner that night, Marty ate the way he had since he'd come home from the hospital and could use a wheelchair to make it to the table. Not much. He pushed the fresh green beans and his favorite chicken casserole around the plate, but he only took a few bites. He kept his eyes down, not paying full attention to what his mom and dad were talking about, but only picking up the keywords—inventory, cleaning crew, and hiring temporary help.

He gripped his fork tighter, and with its edge, mashed a green bean in half. He used to help with the inventory. He used to be the "cleaning crew." He used to do and be a lot of things. He fought back a stab of anger with a big gulp of cold water. Too big. He choked and spurted water through his nose.

"Marty!" His father was by his side in a second, holding a napkin to his mouth and patting him on the back until the choking stopped.

His mom cleared his plate and took away the water-soaked placemat. She had a clean, dry one in front of him by the time he'd recovered. She was about to set a new plate down for him, when he pushed it away. "No. I'm not hungry."

She took her seat and left the plate off to the side.

For a while the room was silent, then his dad said, "What did you do in therapy today?"

Marty shook his head and took his time before saying, "Balance. While sitting in this." He pointed to his wheelchair. He flashed on the balance beam in the gym and how he'd worked his way up from single-leg lift exercises to lunges, to backflips that he could execute perfectly almost each time. Now he had to practice how to sit right while he propelled himself on wheels or transferred from his chair to the bed or the toilet. "It's called independence training or some crap like that."

"Inappropriate language, Marty," his father said, bringing his palms down hard next to his plate, so that it jumped. He made fists of his hands and frowned. "You're suffering, but so are we, and we don't need to suffer more with your cursing at our table."

That was a strong rebuke coming from his dad. It was as sharp as a slap, and Marty straightened suddenly, realizing that he'd slumped forward, his arms resting on the placemat.

"Your mother has cooked your favorite food for weeks. You've barely touched any of it. We understand that you've been stripped of your life as you knew it, but you have to understand that we have, too. And we have to work together to get through this."

"Get through this?" Marty's voice was loud and he stared hard at his dad. "I'm not getting through this, Dad. This is what it is. Forever."

"No." His mom leaned across the table and grabbed his arm. "You can't say that. You're strong. You're young. And you can get better. There are new treatments out there, and I've read about remarkable recoveries from spinal cord injuries. You're remarkable, Marty. I know you can recover."

He was remarkable. If his mom said it, it had to be true. "Sure I am." He should stop talking, because everything he said came out sour and hurtful. He didn't need to punish his parents for something they didn't do.

"I'm going to bed." He pushed away from the table, then wheeled around. "I'm sorry. I can't be who I used to be, and I haven't figured out who I am now. That's hard because I used to have that together once. Now I have to start all over again and make a new me."

His mom rose and wrapped her arms around him. "Get out into the world, Marty. Stop hiding in your room. Being with your friends is going to make a huge difference."

"Maybe. I have to think about it." Marty wheeled

himself down the hall. Once he'd closed the door to his room, he covered his face with his hands. How could he go out into that world and see his friends when he was like this?

Everything he'd worked for was gone. Every dream he'd had, finished. He hadn't cried in a long time. He couldn't remember when that had happened last or why, but now he had a good reason for letting the tears go, so he did until there were no more.

He finally swiped his face with the back of his hands, and he pulled a tissue out of the box on his nightstand and blew his nose. It was at that moment he realized he had an immediate concern. By this time, his bladder was full and he had to do something about it, not think about the past—at least not right now.

He wheeled to his desk and from the folder marked, Therapy, he pulled out the pamphlet the therapist had given him those many weeks ago and studied it. *How to Transfer from the Wheelchair to the Toilet Safely*. He'd been transferring himself for a while, and usually, Akoni was there, hovering. But Akoni wasn't there all the time anymore, so Marty was on his own with the toilet for the first time since the shooting.

He'd wanted privacy, and he'd gotten it. Now all he had to do was remember what the therapist and Akoni had taught him.

****

The next morning, Marty woke up with Akoni humming and tugging at his sheet. "You have an important day. And a Miss Lula to meet."

"I'm not going." Marty snatched the sheet from Akoni's hand and pulled it over his head.

"That ostrich you are pretending to be is not working now, is it?" Akoni pulled the sheet back and set the wheelchair next to the bed. He handed Marty the transfer board, and then walked toward the door. "I will be back."

"Where are you going?" Marty pushed up onto his elbows and glared at him.

"Coffee." Akoni smiled. "And some of your mother's amazing biscuits, which she has prepared because she knows how much I love these."

"And what about me?"

"You may have some coffee and biscuits, too. Just come down the hall. The kitchen is on your left."

"You're a riot, you know that?"

Akoni backed out of the room and shut the door behind him with a soft but firm click.

Marty pounded the mattress and waited, hoping Akoni was kidding. Hoping he was going to pop back and stay nearby while he got out of bed.

"Hey, Akoni! I don't need you anyway," he shouted, then he listened, but there were no footsteps and the door didn't open. "Great. Wonderful. Good riddance!"

With a couple of tries, he'd managed transferring from the bed to the chair last night, so why did he need Akoni now? "I don't."

Slowly, he eased onto his elbows, then up to sitting on the board. He ran through the routine he'd learned in therapy and had practiced with Akoni next to him. It took a while, but he managed to get from the bed to the wheelchair, then to the bathroom. And by the time he'd washed his face and pulled on a clean t-shirt, he felt as if he'd spent hours in the gym. He was exhausted. And for the first time since that day at Blendz and Moore, really hungry.

He yanked open the door and the aroma of his mom's fresh biscuits lured him down the hall and into the kitchen. As he wheeled up to his place, Akoni picked up the last biscuit on the plate.

"Very delicious," he said, holding the biscuit up and inhaling. Then he bit into it, chewed slowly, and grinned at Marty.

"What the—"

His mom patted Marty's hand. "There's more, Marty." She went to the oven and brought out a full pan of hot biscuits and served them.

Marty spread one with butter and jam, and then another.

Mrs. Skolinski poured herself a cup of coffee and took a seat at the table. "Akoni tells me you're going out with friends this morning."

"No. I'm not."

"Marty, you…" His mom stopped, stood up abruptly, and carried her plate to the sink. "I'm working at the store today for a few hours. Your dad has a dentist appointment." She rinsed her plate and left the room.

"You disappoint her," Akoni said.

"Not me! You're the one making up stories. I tell her what's really happening."

"I see." Akoni sipped his coffee and stared across at Marty. Then he said, "I would like to go home and eat the biscuits my mother makes for me."

"I'd say that would be fantastic. Go home. Ask your mother to bake for you. Eat *her* biscuits."

Marty was on a roll. He had a lot of things he wanted to suggest Akoni do, but something in the way Akoni looked at him made him stop.

"My mother is no longer in this world. My family is no longer here either. When you look at me, you are seeing the last of my people." While Akoni's face was clouded with sadness, he said this the way someone on the radio would announce that there was a chance of rain. "It was the war, you see."

Akoni put his plate into the sink, then left Marty to finish his breakfast.

Instead, Marty sat quietly, letting what Akoni had just told him settle into place behind his heart.

Chapter Sixty-Four

Win

Win drove to Marty's and parked across the street. It was a little before ten, so he went to the door and rang the bell.

Mrs. Skolinski opened the door. "Oh, Win. How nice of you to visit. Not many of Marty's friends from school have been by. Please come in. I'm on my way to the store, but Marty's in his room."

Win stepped inside. "I came to pick him up. A bunch of us are going to the gallery in Greenlee."

She looked surprised, but her eyes brightened, and her face flushed with happiness. "He said he wasn't—"

Marty's voice came from down the hall. "I wasn't going, Mom." In his wheelchair, he rolled toward them from the back of the house. "I changed my mind because of..." He jabbed his thumb over his shoulder at Akoni who walked behind him, grinning.

Win had seen Marty in the hospital, but somehow he'd expected he'd be out of the wheelchair and on his feet by now. He'd been stupid. Kate told him what had happened to him, but Win didn't really believe Marty was paralyzed until this moment.

There was a lot he still had to process, but not right now. Right now, he had to get Marty out of the house and into Lula's truck. He glanced over his shoulder to look through the window.

Lula was pulling up to the curb.

"Come on." Win opened the front door and let Marty go past him. Akoni followed close behind, but when Marty's wheels stuck in a crack along the path, he waited until Marty worked his way free by himself.

Win was ready to close the door when Mrs. Skolinski stopped it with her hand. "Is that Lula Banes's truck?"

"Uh, yeah. She's driving. I don't have room for us and the wheelchair. Besides, it was Lula's idea to get Marty to go with us."

"Lula's idea?" Mrs. Skolinski put her hands on her hips and stared at the Tundra idling at the curb. Then with Win in front of her, she started toward the truck. He backed up fast, but even with her much shorter legs, Marty's nom kept up with him.

At the curb, she grabbed the handles of Marty's wheelchair and stopped him. "Just hold on a minute." She stepped in front of him and went to the driver's window.

Lula stared at her through the glass, then slowly let the window down. "Good morning, Mrs. Skolinski. I'm here. Again."

"Yes. I can see that. Where are you headed with my son, Lula?"

"Greenlee's. There's a … Blossom's picture's on display." Lula rubbed her eyes, then went on. "She won first prize for a watercolor or something."

"I see." Mrs. Skolinski glanced right, then left and sniffed before she reached into the open window and put her hand over Lula's, letting it rest there for a few seconds. Then, without saying anything more, she hurried to the garage and backed her car out.

Lula stared after her, then looked at Win.

He shrugged in answer to her silent question. He didn't know what had just happened any more than she did.

"Come now," Akoni said as he opened the passenger door. "Let's be leaving."

He maneuvered Marty up to the open passenger

door. "Set your brake and put that bum of yours onto the seat, my man."

Marty sat very still. He kept his head down and gripped the arms of the wheelchair.

Win stepped forward to give him a hand, but Akoni shook his head.

Lula stared out the front window and bit down on her bottom lip.

In a quick motion, Marty pressed on the brake lever, then pushing on the armrest with his right hand, reached overhead with his left for the handle inside the truck. He brought himself up and out of the chair the way Win had seen him move while practicing in the gym. For a little guy, Marty had some powerful upper body strength.

Akoni held out one arm for him to grasp, and with a small boost from Akoni, Marty pulled himself onto the seat. He took a deep breath, gripped his jeans and pulled his legs to the front. Resting his head against the seat, he took another deep breath before fastening his seatbelt.

Win folded the wheelchair and put it into the truck bed, then he and Akoni got into the back seats.

Lula made a U-turn and started toward Greenlee.

Akoni held out a hand to Win. "I am Akoni. It is my African name that means brave warrior, and I am that." He laughed and tapped Marty on the shoulder. "You can tell them of my bravery."

Marty shook his head. "The worst part of being like this," he said and waved his hand over his legs, "is I am always with a brave warrior."

"Not for always, my good friend," Akoni said.

Akoni laughed and so did Win and Lula. Win thought about how he hadn't made that sound in a very long time. And how he never expected he'd make it again, and yet he just had. With Lula and Marty and

Akoni who said he was brave.

He repeated Akoni's word silently to himself. Brave was something they'd all have to be from now on if they were going to get through their last year of high school without the effects of that day destroying them.

Chapter Sixty-Five

Lula

Lula slowed as they neared the gallery and searched for a place to park, but there were no spaces available in the lot. The street was full, too. Akoni pulled out a handicapped placard and pointed to a curb painted blue.

"Oh, the perks I provide," Marty said, reaching across to plant a hand on Lula's leg.

At his touch, a small dose of joy shot through her. It surprised her how much she'd missed his antics. How much she'd missed the pestering jokester forever in her face, forever there when she needed him or even when she didn't want him to be around. She hadn't expected to hear Marty sounding anything like his former self again, but here he was almost back to the Marty she recognized. With two fingers, she lifted his hand from her thigh and dropped it onto his lap. "Watch the hand. It can't be let loose like that."

This was close to being like it used to be between them. Maybe Mr. Cochran was right. Maybe what he said about getting over the tragedy wasn't all bullshit.

Once she'd parked and Marty was in his wheelchair, they walked toward the gallery. As they came to the entrance, Lula let Akoni open the door, and then waited until Marty went inside before she followed the wheelchair. Win came last. She sensed that like her, he dreaded this visit.

She leaned close to him. "Did you know Blossom entered paintings into shows?"

He shook his head and his lips were pressed tightly together, his jaw clenched.

While the gallery was full and buzzing with conversation, the voices came to her hushed, the way they did when high altitude plugged her ears.

She spotted Mr. Cochran. He smiled at her, and she found it was easy to return his smile because it was just a kind look between a teacher and a student.

Dina stood against one wall and caught her attention with a slight nod, then held her gaze. It was their first real eye contact since they'd been at Blendz and Moore, and between them that day it had all been about sneers. Now none of that was on Dina's face or in Lula's heart. Now they were just two girls who shared a horrible memory. Dina looked past her and suddenly there was something else in her eyes.

Lula looked back to be sure Win had followed her. He had, and the look on Dina's face was all about Baldwin Knight, but it wasn't Dina's sexy come-on expression. What then? Sympathy? That was impossible, but sympathy was exactly what she was picking up.

Marty wheeled his way through the crowd, parting the people and making a path for them. Win stepped ahead of her, but he halted as he reached the end of the room where Blossom's painting hung alone, centered.

Lula stopped just behind and grabbed Win's hand. Or had he grabbed hers? Or had they both reached out to each other the moment they saw Blossom's painting?

Chapter Sixty-Six

Win

Mrs. Henley made her way through the crowd and drew them both close to her for a moment. "Thank you. Blossom's day here at the gallery has been hugely successful. There's a bidding war over that piece." She pointed behind her. "And the gallery owner wants to hang more of her work."

She smiled up at Win. "I almost didn't submit her entry form, Win. I ... but now I'm sure I did the right thing. I hope you think so, too."

Win hadn't let go of Lula's hand, and as Mrs. Henley talked, he tightened his grip and tried to focus on the woman's face, not on his own in the portrait behind her. He'd only passed out once in his life—that day Clifford Mott shot him. But he recognized the signs. At first, his vision narrowed as if a dark curtain were being closed around him, then he grew cold at his center, while perspiration gathered along his hairline.

Lula drew closer to his side. "That's ... great about the gallery wanting to hang more of Blossom's paintings."

More of Blossom's paintings. What would they be? Others of her classmates' portraits? More like ... that one? Win lowered his head and closed his eyes for a moment before he had the courage to look at the painting again.

The picture of the boy that hung on the wall stared out at him with a half-smile, not quite a smirk, not quite a sneer—something in between. This was how Blossom had seen him. He tried to breathe slowly, but each breath became faster and shallower with the acceptance that the image nailed who was. Someone so into himself that he barely put up with those around him. A self-absorbed idiot. He blinked as if that would make it easier to stare at his face. While she'd been honest in this painting, she'd softened the eyes that stared back at him and taken out the contempt he deliberately put into that grin. It was a message from her to him. *This is who I know you can be.*

He brought his gaze back to Mrs. Henley, not wanting to see the truth in face of that boy anymore, trying to stop the light-headedness from dropping him to the floor of the gallery.

"You'll be sure to tell us when more of Blossom's paintings go on display, right?" Lula asked Mrs. Henley. At the same time, she squeezed Win's hand harder.

Lula was making conversation, diverting questions he couldn't answer without blubbering. *Thank you, Lula.* Win shifted from one foot to the next. *Now get me out of here.*

But it was Mr. Cochran who saved him. "I overheard what you said about the gallery." Mr. Cochran spoke over Win's shoulder and gave Win a chance to step aside to let his teacher and Mrs. Henley talk.

Win pulled Lula with him. "I want out of here," he whispered, his quiet voice ragged with the sound of someone who has just taken a hard fist to the midsection. The room was filled with the din of conversations, but he'd gone deaf to everyone around him, and the crowd had become a blur of shadows.

Lula led him through the main door and to the truck where he finally let go of her hand and fell back against the side of the Tundra. He'd never felt this tired or this empty.

Blossom was always staring at him or taking a second look when she thought he wasn't aware. He'd thought that was all about his irresistible charm. Laughable. She was memorizing his face. She was painting him. *Him*. The creep that insulted her with the "pretend" girlfriend plan.

Damn, what a full-of-yourself jerk you were.

He kept his chin to his chest. Once more, that stopped the world from tilting under him, and he was grateful for the Tundra's support at his back, for Lula beside him. He didn't know he was shaking until that moment.

"Stay here. I'll get Marty and Akoni," she said quickly.

He let her go, even more grateful for her again. Grateful that she didn't comfort him. That was the last thing he needed.

Chapter Sixty-Seven

Marty

The four of them rode back from town in silence. And after sitting in front of Win's portrait at the gallery, Marty suddenly had a lot to say, but he knew he'd have to wait until Win wasn't there to hear it.

Seeing the portrait Blossom had created was like someone had ripped a bandage from an open wound. It had inflicted intense and instant pain. A pain that woke up something inside Marty. He hadn't expected to feel anything ever again. His legs were numb. His spine almost fused into a solid rod. It shocked him that he could feel anything now that his dreams were dead and buried.

Yet he did. And he needed to tell Lula that. He'd shut her out of his life for months, and she'd never stopped trying to see him. He thought about that and how upside-down their relationship was now. Well, everything was upside-down, wasn't it? He'd shut everyone out. Mott might as well have killed him that day the way he'd been acting since the shooting. But that was over. He wasn't dead. He was just different.

Lula parked in front of his house, and while Akoni fetched Marty's wheelchair, Win climbed from the Tundra, and without looking at anyone, walked to his T-Bird, and drove away.

"Bad day for the Knight," Marty said to Lula.

She didn't answer for a moment, then turned to face him. "Bad day for all of us."

"I guess so. But I learned something."

She waited, her eyes on him. When he didn't answer right away, she asked, "Well?"

"I learned why my dad always has those tired old sayings saved up. You need them for times like today. You know, times when you keep quiet because what you should say is, 'too close to the bone'. Dad's favorite."

"What would your dad have said at that gallery?"

Marty took in a deep breath and let it out. "Where there's life there's hope."

She nodded, fingering the mangled lucky charm. "How true."

Akoni opened the passenger door and rolled the wheelchair into position. With Akoni's arm to steady him on the way down, Marty maneuvered himself out of his seat and into his chair as if he'd done it his entire life. Then, without waiting for more help, he wheeled himself around the front of the Tundra and up to Lula's window.

"Call me. We need to catch up." With a quick wave, he pushed down on the wheels and rolled himself along the walkway.

"It seems you do not want my propulsion today," Akoni said, walking at his side.

Marty glanced up at him. "You're right, but you can open the door. You're getting paid the big bucks, so you should earn them some way."

"Ah, yes. The big bucks." Akoni pushed the door open and stepped aside for Marty to enter.

Mrs. Skolinski popped her head out from the kitchen when Akoni closed the door. "That was a short outing." She looked at Marty and frowned. "What's wrong? Did that Banes girl—"

"Stop, Mom. Lula didn't do anything but be Lula, and that's nothing like her mother, so I don't want any more bad talk about her."

His mom pulled back, hurt all over her face.

"Well, then," Akoni said. "I have a very important call to place." And he walked down the hall to Marty's room.

Marty wheeled close to his mom and looked up at her. "Without Lula, I wouldn't give a damn about physical therapy or living right now. Be grateful she's sticking with me."

She frowned in thought, then said, "Your father would say, 'Old habits die hard'. I'm sorry."

Marty smiled. "Dad's always got the right saying for every occasion." He took her hand. "Thanks, Mom." He wheeled down the hall to his room, calling loudly, "Akoni, what's all this brave warrior crap?"

Chapter Sixty-Eight

Lula

Lula didn't drive the direct route home. She drove to the lake instead and parked. The water spread out in a calm blue, and she let her head rest against the driver's window while she stared out at a place she'd seen since she could remember. It looked the same, and that confused her because it shouldn't. Nothing in her life was the same, so this lake should be different too.

But it made sense that everything outside of this tiny crucible called Las Animas would remain unchanged. The universe didn't know about Blossom. About the totally altered Win and Marty. About Lucia Banes whose shattered foot had healed but whose heart had been remolded into something unrecognizable.

She fingered the lucky rabbit's foot charm and stroked its misshaped edges. Her heart on a chain.

A huge pressure inside her slowly built. It started in her stomach and rose through her throat. And for the first time in years, Lula cried very hard and very long. She cried because of all she'd lost that Saturday morning. She no longer had faith in being able to take care of herself. Clifford Mott had stripped her of invulnerability. She cried because he'd taken the life of her best friend, and she'd never be able to work on being a real friend the way she wanted to now. She cried because she hated her mother and wished she didn't. She cried because she didn't know what else to do. When she ran out of tears, she started her truck and drove home.

When she arrived, she took a few minutes to stare at the place she'd lived most of her life. It too seemed the same as always, and she wished it wasn't. She shrugged and pushed open the front door, but stopped short when she heard the music. Nobody played music in this house. Nobody except her and that was always sent directly through her earbuds. Silence. That's what The General liked.

And where was Butter? He was always at the front door waiting when Lula was out. For a moment, Lula panicked. Something had happened to her dog. She ran toward the stairs and in a loud voice called. "Here, boy. Come."

At The General's open office door, she skidded to a stop. Inside, Butter lay stretched out on the Persian rug and lifted his head when Lula peered inside. "Butter!"

The General sat at his desk and looked up as her dog trotted across the room to nuzzle her hand. "How was the exhibit?" he said.

Her father hadn't asked her a question like that in forever. So how was she going to answer him? "Fine." was what came out.

"I imagine it was quite difficult, Lucia." He set aside the paperwork in front of him and beckoned her inside.

With Butter alongside, Lula found her usual chair and lowered herself onto it the way she would if she expected spikes. But this time it didn't feel like the hot seat, the place he'd interrogate or threaten her. Something was different here besides the music, but she'd have to wait to find out what. As always, The General set the agenda. She just attended the meetings.

"So, this girl, Blossom Henley, what is her work like?" he asked.

Oh, man. Where is this going? She cleared her throat before she said, "She did a portrait. That's the only thing I've seen of hers. It was good."

"First prize." He nodded. "Impressive."

As always, he knew the details of what was happening in town. She loosened the muscles in her neck a bit with a quick side-to-side roll of her head, and then sat back in the chair. Until that moment she hadn't recognized how she'd been perched on the edge.

"Well, then. Have you eaten?"

Eaten? And since when did he care about my eating schedule? "No."

"I've asked Cook to make something light for lunch. I hope that's good for you."

Now she was really out of what to say, so she let her head move up and down in a yes.

"Butter probably needs his run, so I'll shower while you do that. Lunch is at one." He rose and walked out of the room, leaving her more than speechless.

She was holding her breath, and it was only when her body cried for oxygen that she could exhale, and then could pull more air into her lungs.

****

She ran farther than usual and coming back to the house, even Butter slowed. There had been too much for Lula to deal with today. The gallery. Win. Marty. Oh my God. Marty! And Mrs. Skolinski. *She patted my hand.* Lula looked at her hand, thinking it might be different, like the rest of her. Blessed or something by that pat. There'd been music playing while the General was in his office. And then Butter. Butter on the General's imported rug.

Back at the house, Lula fed her dog and hurried to shower. It was a quarter to one. The General didn't tolerate lateness, and Lula needed no more turmoil. She needed calm waters like the lake.

At exactly one, her hair still damp but "presentable", she entered the dining room. The General already sat at the head of the table, and Lula gave the other end a quick glance to see if Lucille might make an appearance. But they were alone at the long table.

"Here," The General said, and he pointed at the chair to his right. "We need to talk."

Why did she feel so obedient? Tired she guessed. No energy to do combat with the old man. She was relieved Lucille hadn't put in an appearance too. Somehow, the fewer members of her family who gathered around the table, the better. No arguments. No need to think about deals or alibis for her mother or plots and lies to fool her father.

Butter had made his way into the dining room, and Lula reached down to stroke his smooth head. Her dog roaming the house freely was another very different thing in her life. Her father had given Butter free range. What the hell was going on?

Cook served a salmon with rice and roasted vegetables. That was as light as The General allowed, but she was hungry and this was perfect. As she took her first bite of poached salmon, she thought, *Perfect*. It had been a long time since that word had popped into her head.

"I'm sure you're puzzled about this afternoon, Lucia." Her father's voice wasn't its usual generalissimo-in-charge one.

She chewed carefully and swallowed before answering. "Kind of."

"There's no easy way to tell you this, but as you know, I'm direct in all matters. Your mother phoned earlier today." He cleared his throat behind his napkin. "She's no longer part of the family." He held his glass up and sipped his sparkling water. "I wished her the best, and I hope you will understand."

Oh, she understood. Lucille had finally bailed on The General and her daughter. Was it because her daughter hadn't been able to keep that one promise and give Lucille the weekend away? Well, freakin' hell, she hadn't planned on Clifford Mott shattering her foot, had she? She hadn't planned on being in the hospital instead of at Blossom's that night.

Lucille wasn't much as mothers go, but sometimes they could talk, and when they did, Lucille didn't boss her. She'd listen. She was so not like The General.

She suddenly felt the same as she had in the truck today at the lake. Pressure. Pressure that started from deep inside and forced its way up. She was about to explode if she didn't find a valve to open and let all that she felt spew into the room. So she did.

Her voice sounded foreign. Shrill. The way it would if it were being squeezed between tight fists.

"Everybody in town knows about Lucille Banes but you! Or you don't want to. You don't really want to know about me either. You just want to tell me what to do and when to do it. And that's because you couldn't do that to her. Now you want me to 'understand'? What? That this is a hell hole of a place to live? That I'm stuck here with you? That you couldn't keep Lucille here because you didn't know how to love her any more than you know how to love me?"

When the words stopped pouring out of her mouth, she collapsed against the back of her chair and waited for the punishment she knew would follow.

The General stared down the length of the table at Lucille's empty place. When he turned to look at Lula, a single tear traced from one eye to his cheek. He didn't swipe it away, but he stood and before he left the dining room, he said, "Everything you've said is true."

Stunned to silence, Lula watched her father's retreating back. She'd made the General cry, something she had never imagined possible. But what held her

captive and mute in her chair was the fact that she was
sorry.

Chapter Sixty-Nine

Win

Like Lula, Win didn't drive straight to his house after leaving Marty's. Instead, he drove through town, careful not to pass Blendz and Moore. He'd overheard rumors that it had reopened, but business wasn't good, and the owners were thinking of selling.

Good idea, he thought. He'd never go near that place again, and he was sure others in town had to feel the same way.

He glanced out the side window at the stores, almost all of them closed on Sunday. He'd been here uncountable times. He knew each cross street, how the movie house was wedged between Crystal's Fudge Shoppe and the toy store. He knew the meters that didn't work and the place where the raccoons popped up through the storm drains. But now as he rolled slowly through Las Animas, it was as if he'd never seen it before. He'd become a stranger in this place, and with that thought, a stabbing ache in his belly made him pull to the curb.

He leaned his forehead against the steering wheel. "Las Animas," he said, and this time he really listened to the two Spanish words that named the place he lived in. He listened and he paid attention to their meaning for the first time since his mother had told him.

"The Souls," she'd said. "That's what Las Animas means."

"How come?" He didn't get why a town had a name like that.

"I have no idea what the Spanish had in mind, and I read it was once *Las Animas Perdidas,* The Lost Souls.

He looked out his windows again. They should put *Perdidas* back in the name. Lost Souls fit.

Las Animas was the place he'd longed to be free of, but now it seemed foreign, and he felt confused because he missed the sense of home it used to give him. He wondered if he'd ever find that again. And now he wasn't sure if L.A. or London or wherever he landed would welcome him and make him a part of it. He didn't like to think that he'd always be the stranger, a lost soul just passing through. Clifford Mott had robbed him of so much he'd never have again.

So feel sorry for yourself, why don't you?

But he couldn't. Because Mott had robbed Blossom of much more. Over the top of the steering wheel, he cushioned his head with his hands and closed his eyes. She'd been so beautiful. He'd always remember her. He'd always regret not letting her be a part of his life the way she'd wanted. If only he'd admitted earlier that he'd wanted her too. That might have made all the difference in the world.

He waited until the pain of her being gone flushed through him as it had so many times since that moment Kate told him. So many lives gone and Blossom among them.

Win inhaled long and steady before putting his car into gear and driving out of town and to his father's house.

He entered the kitchen and filled a tall glass with water, then took a long gulp. He choked, then took another sip, not as much this time.

"You're back early."

Win whipped around to face his father, who stood in the doorway.

He didn't answer the question, but went to the refrigerator and added ice to his drink.

"I heard about the gallery," his father said. "One of my friends was there this afternoon and called me, so I swung by to see what she was talking about." He took down another glass from the cupboard and filled it from the tap. Then, pulling out a chair from the table, he sat down, at the same time gesturing to a seat opposite him. "Join me?"

Win shook his head and leaned with his back against the counter.

"Okay." He lifted his glass to Win. "Here's to talent."

When he didn't respond, his father drank, then set his glass down and slowly ran his finger around the rim. "I'm sorry, Win. Truly sorry. I wish I could have saved you from this terrible experience—the shooting, the death of that lovely girl…" He rubbed his eyes, every motion signaling weary, not sleepy. He took a slow sip from his glass again. "I've tried to save you from a lot of other bad experiences, and I think I've done a fair job." He looked up at Win, but Win kept his face empty. "Maybe not."

"What do you want?" Win asked.

"I want to talk, to help you."

"I don't need your help."

"Then maybe I need you to help me," his father said. "I need you to meet me somewhere near the middle of this relationship—"

"Relationship? What relationship?" Win hadn't meant to shout.

"I know you hate me, but you don't know my side of the story. You've never given me a chance to explain,"

"Like I care." Win set his glass on the counter with a clunk.

At once, his father was on his feet and in front of him. "I didn't cause your mother to die. She had a bad heart, a congenital condition. I got her the top cardiologists. I stayed with her until the end, and I promised her I'd take care of you the best I could, Win." His father gripped his arm. "I loved her. She just didn't love me."

Win had seen a lot of different emotions on his father's face, but he'd never seen such devastating sorrow until this moment.

"She loved someone else," his father said, and his eyes were wet. "She loved a woman." Kevin Knight sat down again and cradled his head. "I think I could have handled another man in her life. But I couldn't handle Anne O'Brian."

Slowly, Win moved to the table, pulled out the chair next to his father's, and eased into it. He had nothing to say, but he did have a huge shift in his feelings for this man. Maybe today, seeing his own portrait, seeing himself through Blossom's eyes, had swept out a lot of the anger and hate from inside him and left room for understanding. Besides, how could he hate someone who was so like himself? Both self-centered for sure. And very afraid of being hurt by someone they cared for.

"I'm sorry." Win wasn't sure what he was saying sorry for. Maybe it was for a lot of things—a global regret. *I'm sorry my mother didn't love you. I'm sorry I didn't understand. I'm sorry I hated you.*

He didn't try to explain his apology and got up from the chair—a little unsteady from all the new emotions he was feeling—and went to his room.

Chapter Seventy

June
The Following Year
Lula

The morning of graduation, Lula slept late.

Butter finally nudged her awake with a cold nose to the ear.

"Damn!" Lula bolted upright in bed.

Butter hopped next to her and slathered her cheek with a slobbery lick of his tongue.

"No. Stop!" She pulled the covers over her head and rolled onto her side, laughing.

Butter nosed his way under the sheets, and Lula threw her arms around her dog's neck and hugged him close.

A gentle rapping on the door brought Butter to alert and silenced Lula.

"Yes?" she called.

"I'd like to talk to you." It was her father.

Lula got to her feet. She slipped on her robe and went to the door.

The General, dressed and fresh from his shower, stood in the hall. They hadn't talked much since Lucille's disappearance, but they'd listened to music while eating together at the long table, usually with conversations about Butter or how the dinner tasted. So far, they hadn't slipped into the last resort discussion like weather, and there'd been no more reprimands from The General and no more emotional outbreaks from Lula.

She'd said all there was to say, and she still hadn't worked out how to relate to this *new* General, the one who didn't make her sit on the oxblood leather seat in his office and listen to lectures anymore. She was still working on how to understand that single tear the last time they'd talked about Lucille. Well, to be honest, she was trying to make sense of what had happened between them since she'd let the dam of resentment break and hurled words at him until she didn't have any voice left or anything else to get out.

This morning, standing outside her door, his hands at his back, he didn't look anything like that other father. For a moment, she was looking at a handsome, older man hesitant to speak.

"This is your big day," he finally said.

Yes. It was her big day. It was the day that marked the end of her time in Las Animas High, the beginning of something new, and the expectation of that should have been exciting. It just wasn't.

"I have something for you. A graduation present." From behind his back, he took out a large plainly wrapped package and handed it to her. "Return them if it's not what you want."

She took the package and stepped away from her doorway into the hall.

He waited.

"Should I open it now?"

"Whatever you like."

She peeled the paper off and stared at the two books. *Lexicon of Garden and Landscape Architecture* was on top. Under it, *The Principles of Landscaping*.

"You may not need either one of them. Everything's online these days, but I asked a friend who knows about the field, and he said they were good resource books."

"They are." Her voice came out in a whisper. She looked up at him, standing so straight, his hair precise as always, his shirt laundry crisp. "But I thought you weren't paying for a degree in landscape architecture."

"I don't want to. But I've decided you'd be terrible at business. You'd best make your money designing spectacular and unique gardens for people. Then you can afford to hire a good business accountant." He started down the hall. "And that's my advice for the morning."

Before he reached the stairs, she said. "Thank you … Dad."

He looked over his shoulder at her, smiling. "Breakfast in ten."

"You bet."

Chapter Seventy-One

Marty

Akoni hurried to open the hatchback of his car and pulled out Marty's wheelchair. He hadn't been at the Skolinskis' for months, since Marty didn't need his services anymore, but he'd come to see the graduation.

Already, Marty's mom and dad had opened the passenger door, and they stood to the side while Marty settled into his chair. Then, because they were late, Akoni grabbed the handles of Marty's wheelchair and ran, pushing him down the long walk leading to the school. Mr. and Mrs. Skolinski rushed to keep up with them.

Today, the wide front lawn was filled with chairs. Balloons tethered to many of their backs tugged at their strings, the wind teasing them into overhead ballets. Across the entrance, a long platform had been erected with a podium and microphone at the center. At the side by the steps leading to the main entrance, the Las Animas orchestra was tuning up the instruments and a trio of vocalists from the junior class stood next to the microphone. The chairs on the stage were still empty, but those on the lawn had almost filled.

"Where must we go?" Akoni asked Marty.

Marty pointed to the right where his senior class was in a line and already walking single-file up a ramp and onto the stage, their black gowns somber on this warm June day. Many of the students had decorated the flat surfaces of their hats with flowers or flags or college logos, and these bobbed in that sea of black like small, overfilled rafts.

"We'll … catch you after the … ceremony,"

Margie Skolinski said, breathing heavily from her dash across the lawn. Then leaning down, she planted a kiss on Marty's cheek.

His dad gripped his shoulder and held out a folded piece of paper. "I found this and wanted you to have it today."

Marty opened it and read, "'Take the first step in faith. You don't have to see the whole staircase, just take the first step. Martin Luther King.'" Marty glanced up. "This is different from all your other sayings, Dad."

"This is a different kind of day." His dad gripped Marty's shoulder. "It deserved words with some more kick to them. Go get 'em, son." He released his grip and took his wife's hand to lead her to their seats.

Akoni veered to the right and rolled the chair fast over the uneven lawn.

"This thing needs better shocks," Marty said. "You're bruising my butt."

"You may lodge a complaint later, but right now you will have to suffer or not be in the line on time."

They had gone only a few feet when Lula stepped in front of them. "What's this? You get a cushy ride and I have to walk on these?" She pulled up her gown and held out a foot. "Four inches of pure Jimmy Choo hell is what you see."

"All I hear are complaints today? What kind of happy occasion is this anyway?" Akoni smiled.

Lula walked beside Akoni. "I've got him. You can take a break."

"I am only too delighted to let you bruise his butt the rest of the way and listen to all his complaining, too." Akoni turned the handles of the wheelchair over to Lula, and she rolled Marty into his place in line.

"What's with the special attention, Lula?" Marty asked.

"Nothing special. It's the same you're getting every day. You want special, you have to pay."

"I told you no pity. You got that, right?" Marty said.

"Put your hat on and stop being a jerk."

"I love you, Lula. You never change."

"Be thankful," she said. "You have someone stable in your life."

"Oh, yeah. Right."

She pushed Marty toward the ramp, and up onto the stage to the end of the front row. "Okay, Mr. Marty Pants."

Marty covered his ears. "That's Akoni's material, Lula."

"Whatever." She pointed to the back of the stage. "I'm up there in the cheap seats." Lula gave him a quick wave and left to sit with others whose names started with B.

Marty watched her take her place next to Melinda Bailey, and the word fate popped into his head. There they were, two enemies side-by-side, not lashing out at each other, but peacefully sharing one of the most important days of their lives. It all came down to chance. Your last name and the alphabet. Or being in a certain place at a certain time. Change one letter, arrive or leave at a place one minute earlier and a big piece of your life is forever different. If he hadn't planned that trip to see the Gladford coach, if he hadn't wanted Lula to lie so his parents wouldn't find out, if he hadn't run to be with Lula at the front door of the coffee shop—

The first sounds of the orchestra stopped him from more "what ifs".

When the singing group stepped to the microphone, the stage of graduates grew quiet, and the audience of friends and family applauded until the lyrics of the first song were amplified into the air.

My hope is this: may your dreams ever be grand. May your dreams take you to the tallest mountain, the farthest star, the deepest sea. My hope is this...

Marty searched for Lula behind him and when he found her, they locked eyes, listening together to those lyrics about hopes and dreams. As the song came to an end, Marty caught Win's attention and gave him the thumbs up.

Win returned the gesture with a nod.

Nothing about this June's graduation was any different than all those Marty had been to before, except that on the stage, two chairs had no one in them. They were draped with empty gowns and mortarboards. On the first seat, the mortarboard had been decorated with white roses and a large sign. *Brittany, we love you. Always. Your family.*

The other seat held a mortarboard with a towering pile of green orchids, trailing emerald ribbons. These ribbons caught in the breeze, and throughout the speeches and handing out of diplomas, they streamed into the sky. Like everyone else, Marty tracked the delicate ribbons flicking over his head. Like everyone else, he remembered, and his thoughts were all about the special girl who should have been sitting among this graduating class.

One section at a time, students rose, crossed to the podium, and received their diplomas, but before retaking their seats, each one stopped in front of the empty chairs for a moment.

When the principal reached the E's and called Brittany Evers, everyone rose in silence. After that moment, it seemed as if those whose names began with F or G walked more carefully to receive their diplomas—slow and deliberate strides—quiet steps of respect.

And when the principal called Blossom Henley's name, everyone on stage and in the audience again stood in silence. The one exception was Marty. But he closed his eyes and imagined himself on his feet, paying tribute to the girl he'd always remember as being surrounded by light.

The principal called on the R's and Branch and Carter Redford led their group to the podium, then gave Marty a high five and pumped both arms while holding up their diplomas. Their teammates blew horns and whistled.

Marty smiled, letting Blossom slip from his mind. It was good to remember what had been, but it was also good to move on—to enjoy this day. If he'd learned anything from that tragic Saturday, it was that he should appreciate what he had now because he'd never have it again.

When it came time to call up the students whose names started with S, the principal said, "Marty Skolinski."

Marty wheeled crossed the stage, keeping his eyes fixed ahead, not wanting to see the other students looking at him, not wanting to see the families and friends seated on the lawn. He'd come a long way back from that dark place of not wanting to live. He'd doubled down on his exercise and even looked forward to getting out of bed in the mornings. He didn't need a sea of pity washing over him today. As he reached out his hand to take his diploma, everyone cheered.

One voice rose louder than the others. "You've got this, Marty!"

Lula.

Marty glanced up at her and held his diploma overhead, then waved it in the air and faced the audience. He didn't see the pity he'd dreaded would be there. All he saw was pride in his parents' faces.

Chapter Seventy-Two

Win

The knock on the door woke Win. He unburied his head from the pillow to squint at the clock radio on his nightstand. Eleven! He had to be at school in two hours.

"Win? You had better get dressed," Kate said through the door.

"Coming!" Win threw off the covers and groped his way to the bathroom. A quick shower and shave, then into some clothes. In less than half an hour, he was in the kitchen where Kate and his father sat at the table, their dishes empty.

"We couldn't wait any longer, sleepyhead." Kate served him a bowl of cereal and juice. "I figured you'd want breakfast, not lunch." She sat across from him and his father.

"Thanks." He smiled at her and scooped the crunchy cereal into his mouth. For some reason, it tasted better than any he'd eaten in years.

"Are you taking the T-Bird, or would you like me to drive you and Kate to the high school?"

His father hadn't driven him anywhere since Win had taken his driver's test and passed. And it was the first time he remembered any offer from this man to help him get someplace. He had some major getting used to "talking" with him and maybe not hating him as much as he had.

"I'll take my car." But Win didn't like the way that sounded. He needed to say more. "But thanks."

"You've got a big day ahead." It seemed his father wanted to keep this conversation going. "Are you excited?"

Win had stuffed his mouth full, and when he glanced at Kate, he remembered her three-year-old-Win-rule about not talking with your mouth full. Not pretty. Not polite. Win nodded in answer to his father's question and kept his mouth shut.

"Well." His father cleared his throat. "Kate and I have some big news to make it even bigger." He looked across the table at Kate, expectant and waiting. But Kate didn't say anything. She suddenly seemed very involved with the last speck of pancake on her plate.

His father coughed softly into his napkin and looked nervous. "Okay. Well, Kate and I do have some news, Win." Now his father's tone of voice was even more uncertain.

Kate reached across and placed her hand on his father's arm. Smiling, she said, "Okay, Kevin. I'll tell him. Just sit back and relax."

His father did sit back, relief filling his face.

Win pushed his bowl aside and stared first at Kate, then at where her hand still held on to his father's arm.

"You're sitting down, so you won't have far to fall when I tell you this," she said.

"Tell me what?" Something was very wrong. He knew it by the way her mouth pulled into a knot tight enough to keep the dire news from escaping. *Kate's leaving. But that's exactly what I knew was going to happen when I graduated. There's no surprise in that.*

Wait. There could be something else. Kate's got a terminal disease. No. That can't be it.

But it's something serious, something I'm not going to like.

Win inhaled what he was sure would be his last breath before Kate dropped the guillotine. "Okay, tell me what's wrong," he said.

"Nothing's wrong," Kate said. "Everything's absolutely all right." She leaned across the table and grasp his hand. "Your father's asked me to marry him, and I've said I will. But I've agreed on only one condition. That you say it's okay."

Kate had been right. It was a good thing he wasn't standing. *Kate and his father. Married. What happened to her hating him? She'd plotted to poison him and avenge his mother's death. He'd been sure of that for years, but maybe that hadn't been in Kate's mind at all. Only his.*

Win went back through some of his conversations with her, especially the ones on Friday nights when his father brought home dates. *"He's not my favorite person in the world right now."* She'd been jealous. *"Keep in mind some people are good together."* She was talking about her and Kevin Knight.

"It's not such a stretch to imagine me here permanently, is it?" she asked.

He glanced around the kitchen. Now that he thought about it, he couldn't imagine this place without her. But Kate was about a hundred and eighty degrees from the slender blondes he always saw his father with. Kate was … Kate. Generous in every possible way.

"Take some time to wrap your head around the idea, okay?" She stood and placed her hands on his shoulders. "When you've come up with your answer, let us know. In the meantime, focus on getting to the high school and grabbing that diploma before they decide against letting you have it." She bent down and gave him the same hug he remembered forever, only today it felt very different.

Chapter Seventy-Three

The End of Summer
Marty

Doctor McLean sat behind his desk and flipped the papers in front of him one at a time. "Hmm." He nodded and flipped another. Removing his glasses, he leaned back in his swivel chair.

Margie and Dan Skolinski reached for each other's hands but didn't take their eyes from the doctor's face.

"Relax, you two," Marty said. "You're making me tense here."

"These are always tense moments, Marty," the doctor said. "But let me take it down a notch in intensity, okay?" He put his glasses back on.

"You're the ringmaster." Marty folded his hands across his belly, smiling.

"Marty!" Mrs. Skolinski scowled at him.

"The therapy results are positive. Healing's happening. But, Marty, you're in for more years of PT. I want you to be hopeful, but realistic. Does that make sense?"

"I need a timeline, Doc."

"Oh, Marty." Mrs. Skolinski sighed loudly.

"I can't guarantee recovery or partial recovery within any specific time." When Marty leaned forward to say something, Dr. McClean held up a hand. "Wait. You're getting quality medical care." He nodded at the Skolinskis. "You've got intensive physical therapy."

Marty shrugged. Akoni might not be his caregiver anymore, but he came by to wear Marty out with his special "brave warrior" exercises when Marty wasn't at the clinic.

"Now, tell me, do you have the stamina to keep going?" The doctor tented his hands and peered over his glasses at Marty.

"Yes. I want to perform for Cirque, just once."

The doctor did a slow blink.

"I want to at least try out."

"You need realistic goals," the doctor said. "First, concentrate on standing, then walking. The Cirque is out there a bit farther."

"But that's my dream, and I'm not giving up on it." He turned to his parents. "I can't be hurt any more than I've been already, so I'm going for it."

His dad patted Margie Skolinski's hand. "Dreams are the stuff that keep us going."

Marty grinned. "You're right about that, Dad." And Marty flashed on Lula, the girl of his dreams. And he pictured how he'd stand on his feet without the physical therapist's or Akoni's large, supporting hands. One day he'd do a backflip again. He wasn't giving up. Those were his dreams, and like the lyrics of that graduation song, those dreams were *grand*.

He'd read other stories about people who were paralyzed healing and returning to their old lives. If they could do it, so could Marty Skolinski.

Chapter Seventy-Four

Win

Win skirted the topic of Kate's and his father's marriage. It wasn't that he even thought about saying he disapproved. It was that it made him feel awkward to tell them they had his permission to do anything. And he was still having trouble wrapping his head around the idea that Kate would become his stepmother.

They seemed to know he wasn't ready to talk about it, because neither of them said anything to him again. Then early one morning the house phone rang, and when he reached across to the nightstand to answer it, Uncle Marc in L.A. was already talking to his dad. Win hung up and fell back into bed. In a few minutes, the hard rap of his dad's knuckle at his door brought him up to sitting.

"Yeah?"

His dad stuck his head inside the bedroom. "Win. Your uncle's on the line. He wants to talk to you."

Win threw off the sheet and jumped to his feet. "Got it!"

He picked up the phone next to his bed again. "Hey! Thanks for the callback, Uncle Marc."

"It was great to hear from you. Of course, you can stay with me until you get settled. I'd love it." His uncle's voice sounded as happy as he remembered. "But your dad didn't know anything about your plans. What's up with that?"

"I'll tell him as soon as I hang up. I just didn't want to, you know, say anything until I was sure you were okay with the idea."

"All right, then. See you soon. Text me your flight

info."

Uncle Marc was his dad's younger brother by twelve years. Eva had called her brother-in-law The Surprise Child. She said that was why he always played a lot and laughed. "Surprises make people happy," she'd said, holding his chin in her hand and then kissing his cheek. "Like you."

Win nodded at the memory. He needed to be around somebody like that for a while. He needed to play and to laugh again. It had been a long time.

He showered and dressed, then went into the kitchen where Kate and his dad sat with cups of steamy coffee.

His dad looked up. "What's Marc talking about?" His voice was sharp, not exactly angry, but he wanted some straight answers.

"I thought I'd go to L.A. before school started and get a feel for UCLA's campus. I asked Uncle Marc if I could stay with him for a couple of weeks. I didn't know if he'd say yes, so I didn't talk about it."

Kate didn't meet his eyes, and that was a first.

"Look, I'm sorry. I should have talked it over with you both. I didn't."

Kate went to the stove and stirred a simmering pot of what smelled like oatmeal. She kept her back to him.

Pulling out his chair, Win sat and waited. This was the quietest Kate In Her Kitchen had ever been, and he'd been the one who'd hit the mute. It was up to him to break the silence.

He cleared his throat. "I've been thinking a lot about what you asked me. You know, about you two getting married. I haven't said anything because, well, it's just that it took a while to understand."

His dad sipped his coffee but stayed quiet with his eyes fixed on Win's face. His dad's steady gaze made

Win shift in his seat. "Okay. So I guess what I want to tell you is I'd like it if you'd do it. Get married."

"Well, it took you long enough, you little monster." Kate came to him and wrapped her arms around him from behind.

He stood and hugged her, and they held onto each other until his dad clapped him on the back. "Thanks, Win. And I think it's a good idea to go to L.A. early to get a look at the city. Your uncle will be a great tour guide. Just remember he's kind of a wild child, even though he's over thirty." He went to the stove and served three bowls of oatmeal. "And something else. You come home whenever you need to."

Come home whenever you need to. Win repeated his father's words silently, thinking that he would look forward to coming home now.

Chapter Seventy-Five

Lula

The loud knock at the front door brought Lula from upstairs. When she opened it, Win stood there, but he still wasn't the Win she'd known most of her life. No slouch. His hair was swept back from his face, his eyes still dark, but without the mystery or anger that used to drive her crazy. There was none of the Win danger about him. Something like a vast emptiness was there now, a canvas without a single stroke of paint.

She caught the irony of her thoughts. Blossom had captured the real Win in her portrait and the boy at her front door was only a sketch.

"I came to say goodbye." Win stood with one foot on the bottom step of the entrance.

"Where are you going?"

"LA. My uncle says I can stay with him until fall semester." He smiled, looking up at her. "Want to hear a good story?"

"Of course. That's the only kind I want to hear anymore."

"My father's going to marry Kate." Now his smile broadened. "That news set me back on my heels, but I got to thinking about it, and now I'm good with it."

He stepped away, and for a moment she thought he'd leave.

But she didn't want him gone yet. There was always something comforting about talking to someone who'd been there that day, someone who understood the nightmares that came now and then even after more than a year.

Quickly, she said, "I'm leaving for Ohio State, too. But not right now. Not until Marty's better. I want to know if his therapy has a chance to work." She crossed her arms and walked down the steps to stand next to Win. "Meantime, I'm going to Greenlee JC."

Win didn't react, but he kept looking at her as if he didn't want her to stop talking to him.

"He might …walk, you know?" Lula glanced down, blinking away the dampness in her eyes.

They stood in silence for a while, then Win said, "I loved her."

She stared into the eyes that had lost their hooded look, and she didn't have to ask who he was talking about. "Did she know?"

"No. Now I want everyone to know what she meant to me."

Lula understood exactly how he felt. It was too late for either of them. They hadn't been what Blossom needed them to be, but they wanted to make it right in some fashion. And telling others how they felt about her was the only way they had now.

She leaned heavily into the pain of regret. "I should have been a better friend. I should have told her what a great person she was and how much I appreciated her," Lula said. Then, putting her hands on both hips, she looked up at the sky, blinking back the prickly sting of tears, and took a deep breath.

"Win." She swiped at her nose. "Look, I'm sorry I did that knee thing to you in eighth grade. I've always been sorry, okay? But I never said so. I just wanted you to pay attention to me, and you wouldn't. I just wanted you to know I liked you. I'll never not tell someone how much they mean to me again. Never." Lula stressed the never, and in her mind, Marty winked at her.

Win reached out for her hand and pulled her into

his arms. How much she'd longed for him to hold her like this, but now that she stood pressed close to his chest, none of the fire she'd always imagined happening at this moment flickered in her belly. Only a slow, sad heat spread from his arms across her back and into the center of her.

"I was afraid to pay attention to you," he said. "I was afraid of caring for anybody. I'd seen how love destroyed people, but I was wrong, and I won't make that mistake again."

For a moment they stood clutching each other close—two people who held Blossom Henley in their hearts.

The Final Word

The news reports about Clifford Mott came out daily immediately following the shooting at Blendz and Moore. These stories were mostly speculation. Mostly telling the story of a loner nobody knew much about who'd been shot by the police when he exited the coffee shop, gun in hand.

The press dug through the newspaper archives and found police reports about Clifford's father. He'd served jail time for domestic violence. Many times. And twice Mrs. Mott had been hospitalized after her husband's arrest. One reporter found Child Protective Services had stepped in to provide the Mott family counseling, but Clifford had remained in the home and had never been placed in foster care.

He'd gone to school until his senior year, and until that year he'd been in the school photographs, standing in the back and always slightly separate from the group. Now as these pictures were published, alongside the story of the shooting, people asked why no one had noticed how withdrawn from other students he was. They pointed out the strained and dark look in his eyes. After so many domestic violence reports, why hadn't the authorities done more? And how could the convenience store manager allow Mott to work in a place so near their children?

None of them said they should have paid attention.

Later in the month, investigators released more about their findings that revealed Clifford Mott's obsession with Blossom Henley. So many starts to letters, each one a plea for her to come away from Las Animas with him. How he needed her to love him the way he loved her. He'd called her the Sunshine Girl, writing about the way she always glowed—warm and welcoming— when he was with her. They'd found notes in his phone that were about her and about other students at the high school. These notes were random and not exactly threatening unless read in the context of what happened in the coffee shop that Saturday morning.

The sketches of his father were bloody, and in them, he'd killed Harry Mott in as many ways as a life could be ended. The mother only appeared as a ghostly figure, often hovering over the murder scene. Some of these pictures had turned up on his social media, but it seemed nobody noticed. He had five followers and Clifford didn't follow anyone. He was even alone in the online sea of public exposure.

Editorials about mass shootings and their increasing numbers appeared in newspapers around the country. They raised questions about what constituted a mass shooting and why they were on the rise. Once again, people pointed at Congress and the gun lobby and their failure to put stricter gun control laws into effect. The argument over the Second Amendment came up in debates and around dinner tables. Psychologists spoke about the effect of social media and its glorification of gun violence—how much that contributes to these tragedies. But then the editorials dwindled, and the discussions switched to the wars in the world or the next Hollywood high-concept film—a blockbuster for sure.

Lula Banes entered Greenlee Junior College and, with Butter, moved into a small apartment near the campus. She saw Marty every weekend, and her father asked her home for dinner and to talk about what she'd learned in the way of horticulture. He was honestly interested.

Long after Akoni was not officially his caregiver

anymore, Marty called him every week and Akoni came to the house for some of Mrs. Skolinski's homemade biscuits. Marty had come to appreciate Akoni forever bugging him about attitude, and he never missed his appointment at the clinic. A few months later, Marty took his first step alone while holding onto the parallel bars.

Akoni was there with, "Now, I give you a good recommendation."

Marty laughed and risked letting go of one bar long enough to give his friend a high-five.

Win Knight flew to LA and moved in with his uncle until he started the fall semester at UCLA. Mid-semester, he sent Kate and his father a text: "Thinking about pre-med." In June, he returned to Las Animas for his father's and Kate's marriage.

The social worker who'd been assigned to Dina Strong after she recovered from the shooting placed her in a county program where she met other girls with bulimia and started healing. Within a year, she'd lost the skeletal look and had begun to see her reflection in the mirror differently.

She still held onto the idea of high fashion modeling, but she started paying attention to what the counselors were saying about advertisers manipulating their audience by creating what was called *appearance anxiety*.

She didn't like the idea of being manipulated to sell a product. That slowly brought Dina back from her binge and purge destructive behavior and helped her to accept herself for who she was and how she looked. She would always miss her cousin, and she'd never stop regretting that she hadn't left Blendz and Moore earlier that day when Brittany had asked her to.

Margaret Henley sold her home and bought a condo in Oregon. But before she left, she visited Mrs.

Strong and gave her five thousand dollars. It would help Dina with a professional modeling portfolio that Mrs. Strong had said her daughter needed, and there might be some money to give the family a financial boost. Blossom would have approved, of that Mrs. Henley was sure. Her daughter was always a generous and kind girl.

Mr. and Mrs. Skolinski sold their home and moved closer to Greenlee and the hospital where Marty went regularly for therapy. The bikers who'd been renting next door bought the Skolinski home.

After the Greenlee art gallery sold Win's portrait, it hung another of Blossom's pieces. This was a self-portrait of a girl drenched in sunshine. Her eyes were a vivid green, her golden hair tousled, and her lavender dress unbuttoned to reveal a lacy chemise.

The End

Evernight Teen ®

www.evernightteen.com